FAVORITE FAIRY TALES

27 Stories
by The Brothers Grimm,
Andersen, Perrault, and Others

DOVER THRIFT EDITIONS

Edited by

M. C. Waldrep

DOVER PUBLICATIONS, INC.
MINEOLA, NEW YORK

DOVER THRIFT EDITIONS

GENERAL EDITOR: MARY CAROLYN WALDREP

EDITOR OF THIS VOLUME: ALISON DAURIO

Bibliographical Note

Favorite Fairy Tales: 27 Stories by The Brothers Grimm, Andersen, Perrault, and Others is a new compilation of stories selected from the following sources: *The Blue Fairy Book,* 1889, *The Red Fairy Book,* 1890, *The Green Fairy Book,* 1892, *The Yellow Fairy Book,* 1894, *The Pink Fairy Book,* 1897, *The Grey Fairy Book,* 1900, and *The Orange Fairy Book,* 1906, all originally published by Longmans, Green & Co., London.

Library of Congress Cataloging-in-Publication Data

Lang, Andrew, 1844–1912.
    Favorite fairy tales : 27 stories by the Brothers Grimm, Andersen, Perrault, and others.
        p. cm.
    ". . . a new compilation of stories selected from the following sources: The Blue Fairy Book, 1889, The Red Fairy Book, 1890, The Green Fairy Book, 1892, The Yellow Fairy Book, 1894, The Pink Fairy Book, 1897, The Grey Fairy Book, 1900, and The Orange Fairy Book, 1906, all originally published by Longmans, Green & Co., London"—Title page verso.
    ISBN-13: 978-0-486-49878-2
    ISBN-10: 0-486-49878-6
    1. Fairy tales. [1. Fairy tales. 2. Folklore.] I. Title.

PZ8.L15Fav 2012
398.2—dc23
                                                                    2012025666

Manufactured in the United States by LSC Communications
49878606   2019
www.doverpublications.com

Foreword

ANDREW LANG (1844–1912) was a journalist, poet, novelist, historian, and literary critic during the Victorian Era, though he is better known for what he didn't write. Lang's prolific series of collected Fairy Tales, better known as *Andrew Lang's "Color" Fairy Books*, consists of twelve volumes published between 1889 and 1910, and contains over four hundred tales from around the world.

Many children growing up during the Victorian era wouldn't have read these timeless fairy tales; the critics of the time considered their "brutality" to be unfit for children, and instead recommended the more gentle, picturesque, and dreamy stories that were newly published during that time. Lang however, growing up in the small town of Selkirk along the border of England and Scotland, had access to works by The Brothers Grimm, William Shakespeare, and Sir Walter Scott. These authors would spark his initial interest in magic, myth, and folklore, and continue to influence him throughout his career.

When the first book in the series, *The Blue Fairy Book* (1889), quickly sold a satisfactory 5,000 copies, Lang went on to publish the *Red* (1890) and *Green* (1892) *Fairy Books*. The series was initially intended as a trilogy, but Lang hadn't counted on the wild appeal that these tales would have. The subsequent nine books were produced in much larger quantities, and steadily became common favorites with both children and adults alike.

Dover Publications' *Favorite Fairy Tales: 27 Stories by The Brothers Grimm, Andersen, Perrault, and Others* is the definitive collection of fairy tales, carefully plucked from *Andrew Lang's "Color" Fairy Books* and condensed into a single volume—an essential addition to any bookshelf. From the timeless classics like "Beauty and the Beast," "Thumbelina," and "Jack and the Beanstalk," to the perhaps lesser known "Toads and Diamonds," "The Princess on the Glass Hill," and "The Tinder-Box," these stories, complete with the original illustrations by H. J. Ford, present an invaluable opportunity to delve into your imagination and escape into a realm where magic—both good and evil—really exists.

Contents

CINDERELLA; OR, THE LITTLE GLASS SLIPPER

ONCE THERE was a gentleman who married, for his second wife, the proudest and most haughty woman that was ever seen. She had, by a former husband, two daughters of her own humor, who were, indeed, exactly like her in all things. He had likewise, by another wife, a young daughter, but of unparalleled goodness and sweetness of temper, which she took from her mother, who was the best creature in the world.

No sooner were the ceremonies of the wedding over but the mother-in-law began to show herself in her true colors. She could not bear the good qualities of this pretty girl, and the less because they made her own daughters appear the more odious. She employed her in the meanest work of the house: she scoured the dishes, tables, etc., and rubbed madam's chamber, and those of misses, her daughters; she lay up in a sorry garret, upon a wretched straw bed, while her sisters lay in fine rooms, with floors all inlaid, upon beds of the very newest fashion, and where they had looking-glasses so large that they might see themselves at their full length from head to foot.

The poor girl bore all patiently, and dared not tell her father, who would have rattled her off; for his wife governed him entirely. When she had done her work, she used to go into the chimney-corner, and sit down among cinders and ashes, which made her commonly be called *Cinderwench*; but the youngest, who was not so rude and uncivil as the eldest, called her Cinderella. However, Cinderella, notwithstanding her mean apparel, was a hundred times handsomer than her sisters, though they were always dressed very richly.

It happened that the King's son gave a ball, and invited all persons of fashion to it. Our young misses were also invited, for they cut a very grand figure among the quality. They were mightily delighted at this invitation, and wonderfully busy in choosing out such gowns,

1

petticoats, and head-clothes as might become them. This was a new trouble to Cinderella; for it was she who ironed her sisters' linen, and plaited their ruffles; they talked all day long of nothing but how they should be dressed.

"For my part," said the eldest, "I will wear my red velvet suit with French trimming."

"And I," said the youngest, "shall have my usual petticoat; but then, to make amends for that, I will put on my gold-flowered manteau, and my diamond stomacher, which is far from being the most ordinary one in the world."

They sent for the best tire-woman they could get to make up their head-dresses and adjust their double pinners, and they had their red brushes and patches from Mademoiselle de la Poche.

Cinderella was likewise called up to them to be consulted in all these matters, for she had excellent notions, and advised them always for the best, nay, and offered her services to dress their heads, which they were very willing she should do. As she was doing this, they said to her:

"Cinderella, would you not be glad to go to the ball?"

"Alas!" said she, "you only jeer me; it is not for such as I am to go thither."

"Thou art in the right of it," replied they; "it would make the people laugh to see a Cinderwench at a ball."

Anyone but Cinderella would have dressed their heads awry, but she was very good, and dressed them perfectly well. They were almost two days without eating, so much were they transported with joy. They broke above a dozen laces in trying to be laced up close, that they might have a fine slender shape, and they were continually at their looking-glass. At last the happy day came; they went to Court, and Cinderella followed them with her eyes as long as she could, and when she had lost sight of them, she fell a-crying.

Her godmother, who saw her all in tears, asked her what was the matter.

"I wish I could—I wish I could—"; she was not able to speak the rest, being interrupted by her tears and sobbing.

This godmother of hers, who was a fairy, said to her, "Thou wishest thou couldst go to the ball; is it not so?"

"Y—es," cried Cinderella, with a great sigh.

"Well," said her godmother, "be but a good girl, and I will contrive that thou shalt go." Then she took her into her chamber, and said to her, "Run into the garden, and bring me a pumpkin."

Cinderella went immediately to gather the finest she could get, and brought it to her godmother, not being able to imagine how this pumpkin could make her go to the ball. Her godmother scooped out all the inside of it, having left nothing but the rind; which done, she struck it with her wand, and the pumpkin was instantly turned into a fine coach, gilded all over with gold.

She then went to look into her mouse-trap, where she found six mice, all alive, and ordered Cinderella to lift up a little the trapdoor, when, giving each mouse, as it went out, a little tap with her wand, the mouse was that moment turned into a fine horse, which altogether made a very fine set of six horses of a beautiful mouse-colored dapple-grey. Being at a loss for a coachman,

"I will go and see," says Cinderella, "if there is never a rat in the rat-trap—we may make a coachman of him."

"Thou art in the right," replied her godmother; "go and look."

Cinderella brought the trap to her, and in it there were three huge rats. The fairy made choice of one of the three which had the largest beard, and, having touched him with her wand, he was turned into a fat, jolly coachman, who had the smartest whiskers eyes ever beheld. After that, she said to her:

"Go again into the garden, and you will find six lizards behind the watering-pot, bring them to me."

She had no sooner done so but her godmother turned them into six footmen, who skipped up immediately behind the coach, with their liveries all bedaubed with gold and silver, and clung as close behind each other as if they had done nothing else their whole lives. The Fairy then said to Cinderella:

"Well, you see here an equipage fit to go to the ball with; are you not pleased with it?"

"Oh! yes," cried she; "but must I go thither as I am, in these nasty rags?"

Her godmother only just touched her with her wand, and, at the same instant, her clothes were turned into cloth of gold and silver, all beset with jewels. This done, she gave her a pair of glass slippers, the prettiest in the whole world. Being thus decked out, she got up into her coach; but her godmother, above all things, commanded her not to stay till after midnight, telling her, at the same time, that if she stayed one moment longer, the coach would be a pumpkin again, her horses mice, her coachman a rat, her footmen lizards, and her clothes become just as they were before.

She promised her godmother she would not fail of leaving the ball before midnight; and then away she drives, scarce able to contain herself for joy. The King's son, who was told that a great princess, whom nobody knew, was come, ran out to receive her; he gave her his hand as she alighted out of the coach, and led her into the hall, among all the company. There was immediately a profound silence, they left off dancing, and the violins ceased to play, so attentive was everyone to contemplate the singular beauties of the unknown new-comer. Nothing was then heard but a confused noise of:

"Ha! how handsome she is! Ha! how handsome she is!"

The King himself, old as he was, could not help watching her, and telling the Queen softly that it was a long time since he had seen so beautiful and lovely a creature.

All the ladies were busied in considering her clothes and head-dress, that they might have some made next day after the same pattern, provided they could meet with such fine material and as able hands to make them.

The King's son conducted her to the most honorable seat, and afterward took her out to dance with him; she danced so very gracefully that they all more and more admired her. A fine collation was served up, whereof the young prince ate not a morsel, so intently was he busied in gazing on her.

She went and sat down by her sisters, showing them a thousand civilities, giving them part of the oranges and citrons which the Prince had presented her with, which very much surprised them, for they did not know her. While Cinderella was thus amusing her sisters, she heard the clock strike eleven and three-quarters, whereupon she immediately made a courtesy to the company and hasted away as fast as she could.

When she got home she ran to seek out her godmother, and, after having thanked her, she said she could not but heartily wish she might go next day to the ball, because the King's son had desired her.

As she was eagerly telling her godmother whatever had passed at the ball, her two sisters knocked at the door, which Cinderella ran and opened.

"How long you have stayed!" cried she, gaping, rubbing her eyes and stretching herself as if she had been just waked out of her sleep; she had not, however, any manner of inclination to sleep since they went from home.

"If thou hadst been at the ball," said one of her sisters, "thou wouldst not have been tired with it. There came thither the finest princess, the most beautiful ever was seen with mortal eyes; she showed us a thousand civilities, and gave us oranges and citrons."

Cinderella seemed very indifferent in the matter; indeed, she asked them the name of that princess; but they told her they did not know it, and that the King's son was very uneasy on her account and would give all the world to know who she was. At this Cinderella, smiling, replied:

"She must, then, be very beautiful indeed; how happy you have been! Could not I see her? Ah! dear Miss Charlotte, do lend me your yellow suit of clothes which you wear every day."

"Ay, to be sure!" cried Miss Charlotte; "lend my clothes to such a dirty Cinderwench as thou art! I should be a fool."

Cinderella, indeed, expected well such answer, and was very glad of the refusal; for she would have been sadly put to it if her sister had lent her what she asked for jestingly.

The next day the two sisters were at the ball, and so was Cinderella, but dressed more magnificently than before. The King's son was always by her, and never ceased his compliments and kind speeches to her; to whom all this was so far from being tiresome that she quite forgot what her godmother had recommended to her; so that she, at last, counted the clock striking twelve when she took it to be no more than eleven; she then rose up and fled, as nimble as a deer. The Prince followed, but could not overtake her. She left behind one of her glass slippers, which the Prince took up most carefully. She got home but quite out of breath, and in her nasty old clothes, having nothing left her of all her finery but one of the little slippers, fellow to that she dropped. The guards at the palace gate were asked:

If they had not seen a princess go out.

Who said: They had seen nobody go out but a young girl, very meanly dressed, and who had more the air of a poor country wench than a gentlewoman.

When the two sisters returned from the ball Cinderella asked them: If they had been well diverted, and if the fine lady had been there.

They told her: Yes, but that she hurried away immediately when it struck twelve, and with so much haste that she dropped one of her little glass slippers, the prettiest in the world, which the King's son had taken up; that he had done nothing but look at her all the time at the ball, and that most certainly he was very much in love with the beautiful person who owned the glass slipper.

What they said was very true; for a few days after the King's son caused it to be proclaimed, by sound of trumpet, that he would marry her whose foot the slipper would just fit. They whom he employed began to try it upon the princesses, then the duchesses and all the Court, but in vain; it was brought to the two sisters, who did all they possibly could to thrust their foot into the slipper, but they could not effect it. Cinderella, who saw all this, and knew her slipper, said to them, laughing:

"Let me see if it will not fit me."

Her sisters burst out a-laughing, and began to banter her. The gentleman who was sent to try the slipper looked earnestly at Cinderella, and, finding her very handsome, said:

It was but just that she should try, and that he had orders to let everyone make trial.

He obliged Cinderella to sit down, and, putting the slipper to her foot, he found it went on very easily, and fitted her as if it had been made of wax. The astonishment her two sisters were in was excessively great, but still abundantly greater when Cinderella pulled out of her pocket the other slipper, and put it on her foot. Thereupon, in came her godmother, who, having touched with her wand Cinderella's clothes, made them richer and more magnificent than any of those she had before.

And now her two sisters found her to be that fine, beautiful lady whom they had seen at the ball. They threw themselves at her feet to beg pardon for all the ill-treatment they had made her undergo. Cinderella took them up, and, as she embraced them, cried:

That she forgave them with all her heart, and desired them always to love her.

CINDERELLA'S FLIGHT.

She was conducted to the young prince, dressed as she was; he thought her more charming than ever, and, a few days after, married her. Cinderella, who was no less good than beautiful, gave her two sisters lodgings in the palace, and that very same day matched them with two great lords of the Court.

CHARLES PERRAULT

BEAUTY AND THE BEAST

ONCE UPON a time, in a very far-off country, there lived a merchant who had been so fortunate in all his undertakings that he was enormously rich. As he had, however, six sons and six daughters, he found that his money was not too much to let them all have everything they fancied, as they were accustomed to do.

But one day a most unexpected misfortune befell them. Their house caught fire and was speedily burnt to the ground, with all the splendid furniture, the books, pictures, gold, silver, and precious goods it contained; and this was only the beginning of their troubles. Their father, who had until this moment prospered in all ways, suddenly lost every ship he had upon the sea, either by dint of pirates, shipwreck, or fire. Then he heard that his clerks in distant countries, whom he trusted entirely, had proved unfaithful; and at last from great wealth he fell into the direst poverty.

All that he had left was a little house in a desolate place at least a hundred leagues from the town in which he had lived, and to this he was forced to retreat with his children, who were in despair at the idea of leading such a different life. Indeed, the daughters at first hoped that their friends, who had been so numerous while they were rich, would insist on their staying in their houses now they no longer possessed one. But they soon found that they were left alone, and that their former friends even attributed their misfortunes to their own extravagance, and showed no intention of offering them any help. So nothing was left for them but to take their departure to the cottage, which stood in the midst of a dark forest, and seemed to be the most dismal place upon the face of the earth. As they were too poor to have any servants, the girls had to work hard, like peasants, and the sons, for their part, cultivated the fields to earn their living. Roughly clothed, and living in the simplest way, the girls regretted unceasingly the luxuries and amusements of their former life; only the youngest tried to be brave and cheerful. She had been as sad as anyone when misfortune overtook her father, but, soon recovering her natural gaiety, she set to work to make the best of things, to amuse her father and brothers as well as she could, and to try to persuade her sisters to join her in dancing and singing. But they would do nothing of the sort, and, because she was not as doleful as themselves, they declared that this miserable life was all she was fit for. But she was really far prettier and cleverer than they were; indeed, she was so lovely that she was always called Beauty. After two years, when they were all beginning to get used to their new life, something happened to disturb their tranquility. Their father received the news that one of his ships, which he had believed to be lost, had come safely into port with a rich cargo. All the sons and daughters at once thought that their poverty was at an end, and wanted to set out directly for the town; but their father, who was more prudent, begged them to wait a little, and, though it was harvest-time, and he could ill be spared, determined to go himself first, to make inquiries. Only the youngest daughter had any doubt but that they would soon again be as rich as they were before, or at least rich enough to live comfortably in some town where they would find amusement and gay companions once more. So they all loaded their father with commissions for jewels and dresses which it would have taken a fortune to buy; only Beauty, feeling sure that it was of no use, did not ask for anything. Her father, noticing her silence, said: "And what shall I bring for you, Beauty?"

"The only thing I wish for is to see you come home safely," she answered.

But this reply vexed her sisters, who fancied she was blaming them for having asked for such costly things. Her father, however, was pleased, but as he thought that at her age she certainly ought to like pretty presents, he told her to choose something.

"Well, dear father," she said, "as you insist upon it, I beg that you will bring me a rose. I have not seen one since we came here, and I love them so much."

So the merchant set out and reached the town as quickly as possible, but only to find that his former companions, believing him to be dead, had divided between them the goods which the ship had brought; and after six months of trouble and expense he found himself as poor as when he started, having been able to recover only just enough to pay the cost of his journey. To make matters worse, he was obliged to leave the town in the most terrible weather, so that by the time he was within a few leagues of his home he was almost

exhausted with cold and fatigue. Though he knew it would take some hours to get through the forest, he was so anxious to be at his journey's end that he resolved to go on; but night overtook him, and the deep snow and bitter frost made it impossible for his horse to carry him any further. Not a house was to be seen; the only shelter he could get was the hollow trunk of a great tree, and there he crouched all the night which seemed to him the longest he had ever known. In spite of his weariness the howling of the wolves kept him awake, and even when at last the day broke he was not much better off, for the falling snow had covered up every path, and he did not know which way to turn.

At length he made out some sort of track, and though at the beginning it was so rough and slippery that he fell down more than once, it presently became easier, and led him into an avenue of trees which ended in a splendid castle. It seemed to the merchant very strange that no snow had fallen in the avenue, which was entirely composed of orange trees, covered with flowers and fruit. When he reached the first court of the castle he saw before him a flight of agate steps, and went up them, and passed through several splendidly furnished rooms. The pleasant warmth of the air revived him, and he felt very hungry; but there seemed to be nobody in all this vast and splendid palace whom he could ask to give him something to eat. Deep silence reigned everywhere, and at last, tired of roaming through empty rooms and galleries, he stopped in a room smaller than the rest, where a clear fire was burning and a couch was drawn up closely to it. Thinking that this must be prepared for someone who was expected, he sat down to wait till he should come, and very soon fell into a sweet sleep.

When his extreme hunger wakened him after several hours, he was still alone; but a little table, upon which was a good dinner, had been drawn up close to him, and, as he had eaten nothing for twenty-four hours, he lost no time in beginning his meal, hoping that he might soon have an opportunity of thanking his considerate entertainer, whoever it might be. But no one appeared, and even after another long sleep, from which he awoke completely refreshed, there was no sign of anybody, though a fresh meal of dainty cakes and fruit was prepared upon the little table at his elbow. Being naturally timid, the silence began to terrify him, and he resolved to search once more through all the rooms; but it was of no use. Not even a servant was to be seen; there was no sign of life in the palace! He began to wonder what he should do, and to amuse himself by pretending that all the treasures he saw were his own, and considering how he would divide them among his children. Then he went down into the garden, and though it was winter everywhere else, here the sun shone, and the birds sang, and the flowers bloomed, and the air was soft and sweet. The merchant, in ecstasies with all he saw and heard, said to himself:

"All this must be meant for me. I will go this minute and bring my children to share all these delights."

In spite of being so cold and weary when he reached the castle, he had taken his horse to the stable and fed it. Now he thought he would saddle it for his homeward journey, and he turned down the path which led to the stable. This path had a hedge of roses on each side of it, and the merchant thought he had never seen or smelt such exquisite flowers. They reminded him of his promise to Beauty, and he stopped and had just gathered one to take to her when he was startled by a strange noise behind him. Turning round, he saw a frightful Beast, which seemed to be very angry and said, in a terrible voice:

"Who told you that you might gather my roses? Was it not enough that I allowed you to be in my palace and was kind to you? This is the way you show your gratitude, by stealing my flowers! But your insolence shall not go unpunished." The merchant, terrified by these furious words, dropped the fatal rose, and, throwing himself on his knees, cried: "Pardon me, noble sir. I am truly grateful to you for your hospitality, which was so magnificent that I could not imagine that you would be offended by my taking such a little thing as a rose." But the Beast's anger was not lessened by this speech.

"You are very ready with excuses and flattery," he cried; "but that will not save you from the death you deserve."

"Alas!" thought the merchant, "if my daughter could only know what danger her rose has brought me into!"

And in despair he began to tell the Beast all his misfortunes, and the reason of his journey, not forgetting to mention Beauty's request.

"A king's ransom would hardly have procured all that my other daughters asked," he said; "but I thought that I might at least take Beauty her rose. I beg you to forgive me, for you see I meant no harm."

The Beast considered for a moment, and then he said, in a less furious tone:

"I will forgive you on one condition—that is, that you will give me one of your daughters."

"Ah!" cried the merchant, "if I were cruel enough to buy my own life at the expense of one of my children's, what excuse could I invent to bring her here?"

"No excuse would be necessary," answered the Beast. "If she comes at all she must come willingly. On no other condition will I have her. See if any one of them is courageous enough, and loves you well enough to come and save your life. You seem to be an honest man, so I will trust you to go home. I give you a month to see if either of your daughters will come back with you and stay here, to let you go free. If neither of them is willing, you must come alone, after bidding them good-bye forever, for then you will belong to me. And do not imagine that you can hide from me, for if you fail to keep your word I will come and fetch you!" added the Beast grimly.

The merchant accepted this proposal, though he did not really think any of his daughters could be persuaded to come. He promised to return at the time appointed, and then, anxious to escape from the presence of the Beast, he asked permission to set off at once. But the Beast answered that he could not go until the next day.

"Then you will find a horse ready for you," he said. "Now go and eat your supper, and await my orders."

The poor merchant, more dead than alive, went back to his room, where the most delicious supper was already served on the little table which was drawn up before a blazing fire. But he was too terrified to eat, and only tasted a few of the dishes, for fear the Beast should be angry if he did not obey his orders. When he had finished he heard a great noise in the next room, which he knew meant that the Beast was coming. As he could do nothing to escape his visit, the only thing that remained was to seem as little afraid as possible;

so when the Beast appeared and asked roughly if he had supped well, the merchant answered humbly that he had, thanks to his host's kindness. Then the Beast warned him to remember their agreement, and to prepare his daughter exactly for what she had to expect.

"Do not get up tomorrow," he added, "until you see the sun and hear a golden bell ring. Then you will find your breakfast waiting for you here, and the horse you are to ride will be ready in the courtyard. He will also bring you back again when you come with your daughter a month hence. Farewell. Take a rose to Beauty, and remember your promise!"

The merchant was only too glad when the Beast went away, and though he could not sleep for sadness, he lay down until the sun rose. Then, after a hasty breakfast, he went to gather Beauty's rose, and mounted his horse, which carried him off so swiftly that in an instant he had lost sight of the palace, and he was still wrapped in gloomy thoughts when it stopped before the door of the cottage.

His sons and daughters, who had been very uneasy at his long absence, rushed to meet him, eager to know the result of his journey, which, seeing him mounted upon a splendid horse and wrapped in a rich mantle, they supposed to be favorable. He hid the truth from them at first, only saying sadly to Beauty as he gave her the rose:

"Here is what you asked me to bring you; you little know what it has cost."

But this excited their curiosity so greatly that presently he told them his adventures from beginning to end, and then they were all very unhappy. The girls lamented loudly over their lost hopes, and the sons declared that their father should not return to this terrible castle, and began to make plans for killing the Beast if it should come to fetch him. But he reminded them that he had promised to go back. Then the girls were very angry with Beauty, and said it was all her fault, and that if she had asked for something sensible this would never have happened, and complained bitterly that they should have to suffer for her folly.

Poor Beauty, much distressed, said to them:

"I have, indeed, caused this misfortune, but I assure you I did it innocently. Who could have guessed that to ask for a rose in the middle of summer would cause so much misery? But as I did the mischief it is only just that I should suffer for it. I will therefore go back with my father to keep his promise."

At first nobody would hear of this arrangement, and her father and brothers, who loved her dearly, declared that nothing should make them let her go; but Beauty was firm. As the time drew near she divided all her little possessions between her sisters, and said good-bye to everything she loved, and when the fatal day came she encouraged and cheered her father as they mounted together the horse which had brought him back. It seemed to fly rather than gallop, but so smoothly that Beauty was not frightened; indeed, she would have enjoyed the journey if she had not feared what might happen to her at the end of it. Her father still tried to persuade her to go back, but in vain. While they were talking the night fell, and then, to their great surprise, wonderful colored lights began to shine in all directions, and splendid fireworks blazed out before them; all the forest was illuminated by them, and even felt pleasantly warm, though it had been bitterly cold before. This lasted until they reached the avenue of orange trees, where were statues holding flaming torches, and when they got nearer to the palace they saw that it was illuminated from the roof to the ground, and music sounded softly from the courtyard. "The Beast must be very hungry," said Beauty, trying to laugh, "if he makes all this rejoicing over the arrival of his prey."

But, in spite of her anxiety, she could not help admiring all the wonderful things she saw.

The horse stopped at the foot of the flight of steps leading to the terrace, and when they had dismounted her father led her to the little room he had been in before, where they found a splendid fire burning, and the table daintily spread with a delicious supper.

The merchant knew that this was meant for them, and Beauty, who was rather less frightened now that she had passed through so many rooms and seen nothing of the Beast, was quite willing to begin, for her long ride had made her very hungry. But they had hardly finished their meal when the noise of the Beast's footsteps was heard approaching, and Beauty clung to her father in terror, which became all the greater when she saw how frightened he was. But when the Beast really appeared, though she trembled at the sight of him, she made a great effort to hide her horror, and saluted him respectfully.

This evidently pleased the Beast. After looking at her he said, in a tone that might have struck terror into the boldest heart, though he did not seem to be angry:

"Good-evening, old man. Good-evening, Beauty."

The merchant was too terrified to reply, but Beauty answered sweetly:

"Good-evening, Beast."

"Have you come willingly?" asked the Beast. "Will you be content to stay here when your father goes away?"

Beauty answered bravely that she was quite prepared to stay.

"I am pleased with you," said the Beast. "As you have come of your own accord, you may stay. As for you, old man," he added, turning to the merchant, "at sunrise tomorrow you will take your departure. When the bell rings get up quickly and eat your breakfast, and you will find the same horse waiting to take you home; but remember that you must never expect to see my palace again."

Then turning to Beauty, he said:

"Take your father into the next room, and help him to choose everything you think your brothers and sisters would like to have. You will find two traveling-trunks there; fill them as full as you can. It is only just that you should send them something very precious as a remembrance of yourself."

Then he went away, after saying, "Good-bye, Beauty; good-bye, old man"; and though Beauty was beginning to think with great dismay of her father's departure, she was afraid to disobey the Beast's orders; and they went into the next room, which had shelves and cupboards all round it. They were greatly surprised at the riches it contained. There were splendid dresses fit for a queen, with all the ornaments that were to be worn with them; and when Beauty opened the cupboards she was quite dazzled by the gorgeous jewels that lay in heaps upon every shelf. After choosing a vast quantity, which she divided between her sisters—for she had made a heap of the wonderful dresses for each of them—she opened the last chest, which was full of gold.

"I think, father," she said, "that, as the gold will be more useful to you, we had better take out the other things again, and fill the trunks with it." So they did this; but the more they put in the more room there seemed to be, and at last they put back all the jewels and dresses they had taken out, and Beauty even added as many more of the jewels as she could carry at once; and then the trunks were not too full, but they were so heavy that an elephant could not have carried them!

"The Beast was mocking us," cried the merchant; "he must have pretended to give us all these things, knowing that I could not carry them away."

"Let us wait and see," answered Beauty. "I cannot believe that he meant to deceive us. All we can do is to fasten them up and leave them ready."

So they did this and returned to the little room, where, to their astonishment, they found breakfast ready. The merchant ate his with a good appetite, as the Beast's generosity made him believe that he might perhaps venture to come back soon and see Beauty. But she felt sure that her father was leaving her forever, so she was very sad when the bell rang sharply for the second time, and warned them that the time had come for them to part. They went down into the courtyard, where two horses were waiting, one loaded with the two trunks, the other for him to ride. They were pawing the ground in their impatience to start, and the merchant was forced to bid Beauty a hasty farewell; and as soon as he was mounted he went off at such a pace that she lost sight of him in an instant. Then Beauty began to cry, and wandered sadly back to her own room. But she soon found that she was very sleepy, and as she had nothing better to do she lay down and instantly fell asleep. And then she dreamed that she was walking by a brook bordered with trees, and lamenting her sad fate, when a young prince, handsomer than anyone she had ever seen, and with a voice that went straight to her heart, came and said to her, "Ah, Beauty! you are not so unfortunate as you suppose. Here you will be rewarded for all you have suffered elsewhere. Your every wish shall be gratified. Only try to find me out, no matter how I may be disguised, as I love you dearly, and in making me happy you will find your own happiness. Be as true-hearted as you are beautiful, and we shall have nothing left to wish for."

"What can I do, Prince, to make you happy?" said Beauty.

"Only be grateful," he answered, "and do not trust too much to your eyes. And, above all, do not desert me until you have saved me from my cruel misery."

After this she thought she found herself in a room with a stately and beautiful lady, who said to her:

"Dear Beauty, try not to regret all you have left behind you, for you are destined to a better fate. Only do not let yourself be deceived by appearances."

Beauty found her dreams so interesting that she was in no hurry to awake, but presently the clock roused her by calling her name softly twelve times, and then she got up and found her dressing-table set out with everything she could possibly want; and when her toilet was finished she found dinner was waiting in the room next to hers. But dinner does not take very long when you are all by yourself, and very soon she sat down cosily in the corner of a sofa, and began to think about the charming Prince she had seen in her dream.

"He said I could make him happy," said Beauty to herself.

"It seems, then, that this horrible Beast keeps him a prisoner.

How can I set him free? I wonder why they both told me not to trust
to appearances? I don't understand it. But, after all, it was only a
dream, so why should I trouble myself about it? I had better go and
find something to do to amuse myself."

So she got up and began to explore some of the many rooms of
the palace.

The first she entered was lined with mirrors, and Beauty saw
herself reflected on every side, and thought she had never seen such
a charming room. Then a bracelet which was hanging from a chan-
delier caught her eye, and on taking it down she was greatly surprised to find that it held a portrait of her unknown admirer, just as
she had seen him in her dream. With great delight she slipped the
bracelet on her arm, and went on into a gallery of pictures, where
she soon found a portrait of the same handsome Prince, as large as
life, and so well painted that as she studied it he seemed to smile
kindly at her. Tearing herself away from the portrait at last, she
passed through into a room which contained every musical instru-
ment under the sun, and here she amused herself for a long while in
trying some of them, and singing until she was tired. The next room
was a library, and she saw everything she had ever wanted to read,
as well as everything she had read, and it seemed to her that a whole
lifetime would not be enough to even read the names of the books,

there were so many. By this time it was growing dusk, and wax candles in diamond and ruby candlesticks were beginning to light themselves in every room.

Beauty found her supper served just at the time she preferred to have it, but she did not see anyone or hear a sound, and, though her father had warned her that she would be alone, she began to find it rather dull.

But presently she heard the Beast coming, and wondered tremblingly if he meant to eat her up now.

However, as he did not seem at all ferocious, and only said gruffly:

"Good-evening, Beauty," she answered cheerfully and managed to conceal her terror. Then the Beast asked her how she had been amusing herself, and she told him all the rooms she had seen.

Then he asked if she thought she could be happy in his palace; and Beauty answered that everything was so beautiful that she would be very hard to please if she could not be happy. And after about an hour's talk Beauty began to think that the Beast was not nearly so terrible as she had supposed at first. Then he got up to leave her, and said in his gruff voice:

"Do you love me, Beauty? Will you marry me?"

"Oh! what shall I say?" cried Beauty, for she was afraid to make the Beast angry by refusing.

"Say 'yes' or 'no' without fear," he replied.

"Oh! no, Beast," said Beauty hastily.

"Since you will not, good-night, Beauty," he said. And she answered:

"Good-night, Beast," very glad to find that her refusal had not provoked him. And after he was gone she was very soon in bed and asleep, and dreaming of her unknown Prince. She thought he came and said to her:

"Ah, Beauty! why are you so unkind to me? I fear I am fated to be unhappy for many a long day still."

And then her dreams changed, but the charming Prince figured in them all; and when morning came her first thought was to look at the portrait, and see if it was really like him, and she found that it certainly was.

This morning she decided to amuse herself in the garden, for the sun shone, and all the fountains were playing; but she was astonished to find that every place was familiar to her, and presently she came to the brook where the myrtle trees were growing where she had first met the Prince in her dream, and that made her think more than ever that he must be kept a prisoner by the Beast. When she

was tired she went back to the palace, and found a new room full of materials for every kind of work—ribbons to make into bows, and silks to work into flowers. Then there was an aviary full of rare birds, which were so tame that they flew to Beauty as soon as they saw her, and perched upon her shoulders and her head.

"Pretty little creatures," she said, "how I wish that your cage was nearer to my room, that I might often hear you sing!"

So saying she opened a door, and found, to her delight, that it led into her own room, though she had thought it was quite the other side of the palace.

There were more birds in a room farther on, parrots and cockatoos that could talk, and they greeted Beauty by name; indeed, she found them so entertaining that she took one or two back to her room, and they talked to her while she was at supper; after which the Beast paid her his usual visit, and asked her the same questions as before, and then with a gruff "good-night" he took his departure, and Beauty went to bed to dream of her mysterious Prince. The days passed swiftly in different amusements, and after a while Beauty found out another strange thing in the palace, which often pleased her when she was tired of being alone. There was one room which she had not noticed particularly; it was empty, except that under each of the windows stood a very comfortable chair; and the first time she had looked out of the window it had seemed to her that a black curtain prevented her from seeing anything outside. But the second time she went into the room, happening to be tired, she sat down in one of the chairs, when instantly the curtain was rolled aside, and a most amusing pantomime was acted before her; there were dances, and colored lights, and music, and pretty dresses, and it was all so gay that Beauty was in ecstacies. After that she tried the other seven windows in turn, and there was some new and surprising entertainment to be seen from each of them, so that Beauty never could feel lonely any more. Every evening after supper the Beast came to see her, and always before saying good-night asked her in his terrible voice:

"Beauty, will you marry me?"

And it seemed to Beauty, now she understood him better, that when she said, "No, Beast," he went away quite sad. But her happy dreams of the handsome young Prince soon made her forget the poor Beast, and the only thing that at all disturbed her was to be constantly told to distrust appearances, to let her heart guide her, and not her eyes, and many other equally perplexing things, which, consider as she would, she could not understand.

So everything went on for a long time, until at last, happy as she was, Beauty began to long for the sight of her father and her brothers and sisters; and one night, seeing her look very sad, the Beast asked her what was the matter. Beauty had quite ceased to be afraid of him. Now she knew that he was really gentle in spite of his ferocious looks and his dreadful voice. So she answered that she was longing to see her home once more. Upon hearing this the Beast seemed sadly distressed, and cried miserably.

"Ah! Beauty, have you the heart to desert an unhappy Beast like this? What more do you want to make you happy? Is it because you hate me that you want to escape?"

"No, dear Beast," answered Beauty softly, "I do not hate you, and I should be very sorry never to see you any more, but I long to see my father again. Only let me go for two months, and I promise to come back to you and stay for the rest of my life."

The Beast, who had been sighing dolefully while she spoke, now replied:

"I cannot refuse you anything you ask, even though it should cost me my life. Take the four boxes you will find in the room next to your own, and fill them with everything you wish to take with you. But remember your promise and come back when the two months are over, or you may have cause to repent it, for if you do not come in good time you will find your faithful Beast dead. You will not need any chariot to bring you back. Only say good-bye to all your brothers and sisters the night before you come away, and when you have gone to bed turn this ring round upon your finger and say firmly: "I wish to go back to my palace and see my Beast again." Good-night, Beauty. Fear nothing, sleep peacefully, and before long you shall see your father once more."

As soon as Beauty was alone she hastened to fill the boxes with all the rare and precious things she saw about her, and only when she was tired of heaping things into them did they seem to be full.

Then she went to bed, but could hardly sleep for joy. And when at last she did begin to dream of her beloved Prince she was grieved to see him stretched upon a grassy bank, sad and weary, and hardly like himself.

"What is the matter?" she cried.

He looked at her reproachfully, and said:

"How can you ask me, cruel one? Are you not leaving me to my death perhaps?"

"Ah! don't be so sorrowful," cried Beauty; "I am only going to assure my father that I am safe and happy. I have promised the Beast faithfully that I will come back, and he would die of grief if I did not keep my word!"

"What would that matter to you?" said the Prince "Surely you would not care?"

"Indeed, I should be ungrateful if I did not care for such a kind Beast," cried Beauty indignantly. "I would die to save him from pain. I assure you it is not his fault that he is so ugly."

Just then a strange sound woke her—someone was speaking not

very far away; and opening her eyes she found herself in a room she had never seen before, which was certainly not nearly so splendid as those she was used to in the Beast's palace. Where could she be? She got up and dressed hastily, and then saw that the boxes she had packed the night before were all in the room. While she was wondering by what magic the Beast had transported them and herself to this strange place she suddenly heard her father's voice, and rushed out and greeted him joyfully. Her brothers and sisters were all astonished at her appearance, as they had never expected to see her again, and there was no end to the questions they asked her. She had also much to hear about what had happened to them while she was away, and of her father's journey home. But when they heard that she had only come to be with them for a short time, and then must go back to the Beast's palace forever, they lamented loudly. Then Beauty asked her father what he thought could be the meaning of·her strange dreams, and why the Prince constantly begged her not to trust to appearances. After much consideration, he answered: "You tell me yourself that the Beast, frightful as he is, loves you dearly, and deserves your love and gratitude for his gentleness and kindness; I think the Prince must mean you to understand that you ought to reward him by doing as he wishes you to, in spite of his ugliness."

Beauty could not help seeing that this seemed very probable; still, when she thought of her dear Prince who was so handsome, she did not feel at all inclined to marry the Beast. At any rate, for two months she need not decide, but could enjoy herself with her sisters. But though they were rich now, and lived in town again, and had plenty of acquaintances, Beauty found that nothing amused her very much; and she often thought of the palace, where she was so happy, especially as at home she never once dreamed of her dear Prince, and she felt quite sad without him.

Then her sisters seemed to have got quite used to being without her, and even found her rather in the way, so she would not have been sorry when the two months were over but for her father and brothers, who begged her to stay, and seemed so grieved at the thought of her departure that she had not the courage to say goodbye to them. Every day when she got up she meant to say it at night, and when night came she put it off again, until at last she had a dismal dream which helped her to make up her mind. She thought she was wandering in a lonely path in the palace gardens, when she heard groans which seemed to come from some bushes hiding the entrance of a cave, and running quickly to see what could be the matter, she found the Beast stretched out upon his side, apparently dying. He reproached her faintly with being the cause of his distress, and at the same moment a stately lady appeared, and said very gravely:

"Ah! Beauty, you are only just in time to save his life. See what happens when people do not keep their promises! If you had delayed one day more, you would have found him dead."

Beauty was so terrified by this dream that the next morning she announced her intention of going back at once, and that very night she said good-bye to her father and all her brothers and sisters, and as soon as she was in bed she turned her ring round upon her finger, and said firmly:

"I wish to go back to my palace and see my Beast again," as she had been told to do.

Then she fell asleep instantly, and only woke up to hear the clock saying "Beauty, Beauty" twelve times in its musical voice, which told her at once that she was really in the palace once more. Everything was just as before, and her birds were so glad to see her! But Beauty thought she had never known such a long day, for she was so anxious to see the Beast again that she felt as if suppertime would never come.

But when it did come and no Beast appeared she was really frightened; so, after listening and waiting for a long time, she ran down into the garden to search for him. Up and down the paths and avenues ran poor Beauty, calling him in vain, for no one answered, and not a trace of him could she find; until at last, quite tired, she stopped for a minute's rest, and saw that she was standing opposite the shady path she had seen in her dream. She rushed down it, and, sure enough, there was the cave, and in it lay the Beast—asleep, as Beauty thought. Quite glad to have found him, she ran up and stroked his head, but to her horror, he did not move or open his eyes.

"Oh! he is dead; and it is all my fault," said Beauty, crying bitterly.

But then, looking at him again, she fancied he still breathed, and, hastily fetching some water from the nearest fountain, she sprinkled it over his face, and to her great delight he began to revive.

"Oh! Beast, how you frightened me!" she cried. "I never knew how much I loved you until just now, when I feared I was too late to save your life."

"Can you really love such an ugly creature as I am?" said the Beast faintly. "Ah! Beauty, you only came just in time. I was dying because I thought you had forgotten your promise. But go back now and rest, I shall see you again by-and-by."

Beauty, who had half expected that he would be angry with her, was reassured by his gentle voice, and went back to the palace, where supper was awaiting her; and afterwards the Beast came in as usual, and talked about the time she had spent with her father, asking if she had enjoyed herself, and if they had all been very glad to see her.

Beauty answered politely, and quite enjoyed telling him all that had happened to her. And when at last the time came for him to go, and he asked, as he had so often asked before:

"Beauty, will you marry me?" she answered softly:

"Yes, dear Beast."

As she spoke a blaze of light sprang up before the windows of the palace; fireworks crackled and guns banged, and across the avenue of orange trees, in letters all made of fireflies, was written: "Long live the Prince and his Bride."

Turning to ask the Beast what it could all mean, Beauty found that he had disappeared, and in his place stood her long-loved Prince! At the same moment the wheels of a chariot were heard upon the terrace, and two ladies entered the room. One of them Beauty recognized as the stately lady she had seen in her dreams; the other was also so grand and queenly that Beauty hardly knew which to greet first.

But the one she already knew said to her companion:

"Well, Queen, this is Beauty, who has had the courage to rescue your son from the terrible enchantment. They love one another, and only your consent to their marriage is wanting to make them perfectly happy."

"I consent with all my heart," cried the Queen. "How can I ever thank you enough, charming girl, for having restored my dear son to his natural form?"

And then she tenderly embraced Beauty and the Prince, who had meanwhile been greeting the Fairy and receiving her congratulations.

"Now," said the Fairy to Beauty, "I suppose you would like me to send for all your brothers and sisters to dance at your wedding?"

And so she did, and the marriage was celebrated the very next day with the utmost splendor, and Beauty and the Prince lived happily ever after.

MADAME DE VILLENEUVE

SNOWDROP

(Snow White and the Seven Dwarfs)

ONCE UPON a time, in the middle of winter when the snowflakes were falling like feathers on the earth, a Queen sat at a window framed in black ebony and sewed. And as she sewed and gazed out to the white landscape, she pricked her finger with the needle, and three drops of blood fell on the snow outside, and because the red showed out so well against the white she thought to herself:

"Oh! what wouldn't I give to have a child as white as snow, as red as blood, and as black as ebony!"

And her wish was granted, for not long after a little daughter was born to her, with a skin as white as snow, lips and cheeks as red as blood, and hair as black as ebony. They called her Snowdrop, and not long after her birth the Queen died.

After a year the King married again. His new wife was a beautiful woman, but so proud and overbearing that she couldn't stand any rival to her beauty. She possessed a magic mirror, and when she used to stand before it gazing at her own reflection and ask:

> "Mirror, mirror, hanging there,
> Who in all the land's most fair?"

it always replied:

> "You are most fair, my Lady Queen,
> None fairer in the land, I ween."

Then she was quite happy, for she knew the mirror always spoke the truth.

But Snowdrop was growing prettier and prettier every day, and when she was seven years old she was as beautiful as she could be, and fairer even than the Queen herself. One day when the latter asked her mirror the usual question, it replied:

> "My Lady Queen, you are fair, 'tis true,
> But Snowdrop is fairer far than you."

Then the Queen flew into the most awful passion, and turned every shade of green in her jealousy. From this hour she hated poor Snowdrop like poison, and every day her envy, hatred, and malice grew, for envy and jealousy are like evil weeds which spring up and choke the heart. At last she could endure Snowdrop's presence no longer, and, calling a huntsman to her, she said:

"Take the child out into the wood, and never let me see her face again. You must kill her, and bring me back her lungs and liver, that I may know for certain she is dead."

The Huntsman did as he was told and led Snowdrop out into the wood, but as he was in the act of drawing out his knife to slay her, she began to cry, and said:

"Oh, dear Huntsman, spare my life, and I will promise to fly forth into the wide wood and never to return home again."

And because she was so young and pretty the Huntsman had pity on her, and said:

"Well, run along, poor child." For he thought to himself: "The wild beasts will soon eat her up."

And his heart felt lighter because he hadn't had to do the deed himself. And as he turned away a young boar came running past, so he shot it, and brought its lungs and liver home to the Queen as a proof that Snowdrop was really dead. And the wicked woman had them stewed in salt, and ate them up, thinking she had made an end of Snowdrop forever.

Now when the poor child found herself alone in the big wood the very trees around her seemed to assume strange shapes, and she felt so frightened she didn't know what to do. Then she began to run over the sharp stones, and through the bramble bushes, and the wild beasts ran past her, but they did her no harm. She ran as far as her legs would carry her, and as evening approached she saw a little house, and she stepped inside to rest. Everything was very small in the little house, but cleaner and neater than anything you can imagine. In the middle of the room there stood a little table, covered with a white tablecloth, and seven little plates and forks and spoons and knives and tumblers. Side by side against the wall there were seven

little beds, covered with snow-white counterpanes. Snowdrop felt so hungry and so thirsty that she ate a bit of bread and a little porridge from each plate, and drank a drop of wine out of each tumbler. Then feeling tired and sleepy she lay down on one of the beds, but it wasn't comfortable; then she tried all the others in turn, but one was too long, and another too short, and it was only when she got to the seventh that she found one to suit her exactly. So she lay down upon it, said her prayers like a good child, and fell fast asleep.

When it got quite dark the masters of the little house returned. They were seven dwarfs who worked in the mines, right down deep in the heart of the mountain. They lighted their seven little lamps, and as soon as their eyes got accustomed to the glare they saw that someone had been in the room, for all was not in the same order as they had left it.

The first said:

"Who's been sitting on my little chair?"

The second said:

"Who's been eating my little loaf?"

The third said:

"Who's been tasting my porridge?"

The fourth said:

"Who's been eating out of my little plate?"

The fifth said:

"Who's been using my little fork?"

The sixth said:

"Who's been cutting with my little knife?"

The seventh said:

"Who's been drinking out of my little tumbler?"

Then the first Dwarf looked round and saw a little hollow in his bed, and he asked again:

"Who's been lying on my bed?"

The others came running round, and cried when they saw their beds:

"Somebody has lain on ours too."

But when the seventh came to his bed, he started back in amazement, for there he beheld Snowdrop fast asleep. Then he called the others, who turned their little lamps full on the bed, and when they saw Snowdrop lying there they nearly fell down with surprise.

"Goodness gracious!" they cried, "what a beautiful child!"

And they were so enchanted by her beauty that they did not wake her, but let her sleep on in the little bed. But the seventh Dwarf slept with his companions one hour in each bed, and in this way he managed to pass the night.

In the morning Snowdrop awoke, but when she saw the seven little Dwarfs she felt very frightened. But they were so friendly and asked her what her name was in such a kind way, that she replied:

"I am Snowdrop."

"Why did you come to our house?" continued the Dwarfs.

Then she told them how her stepmother had wished her put to death, and how the Huntsman had spared her life, and how she had run the whole day till she had come to their little house. The Dwarfs, when they had heard her sad story, asked her:

"Will you stay and keep house for us, cook, make the beds, do the washing, sew and knit? and if you give satisfaction and keep everything neat and clean, you shall want for nothing."

"Yes," answered Snowdrop, "I will gladly do all you ask."

And so she took up her abode with them. Every morning the Dwarfs went into the mountain to dig for gold, and in the evening, when they returned home, Snowdrop always had their supper ready for them. But during the day the girl was left quite alone, so the good Dwarfs warned her, saying:

"Beware of your stepmother. She will soon find out you are here, and whatever you do don't let anyone into the house."

Now the Queen, after she thought she had eaten Snowdrop's lungs and liver, never dreamed but that she was once more the most beautiful woman in the world; so stepping before her mirror one day she said:

"Mirror, mirror, hanging there,
Who in all the land's most fair?"

and the mirror replied:

> "My Lady Queen, you are fair, 'tis true,
> But Snowdrop is fairer far than you.
> Snowdrop, who dwells with the seven little men,
> Is as fair as you, as fair again."

When the Queen heard these words she was nearly struck dumb with horror, for the mirror always spoke the truth, and she knew now that the Huntsman must have deceived her, and that Snowdrop was still alive. She pondered day and night how she might destroy her, for as long as she felt she had a rival in the land her jealous heart left her no rest. At last she hit upon a plan. She stained her face and dressed herself up as an old peddler wife, so that she was quite unrecognizable. In this guise she went over the seven hills till she came to the house of the seven Dwarfs. There she knocked at the door, calling out at the same time:

"Fine wares to sell, fine wares to sell!"

Snowdrop peeped out of the window, and called out:

"Good-day, mother, what have you to sell?"

"Good wares, fine wares," she answered; "laces of every shade and description," and she held one up that was made of some gay colored silk.

"Surely I can let the honest woman in," thought Snowdrop; so she unbarred the door and bought the pretty lace.

"Good gracious! child," said the old woman, "what a figure you've got. Come! I'll lace you up properly for once."

Snowdrop, suspecting no evil, stood before her and let her lace her bodice up, but the old woman laced her so quickly and so tightly that it took Snowdrop's breath away, and she fell down dead.

"Now you are no longer the fairest," said the wicked old woman, and then she hastened away.

In the evening the seven Dwarfs came home, and you may think what a fright they got when they saw their dear Snowdrop lying on the floor, as still and motionless as a dead person. They lifted her up tenderly, and when they saw how tightly laced she was they cut the lace in two, and she began to breathe a little and gradually came back to life. When the Dwarfs heard what had happened, they said:

"Depend upon it, the old peddler wife was none other than the old Queen. In future you must be sure to let no one in, if we are not at home."

As soon as the wicked old Queen got home she went straight to her mirror, and said:

> "Mirror, mirror, hanging there,
> Who in all the land's most fair?"

and the mirror answered as before:

> "My Lady Queen, you are fair, 'tis true,
> But Snowdrop is fairer far than you.
> Snowdrop, who dwells with the seven little men,
> Is as fair as you, as fair again."

When she heard this she became as pale as death, because she saw at once that Snowdrop must be alive again.

"This time," she said to herself, "I will think of something that will make an end of her once and for all."

And by the witchcraft which she understood so well she made a poisonous comb; then she dressed herself up and assumed the form of another old woman. So she went over the seven hills till she reached the house of the seven Dwarfs, and knocking at the door she called out:

"Fine wares for sale."

Snowdrop looked out of the window and said:

"You must go away, for I may not let anyone in."

"But surely you are not forbidden to look out?" said the old woman, and she held up the poisonous comb for her to see.

It pleased the girl so much that she let herself be taken in, and opened the door. When they had settled their bargain the old woman said:

"Now I'll comb your hair properly for you, for once in the way."

Poor Snowdrop thought no evil, but hardly had the comb touched her hair than the poison worked and she fell down unconscious.

"Now, my fine lady, you're really done for this time," said the wicked woman, and she made her way home as fast as she could.

Fortunately it was now near evening, and the seven Dwarfs returned home. When they saw Snowdrop lying dead on the ground, they at once suspected that her wicked stepmother had been at work again; so they searched till they found the poisonous comb, and the moment they pulled it out of her head Snowdrop came to herself again, and told them what had happened. Then they warned her once more to be on her guard, and to open the door to no one.

As soon as the Queen got home she went straight to her mirror, and asked:

> "Mirror, mirror, hanging there,
> Who in all the land's most fair?"

and it replied as before:

> "My Lady Queen, you are fair, 'tis true,
> But Snowdrop is fairer far than you.
> Snowdrop, who dwells with the seven little men,
> Is as fair as you, as fair again."

When she heard these words she literally trembled and shook with rage.

"Snowdrop shall die," she cried; "yes, though it cost me my own life."

Then she went to a little secret chamber, which no one knew of but herself, and there she made a poisonous apple. Outwardly it looked beautiful, white with red cheeks, so that everyone who saw it longed to eat it, but anyone who might do so would certainly die on the spot. When the apple was quite finished she stained her face and dressed herself up as a peasant, and so she went over the seven hills to the seven Dwarfs'. She knocked at the door, as usual, but Snowdrop put her head out of the window and called out:

"I may not let anyone in, the seven Dwarfs have forbidden me to do so."

"Are you afraid of being poisoned?" asked the old woman. "See, I will cut this apple in half. I'll eat the white cheek and you can eat the red."

But the apple was so cunningly made that only the red cheek was poisonous. Snowdrop longed to eat the tempting fruit, and when she saw that the peasant woman was eating it herself, she couldn't resist the temptation any longer, and stretching out her hand she took the poisonous half. But hardly had the first bite passed her lips than she fell down dead on the ground. Then the eyes of the cruel Queen sparkled with glee, and laughing aloud she cried:

"As white as snow, as red as blood, and as black as ebony, this time the Dwarfs won't be able to bring you back to life."

When she got home she asked the mirror:

"Mirror, mirror, hanging there,
Who in all the land's most fair?"

and this time it replied:

"You are most fair, my Lady Queen,
None fairer in the land, I ween."

Then her jealous heart was at rest—at least, as much at rest as a jealous heart can ever be.

When the little Dwarfs came home in the evening they found Snowdrop lying on the ground, and she neither breathed nor stirred. They lifted her up, and looked round everywhere to see if they could find anything poisonous about. They unlaced her bodice, combed her hair, washed her with water and wine, but all in vain; the child was dead and remained dead. Then they placed her on a bier, and all the seven Dwarfs sat round it, weeping and sobbing for three whole days. At last they made up their minds to bury her, but she looked as blooming as a living being, and her cheeks were still such a lovely color, that they said:

"We can't hide her away in the black ground."

So they had a coffin made of transparent glass, and they laid her in it, and wrote on the lid in golden letters that she was a royal Princess. Then they put the coffin on the top of the mountain, and one of the Dwarfs always remained beside it and kept watch over it. And the very birds of the air came and bewailed Snowdrop's death, first an owl, and then a raven, and last of all a little dove.

Snowdrop lay a long time in the coffin, and she always looked the same, just as if she were fast asleep, and she remained as white as snow, as red as blood, and her hair as black as ebony.

Now it happened one day that a Prince came to the wood and passed by the Dwarfs' house. He saw the coffin on the hill, with the beautiful Snowdrop inside it, and when he had read what was written on it in golden letters, he said to the Dwarf:

"Give me the coffin. I'll give you whatever you like for it."

But the Dwarf said: "No; we wouldn't part with it for all the gold in the world."

"Well, then," he replied, "give it to me, because I can't live without Snowdrop. I will cherish and love it as my dearest possession."

He spoke so sadly that the good Dwarfs had pity on him, and gave him the coffin, and the Prince made his servants bear it away on their shoulders. Now it happened that as they were going down the

hill they stumbled over a bush, and jolted the coffin so violently that
the poisonous bit of apple Snowdrop had swallowed fell out of her
throat. She gradually opened her eyes, lifted up the lid of the coffin,
and sat up alive and well.

"Oh! dear me, where am I?" she cried.

The Prince answered joyfully, "You are with me," and he told her
all that had happened, adding, "I love you better than anyone in the
whole wide world. Will you come with me to my father's palace and
be my wife?"

Snowdrop consented, and went with him, and the marriage was
celebrated with great pomp and splendor.

Now Snowdrop's wicked stepmother was one of the guests invited to the wedding feast. When she had dressed herself very gorgeously for the occasion, she went to the mirror, and said:

> "Mirror, mirror, hanging there,
> Who in all the land's most fair?"

and the mirror answered:

> "My Lady Queen, you are fair, 'tis true,
> But Snowdrop is fairer far than you."

When the wicked woman heard these words she uttered a curse, and was beside herself with rage and mortification. At first she didn't want to go to the wedding at all, but at the same time she felt she would never be happy till she had seen the young Queen. As she entered Snowdrop recognized her, and nearly fainted with fear; but red-hot iron shoes had been prepared for the wicked old Queen, and she was made to get into them and dance till she fell down dead.

THE BROTHERS GRIMM

RAPUNZEL

ONCE UPON a time there lived a man and his wife who were very unhappy because they had no children. These good people had a little window at the back of their house, which looked into the most lovely garden, full of all manner of beautiful flowers and vegetables; but the garden was surrounded by a high wall, and no one dared to enter it, for it belonged to a witch of great power, who was feared by the whole world. One day the woman stood at the window over-looking the garden, and saw there a bed full of the finest rampion: the leaves looked so fresh and green that she longed to eat them. The desire grew day by day, and just because she knew she couldn't possibly get any, she pined away and became quite pale and wretched. Then her husband grew alarmed and said:

"What ails you, dear wife?"

"Oh," she answered, "if I don't get some rampion to eat out of the garden behind the house, I know I shall die."

The man, who loved her dearly, thought to himself, "Come! rather than let your wife die you shall fetch her some rampion, no matter the cost." So at dusk he climbed over the wall into the witch's garden, and, hastily gathering a handful of rampion leaves, he returned with them to his wife. She made them into a salad, which tasted so good that her longing for the forbidden food was greater than ever. If she were to know any peace of mind, there was nothing for it but that her husband should climb over the garden wall again, and fetch her some more. So at dusk over he got, but when he reached the other side he drew back in terror, for there, standing before him, was the old witch.

"How dare you," she said, with a wrathful glance, "climb into my garden and steal my rampion like a common thief? You shall suffer for your foolhardiness."

"Oh!" he implored, "pardon my presumption; necessity alone

40

drove me to the deed. My wife saw your rampion from her window, and conceived such a desire for it that she would certainly have died if her wish had not been gratified." Then the Witch's anger was a little appeased, and she said:

"If it's as you say, you may take as much rampion away with you as you like, but on one condition only—that you give me the child your wife will shortly bring into the world. All shall go well with it, and I will look after it like a mother."

The man in his terror agreed to everything she asked, and as soon as the child was born the Witch appeared, and having given it the name of Rapunzel, which is the same as rampion, she carried it off with her.

Rapunzel was the most beautiful child under the sun. When she was twelve years old the Witch shut her up in a tower, in the middle of a great wood, and the tower had neither stairs nor doors, only high up at the very top a small window. When the old Witch wanted to get in she stood underneath and called out:

> "Rapunzel, Rapunzel,
> Let down your golden hair,"

for Rapunzel had wonderful long hair, and it was as fine as spun gold. Whenever she heard the Witch's voice she unloosed her plaits, and let her hair fall down out of the window about twenty yards below, and the old Witch climbed up by it.

After they had lived like this for a few years, it happened one day that a Prince was riding through the wood and passed by the tower. As he drew near it he heard someone singing so sweetly that he stood still spell-bound, and listened. It was Rapunzel in her loneliness trying to while away the time by letting her sweet voice ring out into the wood. The Prince longed to see the owner of the voice, but he sought in vain for a door in the tower. He rode home, but he was so haunted by the song he had heard that he returned every day to the wood and listened. One day, when he was standing thus behind a tree, he saw the old Witch approach and heard her call out:

> "Rapunzel, Rapunzel,
> Let down your golden hair."

Then Rapunzel let down her plaits, and the Witch climbed up by them.

"So that's the staircase, is it?" said the Prince. "Then I too will climb it and try my luck."

So on the following day, at dusk, he went to the foot of the tower and cried:

"Rapunzel, Rapunzel,
Let down your golden hair,"

and as soon as she had let it down the Prince climbed up.

At first Rapunzel was terribly frightened when a man came in, for she had never seen one before; but the Prince spoke to her so kindly, and told her at once that his heart had been so touched by her singing, that he felt he should know no peace of mind till he had seen her. Very soon Rapunzel forgot her fear, and when he asked her to marry him she consented at once. "For," she thought, "he is young and handsome, and I'll certainly be happier with him than with the old Witch." So she put her hand in his and said:

"Yes, I will gladly go with you, only how am I to get down out of the tower? Every time you come to see me you must bring a skein of silk with you, and I will make a ladder of them, and when it is finished I will climb down by it, and you will take me away on your horse."

They arranged that till the ladder was ready, he was to come to her every evening, because the old woman was with her during the day. The old Witch, of course, knew nothing of what was going on, till one day Rapunzel, not thinking of what she was about, turned to the Witch and said:

"How is it, good mother, that you are so much harder to pull up than the young Prince? He is always with me in a moment."

"Oh! you wicked child," cried the Witch. "What is this I hear? I thought I had hidden you safely from the whole world, and in spite of it you have managed to deceive me."

In her wrath she seized Rapunzel's beautiful hair, wound it round and round her left hand, and then grasping a pair of scissors in her right, snip snap, off it came, and the beautiful plaits lay on the ground. And, worse than this, she was so hard-hearted that she took Rapunzel to a lonely desert place, and there left her to live in loneliness and misery.

But on the evening of the day in which she had driven poor Rapunzel away, the Witch fastened the plaits on to a hook in the window, and when the Prince came and called out:

"Rapunzel, Rapunzel,
Let down your golden hair,"

she let them down, and the Prince climbed up as usual, but instead of his beloved Rapunzel he found the old Witch, who fixed her evil, glittering eyes on him, and cried mockingly:

"Ah, ah! you thought to find your lady love, but the pretty bird has flown and its song is dumb; the cat caught it, and will scratch out your eyes too. Rapunzel is lost to you forever—you will never see her more."

The Prince was beside himself with grief, and in his despair he jumped right down from the tower, and, though he escaped with his life, the thorns among which he fell pierced his eyes out. Then he wandered, blind and miserable, through the wood, eating nothing but roots and berries, and weeping and lamenting the loss of his lovely bride. So he wandered about for some years, as wretched and unhappy as he could well be, and at last he came to the desert place where Rapunzel was living. Of a sudden he heard a voice which seemed strangely familiar to him. He walked eagerly in the direction of the sound, and when he was quite close, Rapunzel recognized him and fell on his neck and wept. But two of her tears touched his eyes, and in a moment they became quite clear again, and he saw as well as he had ever done. Then he led her to his kingdom, where they were received and welcomed with great joy, and they lived happily ever after.

THE BROTHERS GRIMM

RUMPELSTILTZKIN

THERE WAS once upon a time a poor miller who had a very beautiful daughter. Now it happened one day that he had an audience with the King, and in order to appear a person of some importance he told him that he had a daughter who could spin straw into gold. "Now that's a talent worth having," said the King to the miller; "if your daughter is as clever as you say, bring her to my palace tomorrow, and I'll put her to the test." When the girl was brought to him he led her into a room full of straw, gave her a spinning-wheel and spindle, and said: "Now set to work and spin all night till early dawn, and if by that time you haven't spun the straw into gold you shall die." Then he closed the door behind him and left her alone inside.

So the poor miller's daughter sat down, and didn't know what in the world she was to do. She hadn't the least idea of how to spin straw into gold, and became at last so miserable that she began to cry. Suddenly the door opened, and in stepped a tiny little man and said: "Good-evening, Miss Miller-maid; why are you crying so bitterly?" "Oh!" answered the girl, "I have to spin straw into gold, and haven't a notion how it's done." "What will you give me if I spin it for you?" asked the manikin. "My necklace," replied the girl. The little man took the necklace, sat himself down at the wheel, and whir, whir, whir, the wheel went round three times, and the bobbin was full. Then he put on another, and whir, whir, whir, the wheel went round three times, and the second too was full; and so it went on till the morning, when all the straw was spun away, and all the bobbins were full of gold. As soon as the sun rose the King came, and when he perceived the gold he was astonished and delighted, but his heart only lusted more than ever after the precious metal. He had the miller's daughter put into another room full of straw, much bigger than the first, and bade her, if she valued her life, spin it all into gold before the following morning. The girl didn't know what

to do, and began to cry; then the door opened as before, and the tiny
little man appeared and said: "What'll you give me if I spin the straw
into gold for you?" "The ring from my finger," answered the girl.
The manikin took the ring, and whir! round went the spinning-wheel
again, and when morning broke he had spun all the straw into glittering gold. The King was pleased beyond measure at the sights but
his greed for gold was still not satisfied, and he had the miller's
daughter brought into a yet bigger room full of straw, and said: "You

must spin all this away in the night; but if you succeed this time you shall become my wife." "She's only a miller's daughter, it's true," he thought; "but I couldn't find a richer wife if I were to search the whole world over." When the girl was alone the little man appeared for the third time, and said: "What'll you give me if I spin the straw for you once again?" "I've nothing more to give," answered the girl. "Then promise me when you are Queen to give me your first child." "Who knows what may not happen before that?" thought the miller's daughter; and besides, she saw no other way out of it, so she promised the manikin what he demanded, and he set to work once more and spun the straw into gold. When the King came in the morning, and found everything as he had desired, he straightway made her his wife, and the miller's daughter became a queen.

When a year had passed a beautiful son was born to her, and she thought no more of the little man, till all of a sudden one day he stepped into her room and said: "Now give me what you promised." The Queen was in a great state, and offered the little man all the riches in her kingdom if he would only leave her the child. But the manikin said: "No, a living creature is dearer to me than all the treasures in the world." Then the Queen began to cry and sob so bitterly that the little man was sorry for her, and said: "I'll give you three days to guess my name, and if you find it out in that time you may keep your child."

Then the Queen pondered the whole night over all the names she had ever heard, and sent a messenger to scour the land, and to pick up far and near any names he should come across. When the little man arrived on the following day she began with Kasper, Melchior, Belshazzar, and all the other names she knew, in a string, but at each one the manikin called out: "that's not my name." The next day she sent to inquire the names of all the people in the neighborhood, and had a long list of the most uncommon and extraordinary for the little man when he made his appearance. "Is your name, perhaps, Sheepshanks Cruickshanks, Spindleshanks?" but he always replied: "That's not my name." On the third day the messenger returned and announced: "I have not been able to find any new names, but as I came upon a high hill round the corner of the wood, where the foxes and hares bid each other good-night, I saw a little house, and in front of the house burned a fire, and round the fire sprang the most grotesque little man, hopping on one leg and crying:

> "Tomorrow I brew, today I bake,
> And then the child away I'll take;

For little deems my royal dame
That Rumpelstiltzkin is my name!"

You can imagine the Queen's delight at hearing the name, and when the little man stepped in shortly afterward and asked: "Now, my lady Queen, what's my name?" she asked first: "Is your name Conrad?" "No." "Is your name Harry?" "No." "Is your name perhaps, Rumpelstiltzkin?" "Some demon has told you that, some demon has told you that," screamed the little man, and in his rage drove his right foot so far into the ground that it sank in up to his waist; then in a passion he seized the left foot with both hands and tore himself in two.

THE BROTHERS GRIMM

HOW TO TELL A TRUE PRINCESS

(The Princess and the Pea)

THERE WAS once upon a time a Prince who wanted to marry a Princess, but she must be a true Princess. So he traveled through the whole world to find one, but there was always something against each. There were plenty of Princesses, but he could not find out if they were true Princesses. In every case there was some little defect, which showed the genuine article was not yet found. So he came home again in very low spirits, for he had wanted very much to have a true Princess. One night there was a dreadful storm; it thundered and lightened and the rain streamed down in torrents. It was fearful! There was a knocking heard at the Palace gate, and the old King went to open it.

There stood a Princess outside the gate; but oh, in what a sad plight she was from the rain and the storm! The water was running down from her hair and her dress into the points of her shoes and out at the heels again. And yet she said she was a true Princess!

"Well, we shall soon find that!" thought the old Queen. But she said nothing, and went into the sleeping-room, took off all the bed-clothes, and laid a pea on the bottom of the bed. Then she put twenty mattresses on top of the pea, and twenty eider-down quilts on the top of the mattresses. And this was the bed in which the Princess was to sleep.

The next morning she was asked how she had slept.

"Oh, very badly!" said the Princess. "I scarcely closed my eyes all night! I am sure I don't know what was in the bed. I laid on something so hard that my whole body is black and blue. It is dreadful!"

Now they perceived that she was a true Princess, because she had felt the pea through the twenty mattresses and the twenty eider-down quilts.

A · TRUE · PRINCESS

No one but a true Princess could be so sensitive.

So the Prince married her, for now he knew that at last he had got hold of a true Princess. And the pea was put into the Royal Museum, where it is still to be seen if no one has stolen it. Now this is a true story.

HANS CHRISTIAN ANDERSEN

THE TWELVE DANCING PRINCESSES

I

Once upon a time there lived in the village of Montignies-sur-Roc a little cowboy, without either father or mother. His real name was Michael, but he was always called the Star Gazer, because when he drove his cows over the commons to seek for pasture, he went along with his head in the air, gaping at nothing.

As he had a white skin, blue eyes, and hair that curled all over his head, the village girls used to cry after him, "Well, Star Gazer, what are you doing?" and Michael would answer, "Oh, nothing," and go on his way without even turning to look at them.

The fact was he thought them very ugly, with their sunburnt necks, their great red hands, their coarse petticoats and their wooden shoes. He had heard that somewhere in the world there were girls whose necks were white and whose hands were small, who were always dressed in the finest silks and laces, and were called princesses, and while his companions round the fire saw nothing in the flames but common everyday fancies, he dreamed that he had the happiness to marry a princess.

II

One morning about the middle of August, just at mid-day when the sun was hottest, Michael ate his dinner of a piece of dry bread, and went to sleep under an oak. And while he slept he dreamt that there appeared before him a beautiful lady, dressed in a robe of cloth of gold, who said to him: "Go to the castle of Belœil, and there you shall marry a princess."

That evening the little cowboy, who had been thinking a great deal about the advice of the lady in the golden dress, told his dream to the farm people. But, as was natural, they only laughed at the Star Gazer.

The next day at the same hour he went to sleep again under the same tree. The lady appeared to him a second time, and said: "Go to the castle of Belœil, and you shall marry a princess."

In the evening Michael told his friends that he had dreamed the same dream again, but they only laughed at him more than before. "Never mind," he thought to himself; "if the lady appears to me a third time, I will do as she tells me."

The following day, to the great astonishment of all the village, about two o'clock in the afternoon a voice was heard singing:

> "Raleô, raleô,
> How the cattle go!"

It was the little cowboy driving his herd back to the byre.

The farmer began to scold him furiously, but he answered quietly, "I am going away," made his clothes into a bundle, said good-bye to all his friends, and boldly set out to seek his fortunes.

There was great excitement through all the village, and on the top of the hill the people stood holding their sides with laughing, as they watched the Star Gazer trudging bravely along the valley with his bundle at the end of his stick.

It was enough to make anyone laugh, certainly.

III

It was well known for full twenty miles round that there lived in the castle of Belœil twelve princesses of wonderful beauty, and as proud as they were beautiful, and who were besides so very sensitive and of such truly royal blood, that they would have felt at once the presence of a pea in their beds, even if the mattresses had been laid over it.

It was whispered about that they led exactly the lives that princesses ought to lead, sleeping far into the morning, and never getting up till mid-day. They had twelve beds all in the same room, but what was very extraordinary was the fact that though they were locked in by triple bolts, every morning their satin shoes were found worn into holes.

When they were asked what they had been doing all night, they always answered that they had been asleep; and, indeed, no noise was ever heard in the room, yet the shoes could not wear themselves out alone!

At last the Duke of Belœil ordered the trumpet to be sounded, and a proclamation to be made that whoever could discover how his daughters wore out their shoes should choose one of them for his wife.

On hearing the proclamation a number of princes arrived at the castle to try their luck. They watched all night behind the open door of the princesses, but when the morning came they had all disappeared, and no one could tell what had become of them.

IV

When he reached the castle, Michael went straight to the gardener and offered his services. Now it happened that the garden boy had just been sent away, and though the Star Gazer did not look very sturdy, the gardener agreed to take him, as he thought that his pretty face and golden curls would please the princesses.

The first thing he was told was that when the princesses got up he was to present each one with a bouquet, and Michael thought that if he had nothing more unpleasant to do than that he should get on very well.

Accordingly he placed himself behind the door of the princesses' room, with the twelve bouquets in a basket. He gave one to each of the sisters, and they took them without even deigning to look at the lad, except Lina the youngest, who fixed her large black eyes as soft as velvet on him, and exclaimed, "Oh, how pretty he is—our new flower boy!" The rest all burst out laughing, and the eldest pointed out that a princess ought never to lower herself by looking at a garden boy.

Now Michael knew quite well what had happened to all the princes, but notwithstanding, the beautiful eyes of the Princess Lina inspired him with a violent longing to try his fate. Unhappily he did not dare to come forward, being afraid that he should only be jeered at, or even turned away from the castle on account of his impudence.

V

Nevertheless, the Star Gazer had another dream. The lady in the golden dress appeared to him once more, holding in one hand two young laurel trees, a cherry laurel and a rose laurel, and in the other hand a little golden rake, a little golden bucket, and a silken towel. She thus addressed him:

"Plant these two laurels in two large pots, rake them over with the rake, water them with the bucket, and wipe them with the towel. When they have grown as tall as a girl of fifteen, say to each of them, 'My beautiful laurel, with the golden rake I have raked you,

with the golden bucket I have watered you, with the silken towel I have wiped you.' " Then after that ask anything you choose, and the laurels will give it to you."

Michael thanked the lady in the golden dress, and when he woke he found the two laurel bushes beside him. So he carefully obeyed the orders he had been given by the lady.

The trees grew very fast, and when they were as tall as a girl of fifteen he said to the cherry laurel, "My lovely cherry laurel, with the golden rake I have raked thee, with the golden bucket I have watered thee, with the silken towel I have wiped thee. Teach me how to become invisible." Then there instantly appeared on the laurel a pretty white flower, which Michael gathered and stuck into his button-hole.

VI

That evening, when the princesses went upstairs to bed, he followed them barefoot, so that he might make no noise, and hid himself under one of the twelve beds, so as not to take up much room.

The princesses began at once to open their wardrobes and boxes. They took out of them the most magnificent dresses, which they put on before their mirrors, and when they had finished, turned themselves all round to admire their appearances.

Michael could see nothing from his hiding-place, but he could hear everything, and he listened to the princesses laughing and jumping with pleasure. At last the eldest said, "Be quick, my sisters, our partners will be impatient." At the end of an hour, when the Star Gazer heard no more noise, he peeped out and saw the twelve sisters in splendid garments, with their satin shoes on their feet, and in their hands the bouquets he had brought them.

"Are you ready?" asked the eldest.

"Yes," replied the other eleven in chorus, and they took their places one by one behind her.

Then the eldest Princess clapped her hands three times and a trap door opened. All the princesses disappeared down a secret staircase, and Michael hastily followed them.

As he was following on the steps of the Princess Lina, he carelessly trod on her dress.

"There is somebody behind me," cried the Princess; "they are holding my dress."

"You foolish thing," said her eldest sister, "you are always afraid of something. It is only a nail which caught you."

VII

They went down, down, down, till at last they came to a passage with a door at one end, which was only fastened with a latch. The eldest Princess opened it, and they found themselves immediately in a lovely little wood, where the leaves were spangled with drops of silver which shone in the brilliant light of the moon.

They next crossed another wood where the leaves were sprinkled with gold, and after that another still, where the leaves glittered with diamonds.

At last the Star Gazer perceived a large lake, and on the shores of the lake twelve little boats with awnings, in which were seated twelve princes, who, grasping their oars, awaited the princesses.

Each princess entered one of the boats, and Michael slipped into that which held the youngest. The boats glided along rapidly, but Lina's, from being heavier, was always behind the rest. "We never went so slowly before," said the Princess; "what can be the reason?"

"I don't know," answered the Prince. "I assure you I am rowing as hard as I can."

On the other side of the lake the garden boy saw a beautiful castle splendidly illuminated, whence came the lively music of fiddles, kettle-drums, and trumpets.

In a moment they touched land, and the company jumped out of the boats; and the princes, after having securely fastened their barques, gave their arms to the princesses and conducted them to the castle.

VIII

Michael followed, and entered the ball-room in their train. Everywhere were mirrors, lights, flowers, and damask hangings.

The Star Gazer was quite bewildered at the magnificence of the sight.

He placed himself out of the way in a corner, admiring the grace and beauty of the princesses. Their loveliness was of every kind. Some were fair and some were dark; some had chestnut hair, or curls darker still, and some had golden locks. Never were so many beautiful princesses seen together at one time, but the one whom the cowboy thought the most beautiful and the most fascinating was the little Princess with the velvet eyes.

With what eagerness she danced! leaning on her partner's shoulder she swept by like a whirlwind. Her cheeks flushed, her eyes sparkled, and it was plain that she loved dancing better than anything else.

The poor boy envied those handsome young men with whom she danced so gracefully, but he did not know how little reason he had to be jealous of them.

The young men were really the princes who, to the number of fifty at least, had tried to steal the princesses' secret. The princesses had made them drink something of a philter, which froze the heart and left nothing but the love of dancing.

IX

They danced on till the shoes of the princesses were worn into holes. When the cock crowed the third time the fiddles stopped, and a delicious supper was served by negro boys, consisting of sugared orange flowers, crystallized rose leaves, powdered violets, cracknels, wafers, and other dishes, which are, as everyone knows, the favorite food of princesses.

After supper, the dancers all went back to their boats, and this time the Star Gazer entered that of the eldest Princess. They crossed again the wood with the diamond-spangled leaves, the wood with gold-sprinkled leaves, and the wood whose leaves glittered with drops of silver, and as a proof of what he had seen, the boy broke a small branch from a tree in the last wood. Lina turned as she heard the noise made by the breaking of the branch.

"What was that noise?" she said.

"It was nothing," replied her eldest sister; "it was only the screech of the barn-owl that roosts in one of the turrets of the castle."

While she was speaking Michael managed to slip in front, and running up the staircase, he reached the princesses' room first. He flung open the window, and sliding down the vine which climbed up the wall, found himself in the garden just as the sun was beginning to rise, and it was time for him to set to his work.

X

That day, when he made up the bouquets, Michael hid the branch with the silver drops in the nosegay intended for the youngest Princess.

When Lina discovered it she was much surprised. However, she said nothing to her sisters, but as she met the boy by accident while she was walking under the shade of the elms, she suddenly stopped as if to speak to him; then, altering her mind, went on her way.

The same evening the twelve sisters went again to the ball, and the Star Gazer again followed them and crossed the lake in Lina's boat. This time it was the Prince who complained that the boat seemed very heavy.

"It is the heat," replied the Princess. "I, too, have been feeling very warm."

During the ball she looked everywhere for the gardener's boy, but she never saw him.

As they came back, Michael gathered a branch from the wood with the gold-spangled leaves, and now it was the eldest Princess who heard the noise that it made in breaking.

"It is nothing," said Lina; "only the cry of the owl which roosts in the turrets of the castle."

XI

As soon as she got up she found the branch in her bouquet. When the sisters went down she stayed a little behind and said to the cowboy: "Where does this branch come from?"

"Your Royal Highness knows well enough," answered Michael.

"So you have followed us?"

"Yes, Princess."

"How did you manage it? we never saw you."

"I hid myself," replied the Star Gazer quietly.

The Princess was silent a moment, and then said:

"You know our secret!—keep it. Here is the reward of your discretion." And she flung the boy a purse of gold.

"I do not sell my silence," answered Michael, and he went away without picking up the purse.

For three nights Lina neither saw nor heard anything extraordinary; on the fourth she heard a rustling among the diamond-spangled leaves of the wood. That day there was a branch of the trees in her bouquet.

She took the Star Gazer aside, and said to him in a harsh voice:

"You know what price my father has promised to pay for our secret?"

"I know, Princess," answered Michael.

"Don't you mean to tell him?"

"That is not my intention."

"Are you afraid?"

"No, Princess."

"What makes you so discreet, then?"

But Michael was silent.

XII

Lina's sisters had seen her talking to the little garden boy, and jeered at her for it.

"What prevents your marrying him?" asked the eldest, "you would become a gardener too; it is a charming profession. You could live in a cottage at the end of the park, and help your husband to draw up water from the well, and when we get up you could bring us our bouquets."

The Princess Lina was very angry, and when the Star Gazer presented her bouquet, she received it in a disdainful manner.

Michael behaved most respectfully. He never raised his eyes to her, but nearly all day she felt him at her side without ever seeing him.

One day she made up her mind to tell everything to her eldest sister.

"What!" said she, "this rogue knows our secret, and you never told me! I must lose no time in getting rid of him."

"But how?"

"Why, by having him taken to the tower with the dungeons, of course."

For this was the way that in old times beautiful princesses got rid of people who knew too much.

But the astonishing part of it was that the youngest sister did not seem at all to relish this method of stopping the mouth of the gardener's boy, who, after all, had said nothing to their father.

XIII

It was agreed that the question should be submitted to the other ten sisters. All were on the side of the eldest. Then the youngest sister declared that if they laid a finger on the little garden boy, she would herself go and tell their father the secret of the holes in their shoes.

At last it was decided that Michael should be put to the test; that they would take him to the ball, and at the end of supper would give him the philter which was to enchant him like the rest.

They sent for the Star Gazer, and asked him how he had contrived to learn their secret; but still he remained silent.

Then, in commanding tones, the eldest sister gave him the order they had agreed upon.

He only answered:

"I will obey."

He had really been present, invisible, at the council of princesses, and had heard all; but he had made up his mind to drink of the philter, and sacrifice himself to the happiness of her he loved.

Not wishing, however, to cut a poor figure at the ball by the side of the other dancers, he went at once to the laurels, and said:

"My lovely rose laurel, with the golden rake I have raked thee, with the golden bucket I have watered thee, with a silken towel I have dried thee. Dress me like a prince."

A beautiful pink flower appeared. Michael gathered it, and found himself in a moment clothed in velvet, which was as black as the eyes of the little Princess, with a cap to match, a diamond aigrette, and a blossom of the rose laurel in his button-hole.

Thus dressed, he presented himself that evening before the Duke of Belœil, and obtained leave to try and discover his daughters' secret. He looked so distinguished that hardly anyone would have known who he was.

XIV

The twelve princesses went upstairs to bed. Michael followed them, and waited behind the open door till they gave the signal for departure.

This time he did not cross in Lina's boat. He gave his arm to the eldest sister, danced with each in turn, and was so graceful that everyone was delighted with him. At last the time came for him to dance with the little Princess. She found him the best partner in the world, but he did not dare to speak a single word to her.

When he was taking her back to her place she said to him in a mocking voice:

"Here you are at the summit of your wishes: you are being treated like a prince."

"Don't be afraid," replied the Star Gazer gently. "You shall never be a gardener's wife."

The little Princess stared at him with a frightened face, and he left her without waiting for an answer.

When the satin slippers were worn through the fiddles stopped, and the negro boys set the table. Michael was placed next to the eldest sister, and opposite to the youngest.

They gave him the most exquisite dishes to eat, and the most delicate wines to drink; and in order to turn his head more completely, compliments and flattery were heaped on him from every side.

But he took care not to be intoxicated, either by the wine or the compliments.

XV

At last the eldest sister made a sign, and one of the black pages brought in a large golden cup.

"The enchanted castle has no more secrets for you," she said to the Star Gazer. "Let us drink to your triumph."

He cast a lingering glance at the little Princess, and without hesitation lifted the cup.

"Don't drink!" suddenly cried out the little Princess; "I would rather marry a gardener."

And she burst into tears.

Michael flung the contents of the cup behind him, sprang over the table, and fell at Lina's feet. The rest of the princes fell likewise at the knees of the princesses, each of whom chose a husband and raised him to her side. The charm was broken.

The twelve couples embarked in the boats, which crossed back many times in order to carry over the other princes. Then they all went through the three woods, and when they had passed the door of the underground passage a great noise was heard, as if the enchanted castle was crumbling to the earth.

They went straight to the room of the Duke of Belœil, who had just awoke. Michael held in his hand the golden cup, and he revealed the secret of the holes in the shoes.

"Choose, then," said the Duke, "whichever you prefer."

"My choice is already made," replied the garden boy, and he offered his hand to the youngest Princess, who blushed and lowered her eyes.

XVI

The Princess Lina did not become a gardener's wife; on the contrary, it was the Star Gazer who became a Prince: but before the

marriage ceremony the Princess insisted that her lover should tell her how he came to discover the secret.

So he showed her the two laurels which had helped him, and she, like a prudent girl, thinking they gave him too much advantage over his wife, cut them off at the root and threw them in the fire.

And this is why the country girls go about singing:

> Nous n'irons plus au bois,
> Les lauriers sont coupés,

and dancing in summer by the light of the moon.

THE BROTHERS GRIMM, RETOLD BY CHARLES DEULIN

LITTLE RED RIDING-HOOD

ONCE UPON a time there lived in a certain village a little country girl, the prettiest creature that was ever seen. Her mother was excessively fond of her; and her grandmother doted on her still more. This good woman had made for her a little red riding-hood; which became the girl so extremely well that everybody called her Little Red Riding-Hood.

One day her mother, having made some custards, said to her:

"Go, my dear, and see how thy grandmamma does, for I hear she has been very ill; carry her a custard, and this little pot of butter."

Little Red Riding-Hood set out immediately to go to her grandmother, who lived in another village.

As she was going through the wood, she met with Gaffer Wolf, who had a very great mind to eat her up, but he durst not, because of some faggot-makers hard by in the forest. He asked her whither she was going. The poor child, who did not know that it was dangerous to stay and hear a wolf talk, said to him:

"I am going to see my grandmamma and carry her a custard and a little pot of butter from my mamma."

"Does she live far off?" said the Wolf.

"Oh! ay," answered Little Red Riding-Hood; "it is beyond that mill you see there, at the first house in the village."

"Well," said the Wolf, "and I'll go and see her too. I'll go this way and you go that, and we shall see who will be there soonest."

The Wolf began to run as fast as he could, taking the nearest way, and the little girl went by that farthest about, diverting herself in gathering nuts, running after butterflies, and making nosegays of such little flowers as she met with. The Wolf was not long before he got to the old woman's house. He knocked at the door—tap, tap.

"Who's there?"

"Your grandchild, Little Red Riding-Hood," replied the Wolf,

counterfeiting her voice; "who has brought you a custard and a little pot of butter sent you by mamma."

The good grandmother, who was in bed, because she was somewhat ill, cried out:

"Pull the bobbin, and the latch will go up."

The Wolf pulled the bobbin, and the door opened, and then presently he fell upon the good woman and ate her up in a moment, for it was above three days that he had not touched a bit. He then shut the door and went into the grandmother's bed, expecting Little Red Riding-Hood, who came some time afterward and knocked at the door—tap, tap.

"Who's there?"

Little Red Riding-Hood, hearing the big voice of the Wolf, was at first afraid; but believing her grandmother had got a cold and was hoarse, answered:

"'Tis your grandchild, Little Red Riding-Hood, who has brought you a custard and a little pot of butter mamma sends you."

The Wolf cried out to her, softening his voice as much as he could:

"Pull the bobbin, and the latch will go up."

Little Red Riding-Hood pulled the bobbin, and the door opened.

The Wolf, seeing her come in, said to her, hiding himself under the bed-clothes:

"Put the custard and the little pot of butter upon the stool, and come and lie down with me."

Little Red Riding-Hood undressed herself and went into bed, where, being greatly amazed to see how her grandmother looked in her night-clothes, she said to her:

"Grandmamma, what great arms you have got!"

"That is the better to hug thee, my dear."

"Grandmamma, what great legs you have got!"

"That is to run the better, my child."

"Grandmamma, what great ears you have got!"

"That is to hear the better, my child."

"Grandmamma, what great eyes you have got!"

"It is to see the better, my child."

"Grandmamma, what great teeth you have got!"

"That is to eat thee up."

And, saying these words, this wicked wolf fell upon Little Red Riding-Hood, and ate her all up.

CHARLES PERRAULT

THE SNOW-QUEEN

THERE WAS once a dreadfully wicked hobgoblin. One day he was in capital spirits because he had made a looking-glass which reflected everything that was good and beautiful in such a way that it dwindled almost to nothing, but anything that was bad and ugly stood out very clearly and looked much worse. The most beautiful landscapes looked like boiled spinach, and the best people looked repulsive or seemed to stand on their heads with no bodies; their faces were so changed that they could not be recognized, and if anyone had a freckle you might be sure it would be spread over the nose and mouth.

That was the best part of it, said the hobgoblin.

But one day the looking-glass was dropped, and it broke into a million-billion and more pieces.

And now came the greatest misfortune of all, for each of the pieces was hardly as large as a grain of sand and they flew about all over the world, and if anyone had a bit in his eye there it stayed, and then he would see everything awry, or else could only see the bad sides of a case. For every tiny splinter of the glass possessed the same power that the whole glass had.

Some people got a splinter in their hearts, and that was dreadful, for then it began to turn into a lump of ice.

The hobgoblin laughed till his sides ached, but still the tiny bits of glass flew about.

And now we will hear all about it.

In a large town, where there were so many people and houses that there was not room enough for everybody to have gardens, lived two poor children. They were not brother and sister, but they loved each other just as much as if they were. Their parents lived opposite one another in two attics, and out on the leads they had put two boxes filled with flowers. There were sweet peas in it, and two rose

The Hobgoblin laughed till his sides ached

trees, which grew beautifully, and in summer the two children were allowed to take their little chairs and sit out under the roses. Then they had splendid games.

In the winter they could not do this, but then they put hot pennies against the frozen window-panes, and made round holes to look at each other through.

His name was Kay, and hers was Gerda.

Outside it was snowing fast.

"Those are the white bees swarming," said the old grandmother.

"Have they also a queen bee?" asked the little boy, for he knew that the real bees have one.

"To be sure," said the grandmother. "She flies wherever they swarm the thickest. She is larger than any of them, and never stays upon the earth, but flies again up into the black clouds. Often at midnight she flies through the streets, and peeps in at all the windows, and then they freeze in such pretty patterns and look like flowers."

"Yes, we have seen that," said both children; they knew that it was true.

"Can the Snow-Queen come in here?" asked the little girl.

"Just let her!" cried the boy, "I would put her on the stove, and melt her!"

But the grandmother stroked his hair, and told some more stories.

In the evening, when little Kay was going to bed, he jumped on the chair by the window, and looked through the little hole. A few snowflakes were falling outside, and one of them, the largest, lay on the edge of one of the window-boxes. The snow-flake grew larger and larger till it took the form of a maiden, dressed in finest white gauze.

She was so beautiful and dainty, but all of ice, hard bright ice.

Still she was alive; her eyes glittered like two clear stars, but there was no rest or peace in them. She nodded at the window, and beckoned with her hand. The little boy was frightened, and sprang down from the chair. It seemed as if a great white bird had flown past the window.

The next day there was a harder frost than before.

Then came the spring, then the summer, when the roses grew and smelt more beautifully than ever.

Kay and Gerda were looking at one of their picture-books—the clock in the great church-tower had just struck five, when Kay exclaimed, "Oh! something has stung my heart, and I've got something in my eye!"

The little girl threw her arms round his neck; he winked hard with both his eyes; no, she could see nothing in them.

"I think it is gone now," said he; but it had not gone. It was one of the tiny splinters of the glass of the magic mirror which we have heard about, that turned everything great and good reflected in it small and ugly. And poor Kay had also a splinter in his heart, and it began to change into a lump of ice. It did not hurt him at all, but the splinter was there all the same.

"Why are you crying?" he asked; "it makes you look so ugly!

THE SNOW QUEEN APPEARS TO LITTLE KAY

There's nothing the matter with me. Just look! that rose is all slug-eaten, and this one is stunted! What ugly roses they are!"

And he began to pull them to pieces.

"Kay, what *are* you doing?" cried the little girl.

And when he saw how frightened she was, he pulled off another rose, and ran in at his window away from dear little Gerda.

When she came later on with the picture book, he said that it was only fit for babies, and when his grandmother told them stories, he was always interrupting with, "But—" and then he would get behind her and put on her spectacles, and speak just as she did. This he did very well, and everybody laughed. Very soon he could imitate the way all the people in the street walked and talked.

His games were now quite different. On a winter's day he would take a burning glass and hold it out on his blue coat and let the snow-flakes fall on it.

"Look in the glass, Gerda! Just see how regular they are! They are much more interesting than real flowers. Each is perfect; they are all made according to rule. If only they did not melt!"

One morning Kay came out with his warm gloves on, and his little sledge hung over his shoulder. He shouted to Gerda, "I am going to the market-place to play with the other boys," and away he went.

In the market-place the boldest boys used often to fasten their sledges to the carts of the farmers, and then they got a good ride.

When they were in the middle of their games there drove into the square a large sledge, all white, and in it sat a figure dressed in a rough white fur pelisse with a white fur cap on.

The sledge drove twice round the square, and Kay fastened his little sledge behind it and drove off. It went quicker and quicker into the next street. The driver turned round, and nodded to Kay in a friendly way as if they had known each other before. Every time that Kay tried to unfasten his sledge the driver nodded again, and Kay sat still once more. Then they drove out of the town, and the snow began to fall so thickly that the little boy could not see his hand before him, and on and on they went. He quickly unfastened the cord to get loose from the big sledge, but it was of no use; his little sledge hung on fast, and it went on like the wind.

Then he cried out, but nobody heard him. He was dreadfully frightened.

The snowflakes grew larger and larger till they looked like great white birds. All at once they flew aside, the large sledge stood still, and the figure who was driving stood up. The fur cloak and cap were all of snow. It was a lady, tall and slim, and glittering. It was the Snow-Queen.

"We have come at a good rate," she said; "but you are almost frozen. Creep in under my cloak."

And she set him close to her in the sledge and drew the cloak over him. He felt as though he were sinking into a snow-drift.

"Are you cold now?" she asked, and kissed his forehead. The kiss was cold as ice and reached down to his heart, which was already half a lump of ice.

"My sledge! Don't forget my sledge!" He thought of that first, and it was fastened to one of the great white birds who flew behind with the sledge on its back.

The Snow-Queen kissed Kay again, and then he forgot all about little Gerda, his grandmother, and everybody at home.

"Now I must not kiss you any more," she said, "or else I should kiss you to death."

Then away they flew over forests and lakes, over sea and land. Round them whistled the cold wind, the wolves howled, and the snow hissed; over them flew the black shrieking crows. But high up the moon shone large and bright, and thus Kay passed the long winter night. In the day he slept at the Snow-Queen's feet.

But what happened to little Gerda when Kay did not come back?

What had become of him? Nobody knew. The other boys told how they had seen him fasten his sledge on to a large one which had driven out of the town gate.

Gerda cried a great deal. The winter was long and dark to her.

Then the spring came with warm sunshine. "I will go and look for Kay," said Gerda.

So she went down to the river and got into a little boat that was there. Presently the stream began to carry it away.

"Perhaps the river will take me to Kay," thought Gerda. She glided down, past trees and fields, till she came to a large cherry garden, in which stood a little house with strange red and blue windows and a straw roof. Before the door stood two wooden soldiers, who were shouldering arms.

Gerda called to them, but they naturally did not answer. The river carried the boat on to the land.

Gerda called out still louder, and there came out of the house a very old woman. She leant upon a crutch, and she wore a large sun-hat which was painted with the most beautiful flowers.

"You poor little girl!" said the old woman.

· THE · SNOW · QUEEN · TAKES · KAY · IN · HER · SLEDGE ·

And then she stepped into the water, brought the boat in close with her crutch, and lifted little Gerda out.

"And now come and tell me who you are, and how you came here," she said.

Then Gerda told her everything, and asked her if she had seen Kay. But she said he had not passed that way yet, but he would soon come.

She told Gerda not to be sad, and that she should stay with her and take of the cherry trees and flowers, which were better than any picture-book, as they could each tell a story.

She then took Gerda's hand and led her into the little house and shut the door.

The windows were very high, and the panes were red, blue, and yellow, so that the light came through in curious colors. On the table were the most delicious cherries, and the old woman let Gerda eat as many as she liked, while she combed her hair with a gold comb as she ate.

The beautiful sunny hair rippled and shone round the dear little face, which was so soft and sweet. "I have always longed to have a dear little girl just like you, and you shall see how happy we will be together."

And as she combed Gerda's hair, Gerda thought less and less about Kay, for the old woman was a witch, but not a wicked witch, for she only enchanted now and then to amuse herself, and she did want to keep little Gerda very much.

So she went into the garden and waved her stick over all the rose bushes and blossoms and all; they sank down into the black earth, and no one could see where they had been.

The old woman was afraid that if Gerda saw the roses she would begin to think about her own, and then would remember Kay and run away.

Then she led Gerda out into the garden. How glorious it was, and what lovely scents filled the air! All the flowers you can think of blossomed there all the year round.

Gerda jumped for joy and played there till the sun set behind the tall cherry trees, and then she slept in a beautiful bed with red silk pillows filled with violets, and she slept soundly and dreamed as a queen does on her wedding day.

The next day she played again with the flowers in the warm sunshine, and so many days passed by. Gerda knew every flower, but although there were so many, it seemed to her as if *one* were not there, though she could not remember which.

She was looking one day at the old woman's sun-hat which had the painted flowers on it, and there she saw a rose.

The witch had forgotten to make that vanish when she had made the other roses disappear under the earth. It is so difficult to think of everything.

"Why, there are no roses here!" cried Gerda, and she hunted amongst all the flowers, but not one was to be found. Then she sat down and cried, but her tears fell just on the spot where a rose bush had sunk, and when her warm tears watered the earth, the bush came up in full bloom just as it had been before. Gerda kissed the roses and thought of the lovely roses at home, and with them came the thought of little Kay.

"Oh, what have I been doing!" said the little girl. "I wanted to look for Kay."

She ran to the end of the garden. The gate was shut, but she pushed against the rusty lock so that it came open.

She ran out with her little bare feet. No one came after her. At last she could not run any longer, and she sat down on a large stone. When she looked round she saw that the summer was over; it was late autumn. It had not changed in the beautiful garden, where were sunshine and flowers all the year round.

"Oh, dear, how late I have made myself!" said Gerda. "It's autumn already! I cannot rest!" And she sprang up to run on.

Oh, how tired and sore her little feet grew, and it became colder and colder.

She had to rest again, and there on the snow in front of her was a large crow.

It had been looking at her for some time, and it nodded its head and said, "Caw! caw! good day." Then it asked the little girl why she was alone in the world. She told the crow her story, and asked if he had seen Kay.

The crow nodded very thoughtfully and said, "It might be! It *might* be!"

"What! Do you think you have?" cried the little girl, and she almost squeezed the crow to death as she kissed him.

"Gently, gently!" said the crow. "I think—I know—I think—it might be little Kay, but now he has forgotten you for the princess!"

"Does he live with a princess?" asked Gerda.

"Yes, listen," said the crow.

Then he told her all he knew.

"In the kingdom in which we are now sitting lives a princess who is dreadfully clever. She has read all the newspapers in the world and has forgotten them again. She is as clever as that. The other day she came to the throne, and that is not so pleasant as people think. Then she began to say, "Why should I not marry?" But she wanted a husband who could answer when he was spoken to, not one who would stand up stiffly and look respectable—that would be too dull.

"When she told all the Court ladies, they were delighted. You can believe every word I say," said the crow, "I have a tame sweetheart in the palace, and she tells me everything."

Of course his sweetheart was a crow.

"The newspapers came out next morning with a border of hearts round it, and the princess's monogram on it, and inside you could read that every good-looking young man might come into the palace and speak to the princess, and whoever should speak loud enough to be heard would be well fed and looked after, and the one who spoke best should become the princess's husband. Indeed," said the crow, "you can quite believe me. It is as true as that I am sitting here.

"Young men came in streams, and there was such a crowding and a mixing together! But nothing came of it on the first nor on the second day. They could all speak quite well when they were in the street, but as soon as they came inside the palace door, and saw the guards in silver, and upstairs the footmen in gold, and the great hall all lighted up, then their wits left them! And when they stood in front of the throne where the princess was sitting, then they could not think of anything to say except to repeat the last word she had spoken, and she did not much care to hear that again. It seemed as if they were walking in their sleep until they came out into the street again, when they could speak once more. There was a row stretching from the gate of the town up to the castle.

"They were hungry and thirsty, but in the palace they did not even get a glass of water.

"A few of the cleverest had brought some slices of bread and butter with them, but they did not share them with their neighbors, for they thought, 'If he looks hungry, the princess will not take him!' "

"But what about Kay?" asked Gerda. "When did he come? Was he in the crowd?"

"Wait a bit; we are coming to him! On the third day a little figure came without horse or carriage and walked jauntily up to the palace. His eyes shone as yours do; he had lovely curling hair, but quite poor clothes."

"That was Kay!" cried Gerda with delight. "Oh, then I have found him!" and she clapped her hands.

"He had a little bundle on his back," said the crow.

"No, it must have been his skates, for he went away with his skates!"

"Very likely," said the crow, "I did not see for certain. But I know this from my sweetheart, that when he came to the palace door and saw the royal guards in silver, and on the stairs the footmen in gold, he was not the least bit put out. He nodded to them, saying, "It must be rather dull standing on the stairs; I would rather go inside!"

"The halls blazed with lights; councilors and ambassadors were walking about in noiseless shoes carrying gold dishes. It was enough to make one nervous! His boots creaked dreadfully loud, but he was not frightened."

"That *must* be Kay!" said Gerda. "I know he had new boots on; I have heard them creaking in his grandmother's room!"

"They *did* creak, certainly!" said the crow. "And, not one bit afraid, up he went to the princess, who was sitting on a large pearl

'HE HAD NOT COME TO WOO' HE SAID.

as round as a spinning wheel. All the ladies-in-waiting were standing round, each with their attendants, and the lords-in-waiting with
their attendants. The nearer they stood to the door the prouder they
were."

"It must have been dreadful!" said little Gerda. "And Kay did win
the princess?"

"I heard from my tame sweetheart that he was merry and
quick-witted; he had not come to woo, he said, but to listen to the
princess's wisdom. And the end of it was that they fell in love with
each other."

"Oh, yes; that was Kay!" said Gerda. "He was so clever; he could
do sums with fractions. Oh, do lead me to the palace!"

"That's easily said!" answered the crow, "but how are we to manage that? I must talk it over with my tame sweetheart. She may be
able to advise us, for I must tell you that a little girl like you could
never get permission to enter it."

"Yes, I will get it!" said Gerda. "When Kay hears that I am there
he will come out at once and fetch me!"

"Wait for me by the railings," said the crow, and he nodded his
head and flew away.

It was late in the evening when he came back.

"Caw, caw!" he said, "I am to give you her love, and here is a little
roll for you. She took it out of the kitchen; there's plenty there, and
you must be hungry. You cannot come into the palace. The guards in
silver and the footmen in gold would not allow it. But don't cry! You
shall get in all right. My sweetheart knows a little back-stairs which
leads to the sleeping-room, and she knows where to find the key."

They went into the garden, and when the lights in the palace
were put out one after the other, the crow led Gerda to a back-door.

Oh, how Gerda's heart beat with anxiety and longing! It seemed
as if she were going to do something wrong, but she only wanted to
know if it were little Kay. Yes, it must be he! She remembered so
well his clever eyes, his curly hair. She could see him smiling as he
did when they were at home under the rose trees! He would be so
pleased to see her, and to hear how they all were at home.

Now they were on the stairs; a little lamp was burning, and on
the landing stood the tame crow. She put her head on one side and
looked at Gerda, who bowed as her grandmother had taught her.

"My betrothed has told me many nice things about you, my dear
young lady," she said. "Will you take the lamp while I go in front?
We go this way so as to meet no one."

Through beautiful rooms they came to the sleeping-room. In the middle of it, hung on a thick rod of gold, were two beds, shaped like lilies, one all white, in which lay the princess, and the other red, in which Gerda hoped to find Kay. She pushed aside the curtain, and saw a brown neck. Oh, it *was* Kay! She called his name out loud, holding the lamp towards him.

He woke up, turned his head and—it was *not* Kay!

It was only his neck that was like Kay's, but he was young and handsome. The princess sat up in her lily-bed and asked who was there.

Then Gerda cried, and told her story and all that the crows had done.

"You poor child!" said the prince and princess, and they praised the crows, and said that they were not angry with them, but that they must not do it again. Now they should have a reward.

"Would you like to fly away free?" said the princess, "or will you have a permanent place as court crows with what you can get in the kitchen?"

And both crows bowed and asked for a permanent appointment, for they thought of their old age.

And they put Gerda to bed, and she folded her hands, thinking, as she fell asleep, "How good people and animals are to me!"

The next day she was dressed from head to foot in silk and satin. They wanted her to stay on in the palace, but she begged for a little carriage and a horse, and a pair of shoes so that she might go out again into the world to look for Kay.

They gave her a muff as well as some shoes; she was warmly dressed, and when she was ready, there in front of the door stood a coach of pure gold, with a coachman, footmen and postilions with gold crowns on.

The prince and princess helped her into the carriage and wished her good luck.

The wild crow who was now married drove with her for the first three miles; the other crow could not come because she had a bad headache.

"Good-bye, good-bye!" called the prince and princess; and little Gerda cried, and the crow cried.

When he said good-bye, he flew on to a tree and waved with his black wings as long as the carriage, which shone like the sun, was in sight.

They came at last to a dark wood, but the coach lit it up like a torch. When the robbers saw it, they rushed out, exclaiming, "Gold! gold!"

They seized the horses, killed the coachman, footmen and postilions, and dragged Gerda out of the carriage.

"She is plump and tender! I will eat her!" said the old robber-queen, and she drew her long knife, which glittered horribly.

"You shall not kill her!" cried her little daughter. "She shall play with me. She shall give me her muff and her beautiful dress, and she shall sleep in my bed."

The little robber-girl was as big as Gerda, but was stronger, broader, with dark hair and black eyes. She threw her arms round Gerda and said, "They shall not kill you, so long as you are not naughty. Aren't you a princess?"

"No," said Gerda, and she told all that had happened to her, and how dearly she loved little Kay.

The robber-girl looked at her very seriously, and nodded her head, saying, "They shall not kill you, even if you are naughty, for then I will kill you myself!"

And she dried Gerda's eyes, and stuck both her hands in the beautiful warm muff.

The little robber-girl took Gerda to a corner of the robbers' camp where she slept.

All round were more than a hundred wood-pigeons which seemed to be asleep, but they moved a little when the two girls came up.

There was also, near by, a reindeer which the robber-girl teased by tickling it with her long sharp knife.

Gerda lay awake for some time.

"Coo, coo!" said the wood-pigeons. "We have seen little Kay. A white bird carried his sledge; he was sitting in the Snow-Queen's carriage which drove over the forest when our little ones were in the nest. She breathed on them, and all except we two died. Coo, coo!"

"What are you saying over there?" cried Gerda. "Where was the Snow-Queen going to? Do you know at all?"

"She was probably traveling to Lapland, where there is always ice and snow. Ask the reindeer."

"There is capital ice and snow there!" said the reindeer. "One can jump about there in the great sparkling valleys. There the Snow-Queen has her summer palace, but her best palace is up by the North Pole, on the island called Spitzbergen."

"O Kay, my little Kay!" sobbed Gerda.

"You must lie still," said the little robber-girl, "or else I shall stick my knife into you!"

In the morning Gerda told her all that the wood-pigeons had said. She nodded. "Do you know where Lapland is?" she asked the reindeer.

"Who should know better than I?" said the beast, and his eyes sparkled. "I was born and bred there on the snow-fields."

"Listen!" said the robber-girl to Gerda; "you see that all the robbers have gone; only my mother is left, and she will fall asleep in the afternoon—then I will do something for you!"

When her mother had fallen asleep, the robber-girl went up to the reindeer and said, "I am going to set you free so that you can run to Lapland. But you must go quickly and carry this little girl to the Snow-Queen's palace, where her playfellow is. You must have heard all that she told about it, for she spoke loud enough!"

The reindeer sprang high for joy. The robber-girl lifted little Gerda up, and had the foresight to tie her on firmly, and even gave her a little pillow for a saddle. "You must have your fur boots," she said, "for it will be cold; but I shall keep your muff, for it is so cosy! But, so that you may not freeze, here are my mother's great fur gloves; they will come up to your elbows. Creep into them!"

And Gerda cried for joy.

"Don't make such faces!" said the little robber-girl. "You must look very happy. And here are two loaves and a sausage; now you won't be hungry!"

They were tied to the reindeer, the little robber-girl opened the door, made all the big dogs come away, cut through the halter with her sharp knife, and said to the reindeer, "Run now! But take great care of the little girl."

And Gerda stretched out her hands with the large fur gloves towards the little robber-girl and said, "Good-bye!"

Then the reindeer flew over the ground, through the great forest, as fast as he could.

The wolves howled, the ravens screamed, the sky seemed on fire. "Those are my dear old northern lights," said the reindeer; "see how they shine!"

And then he ran faster still, day and night.

The loaves were eaten, and the sausage also, and then they came to Lapland.

They stopped by a wretched little house; the roof almost touched the ground, and the door was so low that you had to creep in and out.

There was no one in the house except an old Lapland woman who was cooking fish over an oil-lamp. The reindeer told Gerda's whole history, but first he told his own, for that seemed to him much more important, and Gerda was so cold that she could not speak.

"Ah, you poor creatures!" said the Lapland woman; "you have still further to go! You must go over a hundred miles into Finland,

The Robber-girl sends Gerda off on the Reindeer

for there the Snow-Queen lives, and every night she burns Bengal lights. I will write some words on a dried stock-fish, for I have no paper, and you must give it to the Finland woman, for she can give you better advice than I can."

And when Gerda was warmed and had had something to eat and drink, the Lapland woman wrote on a dried stock-fish, and begged Gerda to take care of it, tied Gerda securely on the reindeer's back, and away they went again.

The whole night was ablaze with northern lights, and then they came to Finland and knocked at the Finland woman's chimney, for door she had none.

Inside it was so hot that the Finland woman wore very few clothes; she loosened Gerda's clothes and drew off her fur gloves and boots. She laid a piece of ice on the reindeer's head, and then read what was written on the stock-fish. She read it over three times till she knew it by heart, and then put the fish in the saucepan, for she never wasted anything.

Then the reindeer told his story, and afterwards little Gerda's and the Finland woman blinked her eyes but said nothing.

"You are very clever," said the reindeer. "I know. Cannot you give the little girl a drink so that she may have the strength of twelve men and overcome the Snow-Queen?"

"The strength of twelve men!" said the Finland woman; "that would not help much. Little Kay is with the Snow-Queen and he likes everything there very much and thinks it the best place in the world. But that is because he has a splinter of glass in his heart and a bit in his eye. If these do not come out, he will never be free, and the Snow-Queen will keep her power over him."

"But cannot you give little Gerda something so that she can have power over her?"

"I can give her no greater power than she has already; don't you see how great it is? Don't you see how men and beasts must help her when she wanders into the wide world with her bare feet? She is powerful already, because she is a dear little innocent child. If she cannot by herself conquer the Snow-Queen and take away the glass splinters from little Kay, *we* cannot help her! The Snow-Queen's garden begins two miles from here. You can carry the little maiden so far; put her down by the large bush with red berries growing in the snow. Then you must come back here as fast as you can."

Then the Finland woman lifted little Gerda on the reindeer and away he sped.

"Oh, I have left my gloves and boots behind!" cried Gerda. She missed them in the piercing cold, but the reindeer did not dare to stop. On he ran till he came to the bush with red berries. Then he set Gerda down and kissed her mouth, and great big tears ran down his cheeks, and then he ran back. There stood poor Gerda, without shoes or gloves in the middle of the bitter cold of Finland.

She ran on as fast as she could. A regiment of gigantic snowflakes came against her, but they melted when they touched her, and she went on with fresh courage.

And now we must see what Kay was doing. He was not thinking of Gerda, and never dreamt that she was standing outside the palace.

The walls of the palace were built of driven snow, and the doors and windows of piercing winds. There were more than a hundred halls in it all of frozen snow. The largest was several miles long; the bright Northern lights lit them up, and very large and empty and cold and glittering they were! In the middle of the great hall was a frozen lake which had cracked in a thousand pieces; each piece was exactly like the other. Here the Snow-Queen used to sit when she was at home.

Little Kay was almost blue and black with cold, but he did not feel it, for she had kissed away his feelings and his heart was a lump of ice.

He was pulling about some sharp, flat pieces of ice, and trying to fit one into the other. He thought each was most beautiful, but that was because of the splinter of glass in his eye. He fitted them into a great many shapes, but he wanted to make them spell the word "Love." The Snow-Queen had said, "If you can spell out that word you shall be your own master. I will give you the whole world and a new pair of skates."

But he could not do it.

"Now I must fly to warmer countries," said the Snow-Queen. "I must go and powder my black kettles!" (This was what she called Mount Etna and Mount Vesuvius.) "It does the lemons and grapes good."

And off she flew, and Kay sat alone in the great hall trying to do his puzzle.

He sat so still that you would have thought he was frozen.

Then it happened that little Gerda stepped into the hall. The biting cold winds became quiet as if they had fallen asleep when she appeared in the great, empty, freezing hall.

She caught sight of Kay; she recognized him, and ran and put her arms round his neck, crying, "Kay! dear little Kay! I have found you at last!"

But he sat quite still and cold. Then Gerda wept hot tears which fell on his neck and thawed his heart and swept away the bit of the looking-glass. He looked at her and then he burst into tears. He cried so much that the glass splinter swam out of his eye; then he knew her, and cried out, "Gerda! dear little Gerda! Where have you been so long? and where have I been?"

And he looked round him.

"How cold it is here! How wide and empty!" and he threw himself on Gerda, and she laughed and wept for joy. It was such a happy time that the pieces of ice even danced round them for joy, and when they were tired and lay down again they formed themselves into the letters that the Snow-Queen had said he must spell in order to become his own master and have the whole world and a new pair of skates.

And Gerda kissed his cheeks and they grew rosy; she kissed his eyes and they sparkled like hers; she kissed his hands and feet and he

became warm and glowing. The Snow-Queen might come home now; his release—the word "Love"—stood written in sparkling ice.

They took each other's hands and wandered out of the great palace; they talked about the grandmother and the roses on the leads, wherever they came the winds hushed and the sun came out. When they reached the bush with red berries there stood the reindeer waiting for them.

He carried Kay and Gerda first to the Finland woman, who warmed them in her hot room and gave them advice for their journey home.

Then they went to the Lapland woman, who gave them new clothes and mended their sleigh. The reindeer ran with them until they came to the green fields fresh with the spring green. Here he said good-bye.

They came to the forest, which was bursting into bud, and out of it came a splendid horse which Gerda knew; it was the one which had drawn the gold coach ridden by a young girl with a red cap on and pistols in her belt. It was the little robber girl who was tired of being at home and wanted to go out into the world. She and Gerda knew each other at once.

"You are a nice fellow!" she said to Kay. "I should like to know if you deserve to be run all over the world!"

But Gerda patted her cheeks and asked after the prince and princess.

"They are traveling about," said the robber girl.

"And the crow?" asked Gerda.

"Oh, the crow is dead!" answered the robber-girl. "His tame sweetheart is a widow and hops about with a bit of black crape round her leg. She makes a great fuss, but that's all nonsense. But tell me what happened to you, and how you caught him."

And Kay and Gerda told her all.

"Dear, dear!" said the robber-girl, shook both their hands, and promised that if she came to their town she would come and see them. Then she rode on.

But Gerda and Kay went home hand in hand. There they found the grandmother and everything just as it had been, but when they went through the doorway they found they were grown-up.

There were the roses on the leads; it was summer, warm, glorious summer.

HANS CHRISTIAN ANDERSEN

THUMBELINA

THERE WAS once a woman who wanted to have quite a tiny, little child, but she did not know where to get one from. So one day she went to an old Witch and said to her: "I should so much like to have a tiny, little child; can you tell me where I can get one?"

"Oh, we have just got one ready!" said the Witch. "Here is a barley-corn for you, but it's not the kind the farmer sows in his field, or feeds the cocks and hens with, I can tell you. Put it in a flower-pot, and then you will see something happen."

"Oh, thank you!" said the woman, and gave the Witch a shilling, for that was what it cost. Then she went home and planted the barley-corn; immediately there grew out of it a large and beautiful flower, which looked like a tulip, but the petals were tightly closed as if it were still only a bud.

"What a beautiful flower!" exclaimed the woman, and she kissed the red and yellow petals; but as she kissed them the flower burst open. It was a real tulip, such as one can see any day; but in the middle of the blossom, on the green velvety petals, sat a little girl, quite tiny, trim, and pretty. She was scarcely half a thumb in height; so they called her Thumbelina. An elegant polished walnut-shell served Thumbelina as a cradle, the blue petals of a violet were her mattress, and a rose-leaf her coverlid. There she lay at night, but in the day-time she used to play about on the table; here the woman had put a bowl, surrounded by a ring of flowers, with their stalks in water, in the middle of which floated a great tulip pedal, and on this Thumbelina sat, and sailed from one side of the bowl to the other, rowing herself with two white horse-hairs for oars. It was such a pretty sight! She could sing, too, with a voice more soft and sweet than had ever been heard before.

One night, when she was lying in her pretty little bed, an old toad crept in through a broken pane in the window. She was very ugly,

CROAK CROAK CROAK was all he could say.

clumsy, and clammy; she hopped on to the table where Thumbelina lay asleep under the red rose-leaf.

"This would make a beautiful wife for my son," said the toad, taking up the walnut-shell, with Thumbelina inside, and hopping with it through the window into the garden.

There flowed a great wide stream, with slippery and marshy banks; here the toad lived with her son. Ugh! how ugly and clammy he was, just like his mother! "Croak, croak, croak!" was all he could say when he saw the pretty little girl in the walnut-shell.

"Don't talk so loud, or you'll wake her," said the old toad. "She might escape us even now; she is as light as a feather. We will put her at once on a broad water-lily leaf in the stream. That will be quite an island for her; she is so small and light. She can't run away from us there, whilst we are preparing the guest-chamber under the marsh where she shall live."

Outside in the brook grew many water-lilies, with broad green leaves, which looked as if they were swimming about on the water. The leaf farthest away was the largest, and to this the old toad swam with Thumbelina in her walnut-shell.

The tiny Thumbelina woke up very early in the morning, and when she saw where she was she began to cry bitterly; for on every side of the great green leaf was water, and she could not get to the land.

The old toad was down under the marsh, decorating her room

Thumbelina rides on the water lily-leaf

with rushes and yellow marigold leaves, to make it very grand for
her new daughter-in-law; then she swam out with her ugly son to
the leaf where Thumbelina lay. She wanted to fetch the pretty cradle
to put it into her room before Thumbelina herself came there. The
old toad bowed low in the water before her, and said: "Here is my
son; you shall marry him, and live in great magnificence down
under the marsh."

"Croak, croak, croak!" was all that the son could say. Then they
took the neat little cradle and swam away with it; but Thumbelina
sat alone on the great green leaf and wept, for she did not want to
live with the clammy toad, or marry her ugly son. The little fishes
swimming about under the water had seen the toad quite plainly,
and heard what she had said; so they put up their heads to see the
little girl. When they saw her, they thought her so pretty that they
were very sorry she should go down with the ugly toad to live. No;
that must not happen. They assembled in the water round the green
stalk which supported the leaf on which she was sitting, and nibbled
the stem in two. Away floated the leaf down the stream, bearing
Thumbelina far beyond the reach of the toad.

On she sailed past several towns, and the little birds sitting in the
bushes saw her, and sang, "What a pretty little girl!" The leaf floated
farther and farther away; thus Thumbelina left her native land.

A beautiful little white butterfly fluttered above her, and at last settled on the leaf. Thumbelina pleased him, and she, too, was delighted, for now the toads could not reach her, and it was so beautiful where she was traveling; the sun shone on the water and made it sparkle like the brightest silver. She took off her sash, and tied one end round the butterfly; the other end she fastened to the leaf, so that now it glided along with her faster than ever.

A great cockchafer came flying past; he caught sight of Thumbelina, and in a moment had put his arms round her slender waist, and had flown off with her to a tree. The green leaf floated away down the stream, and the butterfly with it, for he was fastened to the leaf and could not get loose from it. Oh, dear! how terrified poor little Thumbelina was when the cockchafer flew off with her to the tree! But she was especially distressed on the beautiful white butterfly's account, as she had tied him fast, so that if he could not get away he must starve to death. But the cockchafer did not trouble himself about that; he sat down with her on a large green leaf, gave her the honey out of the flowers to eat, and told her that she was very pretty, although she wasn't in the least like a cockchafer. Later on, all the other cockchafers who lived in the same tree came to pay calls; they examined Thumbelina closely, and remarked, "Why, she has only two legs! How very miserable!"

"She has no feelers!" cried another.

"How ugly she is!" said all the lady chafers—and yet Thumbelina was really very pretty.

The cockchafer who had stolen her knew this very well; but when he heard all the ladies saying she was ugly, he began to think so too, and would not keep her; she might go wherever she liked. So he flew down from the tree with her and put her on a daisy. There she sat and wept, because she was so ugly that the cockchafer would have nothing to do with her; and yet she was the most beautiful creature imaginable, so soft and delicate, like the loveliest rose-leaf.

The whole summer poor little Thumbelina lived alone in the great wood. She plaited a bed for herself of blades of grass, and hung it up under a clover-leaf, so that she was protected from the rain; she gathered honey from the flowers for food, and drank the dew on the leaves every morning. Thus the summer and autumn passed, but then came winter—the long, cold winter. All the birds who had sung so sweetly about her had flown away; the trees shed their leaves, the flowers died; the great clover-leaf under which she had lived curled up, and nothing remained of it but the withered stalk. She was terribly cold, for her clothes were ragged, and she herself was so small and thin. Poor little Thumbelina! she would surely be frozen to death. It began to snow, and every snowflake that fell on her was to her as a whole shovelful thrown on one of us, for we are so big, and she was only an inch high. She wrapt herself round in a dead leaf, but it was torn in the middle and gave her no warmth; she was trembling with cold.

Just outside the wood where she was now living lay a great corn-field. But the corn had been gone a long time; only the dry, bare stubble was left standing in the frozen ground. This made a forest for her to wander about in. All at once she came across the door of a field mouse, who had a little hole under a corn-stalk. There the mouse lived warm and snug, with a storeroom full of corn, a splendid kitchen and dining room. Poor little Thumbelina went up to the door and begged for a little piece of barley, for she had not had anything to eat for the last two days.

"Poor little creature!" said the field mouse, for she was a kind-hearted old thing at the bottom. "Come into my warm room and have some dinner with me."

As Thumbelina pleased her, she said: "As far as I am concerned you may spend the winter with me; but you must keep my room clean and tidy, and tell me stories, for I like that very much."

And Thumbelina did all that the kind old field mouse asked, and did it remarkably well too.

"Now I am expecting a visitor," said the field mouse; "my neighbor comes to call on me once a week. He is in better circumstances than I am, has great, big rooms, and wears a fine black-velvet coat. If you could only marry him, you would be well provided for. But he is blind. You must tell him all the prettiest stories you know."

But Thumbelina did not trouble her head about him, for he was only a mole. He came and paid them a visit in his black-velvet coat.

"He is so rich and so accomplished," the field mouse told her.

"His house is twenty times larger than mine; he possesses great knowledge, but he cannot bear the sun and the beautiful flowers, and speaks slightingly of them, for he has never seen them."

Thumbelina had to sing to him, so she sang "Lady-bird, lady-bird, fly away home!" and other songs so prettily that the mole fell in love with her; but he did not say anything, he was a very cautious man. A short time before he had dug a long passage through the ground from his own house to that of his neighbor; in this he gave the field-mouse and Thumbelina permission to walk as often as they liked. But he begged them not to be afraid of the dead bird that lay in the passage: it was a real bird with beak and feathers, and must have died a little time ago, and now laid buried just where he had made his tunnel. The mole took a piece of rotten wood in his mouth, for that glows like fire in the dark, and went in front, lighting them through the long dark passage. When they came to the place where the dead bird lay, the mole put his broad nose against the ceiling and pushed a hole through, so that the daylight could shine down. In the middle of the path lay a dead swallow, his pretty wings pressed close to his sides, his claws and head drawn under his feathers; the poor bird had evidently died of cold. Thumbelina was very sorry, for she was very fond of all little birds; they had sung and twittered so beautifully to her all through the summer. But the mole kicked him with his bandy legs and said:

"Now he can't sing any more! It must be very miserable to be a little bird! I'm thankful that none of my little children are; birds always starve in winter."

"Yes, you speak like a sensible man," said the field mouse. "What has a bird, in spite of all his singing, in the winter-time? He must starve and freeze, and that must be very pleasant for him, I must say!"

Thumbelina did not say anything; but when the other two had passed on she bent down to the bird, brushed aside the feathers from his head, and kissed his closed eyes gently. "Perhaps it was he that sang to me so prettily in the summer," she thought. "How much pleasure he did give me, dear little bird!"

The mole closed up the hole again which let in the light, and then escorted the ladies home. But Thumbelina could not sleep that night; so she got out of bed, and plaited a great big blanket of straw, and carried it off, and spread it over the dead bird, and piled upon it thistle-down as soft as cotton-wool, which she had found in the field-mouse's room, so that the poor little thing should lie warmly buried.

"Farewell, pretty little bird!" she said. "Farewell, and thank you for your beautiful songs in the summer, when the trees were green, and the sun shone down warmly on us!" Then she laid her head against the bird's heart. But the bird was not dead: he had been frozen, but now that she had warmed him, he was coming to life again.

In autumn the swallows fly away to foreign lands; but there are some who are late in starting, and then they get so cold that they drop down as if dead, and the snow comes and covers them over.

Thumbelina trembled, she was so frightened; for the bird was very large in comparison with herself—only an inch high. But she took courage, piled up the down more closely over the poor swallow, fetched her own coverlid and laid it over his head.

Next night she crept out again to him. There he was alive, but

Thumbelina brings thistledown for the Swallow

very weak; he could only open his eyes for a moment and look at Thumbelina, who was standing in front of him with a piece of rotten wood in her hand, for she had no other lantern.

"Thank you, pretty little child!" said the swallow to her. "I am so beautifully warm! Soon I shall regain my strength, and then I shall be able to fly out again into the warm sunshine."

"Oh!" she said, "it is very cold outside; it is snowing and freezing! stay in your warm bed; I will take care of you!"

Then she brought him water in a petal, which he drank, after which he related to her how he had torn one of his wings on a bramble, so that he could not fly as fast as the other swallows, who had flown far away to warmer lands. So at last he had dropped down exhausted, and then he could remember no more. The whole winter he remained down there, and Thumbelina looked after him and nursed him tenderly. Neither the mole nor the field mouse learnt anything of this, for they could not bear the poor swallow.

When the spring came, and the sun warmed the earth again, the swallow said farewell to Thumbelina, who opened the hole in the roof for him which the mole had made. The sun shone brightly down upon her, and the swallow asked her if she would go with him; she could sit upon his back. Thumbelina wanted very much to fly far away into the green wood, but she knew that the old field mouse would be sad if she ran away. "No, I mustn't come!" she said.

"Farewell, dear good little girl!" said the swallow, and flew off into the sunshine. Thumbelina gazed after him with the tears standing in her eyes, for she was very fond of the swallow.

"Tweet, tweet!" sang the bird, and flew into the green wood.

Thumbelina was very unhappy. She was not allowed to go out into the warm sunshine. The corn which had been sowed in the field over the field mouse's home grew up high into the air, and made a thick forest for the poor little girl, who was only an inch high.

"Now you are to be a bride, Thumbelina!" said the field mouse, "for our neighbor has proposed for you! What a piece of fortune for a poor child like you! Now you must set to work at your linen for your dowry, for nothing must be lacking if you are to become the wife of our neighbor, the mole!"

Thumbelina had to spin all day long, and every evening the mole visited her, and told her that when the summer was over the sun would not shine so hot; now it was burning the earth as hard as a stone. Yes, when the summer had passed, they would keep the wedding.

But she was not at all pleased about it, for she did not like the stupid mole. Every morning when the sun was rising, and every evening when it was setting, she would steal out of the house-door, and when the breeze parted the ears of corn so that she could see the blue sky through them, she thought how bright and beautiful it must be outside, and longed to see her dear swallow again. But he never came; no doubt he had flown away far into the great green wood.

By the autumn Thumbelina had finished the dowry.

"In four weeks you will be married!" said the field mouse; "don't

Thumbelina had to spin

be obstinate, or I shall bite you with my sharp white teeth! You will get a fine husband! The King himself has not such a velvet coat. His store-room and cellar are full, and you should be thankful for that."

Well, the wedding-day arrived. The mole had come to fetch Thumbelina to live with him deep down under the ground, never to come out into the warm sun again, for that was what he didn't like. The poor little girl was very sad; for now she must say good-bye to the beautiful sun.

"Farewell, bright sun!" she cried, stretching out her arms towards it, and taking another step outside the house; for now the corn had been reaped, and only the dry stubble was left standing. "Farewell, farewell!" she said, and put her arms round a little red flower that grew there. "Give my love to the dear swallow when you see him!"

"Tweet, tweet!" sounded in her ear all at once. She looked up. There was the swallow flying past! As soon as he saw Thumbelina, he was very glad. She told him how unwilling she was to marry the ugly mole, as then she had to live underground where the sun never shone, and she could not help bursting into tears.

"The cold winter is coming now," said the swallow. "I must fly away to warmer lands: will you come with me? You can sit on my back, and we will fly far away from the ugly mole and his dark house, over the mountains, to the warm countries where the sun shines more brightly than here, where it is always summer, and there are always beautiful flowers. Do come with me, dear little Thumbelina, who saved my life when I lay frozen in the dark tunnel!"

"Yes, I will go with you," said Thumbelina, and got on the swallow's back, with her feet on one of his outstretched wings. Up he flew into the air, over woods and seas, over the great mountains where the snow is always lying. And if she was cold she crept under his warm feathers, only keeping her little head out to admire all the beautiful things in the world beneath. At last they came to warm lands; there the sun was brighter, the sky seemed twice as high, and in the hedges hung the finest green and purple grapes; in the woods grew oranges and lemons: the air was scented with myrtle and mint, and on the roads were pretty little children running about and playing with great gorgeous butterflies. But the swallow flew on farther, and it became more and more beautiful. Under the most splendid green trees besides a blue lake stood a glittering white-marble castle. Vines hung about the high pillars; there were many swallows' nests, and in one of these lived the swallow who was carrying Thumbelina.

"Here is my house!" said he. "But it won't do for you to live with me; I am not tidy enough to please you. Find a home for yourself in one of the lovely flowers that grow down there; now I will set you down, and you can do whatever you like."

"That will be splendid!" said she, clapping her little hands.

There lay a great white marble column which had fallen to the ground and broken into three pieces, but between these grew the most beautiful white flowers. The swallow flew down with Thumbelina, and set her upon one of the broad leaves. But there, to her astonishment, she found a tiny little man sitting in the middle of the flower, as white and transparent as if he were made of glass; he had the prettiest golden crown on his head, and the most beautiful wings on his shoulders; he himself was no bigger than Thumbelina. He was the spirit of the flower. In each blossom there dwelt a tiny man or woman; but this one was the King over the others.

"How handsome he is!" whispered Thumbelina to the swallow.

The little Prince was very much frightened at the swallow, for in comparison with one so tiny as himself he seemed a giant. But when he saw Thumbelina, he was delighted, for she was the most beautiful girl he had ever seen. So he took his golden crown from off his head and put it on hers, asking her her name, and if she would be his wife, and then she would be Queen of all the flowers. Yes! he was a different kind of husband to the son of the toad and the mole with the black-velvet coat. So she said "Yes" to the noble Prince. And out of each flower came a lady and gentleman, each so tiny and pretty that it was a pleasure to see them. Each brought Thumbelina a present, but the best of all was a beautiful pair of wings which were fastened on to her back, and now she too could fly from flower to flower. They all wished her joy, and the swallow sat above in his nest and sang the wedding march, and that he did as well as he could; but he was sad, because he was very fond of Thumbelina and did not want to be separated from her.

"You shall not be called Thumbelina!" said the spirit of the flower to her; "that is an ugly name, and you are much too pretty for that. We will call you May Blossom."

"Farewell, farewell!" said the little swallow with a heavy heart, and flew away to farther lands, far, far away, right back to Denmark. There he had a little nest above a window, where his wife lived, who can tell fairy-stories. "Tweet, tweet!" he sang to her. And that is the way we learnt the whole story.

HANS CHRISTIAN ANDERSEN

THE SIX SWANS

A KING was once hunting in a great wood, and he hunted the game so eagerly that none of his courtiers could follow him. When evening came on he stood still and looked round him, and he saw that he had quite lost himself. He sought a way out, but could find none. Then he saw an old woman with a shaking head coming towards him; but she was a witch.

"Good woman," he said to her, "can you not show me the way out of the wood?"

"Oh, certainly, Sir King," she replied, "I can quite well do that, but on one condition, which if you do not fulfill you will never get out of the wood, and will die of hunger."

"What is the condition?" asked the King.

"I have a daughter," said the old woman, "who is so beautiful that she has not her equal in the world, and is well fitted to be your wife; if you will make her lady-queen I will show you the way out of the wood."

The King in his anguish of mind consented, and the old woman led him to her little house where her daughter was sitting by the fire. She received the King as if she were expecting him, and he saw that she was certainly very beautiful; but she did not please him, and he could not look at her without a secret feeling of horror. As soon as he had lifted the maiden on to his horse the old woman showed him the way, and the King reached his palace, where the wedding was celebrated.

The King had already been married once, and had by his first wife seven children, six boys and one girl, whom he loved more than anything in the world. And now, because he was afraid that their stepmother might not treat them well and might do them harm, he put them in a lonely castle that stood in the middle of a wood. It lay so hidden, and the way to it was so hard to find, that he himself could not have found it out had not a wise-woman given him a reel of thread which possessed a marvelous property: when he threw it before him it unwound itself and showed him the way. But the King went so often to his dear children that the Queen was offended at his absence. She grew curious, and wanted to know what he had to do quite alone in the wood. She gave his servants a great deal of money, and they betrayed the secret to her, and also told her of the reel which alone could point out the way. She had no rest now till she had found out where the King guarded the reel, and then she made some little white shirts, and, as she had learnt from her witch-mother, sewed an enchantment in each of them.

And when the King had ridden off she took the little shirts and went into the wood, and the reel showed her the way. The children, who saw someone coming in the distance, thought it was their dear father coming to them, and sprang to meet him very joyfully. Then she threw over each one a little shirt, which when it had touched their bodies changed them into swans, and they flew away over the forest. The Queen went home quite satisfied, and thought she had got rid of her step-children; but the girl had not run to meet her with her brothers, and she knew nothing of her.

The next day the King came to visit his children, but he found no one but the girl.

"Where are your brothers?" asked the King.

"Alas! dear father," she answered, "they have gone away and left me all alone." And she told him that looking out of her little window she had seen her brothers flying over the wood in the shape of swans, and she showed him the feathers which they had let fall in the yard, and which she had collected. The King mourned, but he did not think that the Queen had done the wicked deed, and as he was afraid the maiden would also be taken from him, he wanted to take her with him. But she was afraid of the stepmother, and begged the King to let her stay just one night more in the castle in the wood. The poor maiden thought, "My home is no longer here; I will go and seek my brothers." And when night came she fled away into the forest. She ran all through the night and the next day, till she could go no farther for weariness. Then she saw a little hut, went in, and found a room with six little beds. She was afraid to lie down on one, so she crept under one of them, lay on the hard floor, and was going to spend the night there. But when the sun had set she heard a noise, and saw six swans flying in at the window. They stood on the floor and blew at one another, and blew all their feathers off, and their swan-skin came off like a shirt. Then the maiden recognized her

brothers, and overjoyed she crept out from under the bed. Her
brothers were not less delighted than she to see their little sister
again, but their joy did not last long.

"You cannot stay here," they said to her. "This is a den of robbers;
if they were to come here and find you they would kill you."

"Could you not protect me?" asked the little sister.

"No," they answered, "for we can only lay aside our swan skins
for a quarter of an hour every evening. For this time we regain our
human forms, but then we are changed into swans again."

Then the little sister cried and said, "Can you not be freed?"

"Oh, no," they said, "the conditions are too hard. You must not speak or laugh for six years, and must make in that time six shirts for us out of star-flowers. If a single word comes out of your mouth, all your labor is vain." And when the brothers had said this the quarter of an hour came to an end, and they flew away out of the window as swans.

But the maiden had determined to free her brothers even if it should cost her her life. She left the hut, went into the forest, climbed a tree, and spent the night there. The next morning she went out, collected star-flowers, and began to sew. She could speak to no one, and she had no wish to laugh, so she sat there, looking only at her work.

When she had lived there some time, it happened that the King of the country was hunting in the forest, and his hunters came to the tree on which the maiden sat. They called to her and said "Who are you?"

But she gave no answer.

"Come down to us," they said, "we will do you no harm."

But she shook her head silently. As they pressed her further with questions, she threw them the golden chain from her neck. But they did not leave off, and she threw them her girdle, and when this was no use, her garters, and then her dress. The huntsmen would not leave her alone, but climbed the tree, lifted the maiden down, and led her to the King. The King asked, "Who are you? What are you doing up that tree?"

But she answered nothing.

He asked her in all the languages he knew, but she remained as dumb as a fish. Because she was so beautiful, however, the King's heart was touched, and he was seized with a great love for her. He wrapped her up in his cloak, placed her before him on his horse, and brought her to his castle. There he had her dressed in rich clothes, and her beauty shone out as bright as day, but not a word could be drawn from her. He set her at table by his side, and her modest ways and behavior pleased him so much that he said, "I will marry this maiden and none other in the world," and after some days he married her. But the King had a wicked mother who was displeased with the marriage, and said wicked things of the young Queen. "Who knows who this girl is?" she said; "she cannot speak, and is not worthy of a king."

After a year, when the Queen had her first child, the old mother took it away from her. Then she went to the King and said that the Queen had killed it. The King would not believe it, and would not

The Six Brothers Changed Into Swans By Their Stepmother.

allow any harm to be done her. But she sat quietly sewing at the shirts and troubling herself about nothing. The next time she had a child the wicked mother did the same thing, but the King could not make up his mind to believe her. He said, "She is too sweet and good to do such a thing as that. If she were not dumb and could defend herself, her innocence would be proved." But when the third child was taken away, and the Queen was again accused, and could not utter a word in her own defense, the King was obliged to give her over to the law, which decreed that she must be burnt to death. When the day came on which the sentence was to be executed, it was the last day of the six years in which she must not speak or laugh, and now she had freed her dear brothers from the power of the enchantment. The six shirts were done; there was only the left sleeve wanting to the last.

When she was led to the stake, she laid the shirts on her arm, and as she stood on the pile and the fire was about to be lighted, she looked around her and saw six swans flying through the air. Then she knew that her release was at hand and her heart danced for joy. The swans fluttered round her, and hovered low so that she could throw the shirts over them. When they had touched them the swan-skins fell off, and her brothers stood before her living, well and beautiful. Only the youngest had a swan's wing instead of his left arm. They embraced and kissed each other, and the Queen went to the King, who was standing by in great astonishment, and began to speak to him, saying, "Dearest husband, now I can speak and tell you openly that I am innocent and have been falsely accused."

She told him of the old woman's deceit, and how she had taken the three children away and hidden them. Then they were fetched, to the great joy of the King, and the wicked mother came to no good end.

But the King and the Queen with their six brothers lived many years in happiness and peace.

THE BROTHERS GRIMM

THE NIGHTINGALE

IN CHINA, as I daresay you know, the Emperor is a Chinaman, and all his courtiers are also Chinamen. The story I am going to tell you happened many years ago, but it is worthwhile for you to listen to it, before it is forgotten.

The Emperor's Palace was the most splendid in the world, all made of priceless porcelain, but so brittle and delicate that you had to take great care how you touched it. In the garden were the most beautiful flowers, and on the loveliest of them were tied silver bells which tinkled, so that if you passed you could not help looking at the flowers. Everything in the Emperor's garden was admirably arranged with a view to effect; and the garden was so large that even the gardener himself did not know where it ended. If you ever got beyond it, you came to a stately forest with great trees and deep lakes in it. The forest sloped down to the sea, which was a clear blue. Large ships could sail under the boughs of the trees, and in these trees there lived a Nightingale. She sang so beautifully that even the poor fisherman who had so much to do stood and listened when he came at night to cast his nets. "How beautiful it is!" he said; but he had to attend to his work, and forgot about the bird. But when she sang the next night and the fisherman came there again, he said the same thing, "How beautiful it is!"

From all the countries round came travelers to the Emperor's town, who were astonished at the Palace and the garden. But when they heard the Nightingale they all said, "This is the finest thing after all!"

The travelers told all about it when they went home, and learned scholars wrote many books upon the town, the Palace, and the garden. But they did not forget the Nightingale; she was praised the most, and all the poets composed splendid verses on the Nightingale in the forest by the deep sea.

The books were circulated throughout the world, and some of them reached the Emperor. He sat in his golden chair, and read and read. He nodded his head every moment, for he liked reading the brilliant accounts of the town, the Palace, and the garden. "But the Nightingale is better than all," he saw written.

"What is that?" said the Emperor. "I don't know anything about the Nightingale! Is there such a bird in my empire, and so near as in my garden? I have never heard it! Fancy reading for the first time about it in a book!"

And he called his First Lord to him. He was so proud that if anyone of lower rank than his own ventured to speak to him or ask him anything, he would say nothing but "P!" and that does not mean anything.

."Here is a most remarkable bird which is called a Nightingale!" said the Emperor. "They say it is the most glorious thing in my kingdom. Why has no one ever said anything to me about it?"

"I have never before heard it mentioned!" said the First Lord. "I will look for it and find it!"

But where was it to be found? The First Lord ran up and down stairs, through the halls and corridors; but none of those he met had ever heard of the Nightingale. And the First Lord ran again to the Emperor, and told him that it must be an invention on the part of those who had written the books.

"Your Imperial Majesty cannot really believe all that is written! There are some inventions called the Black Art!"

"But the book in which I read this," said the Emperor, "is sent me by His Great Majesty the Emperor of Japan; so it cannot be untrue, and I will hear the Nightingale! She must be here this evening! She has my gracious permission to appear, and if she does not, the whole Court shall be trampled under foot after supper!"

"Tsing pe!" said the First Lord; and he ran up and down stairs, through the halls and corridors, and half the Court ran with him, for they did not want to be trampled under foot. Everyone was asking after the wonderful Nightingale which all the world knew of, except those at Court.

At last they met a poor little girl in the kitchen, who said, "Oh! I know the Nightingale well. How she sings! I have permission to carry the scraps over from the Court meals to my poor sick mother, and when I am going home at night, tired and weary, and rest for a little in the wood, then I hear the Nightingale singing! It brings tears to my eyes, and I feel as if my mother were kissing me!"

"Little kitchenmaid!" said the First Lord, "I will give you a place

THE KITCHEN MAID LISTENS TO THE NIGHTINGALE

in the kitchen, and you shall have leave to see the Emperor at dinner, if you can lead us to the Nightingale, for she is invited to come to Court this evening."

And so they all went into the wood where the Nightingale was wont to sing, and half the Court went too.

When they were on the way there they heard a cow mooing.

"Oh!" said the Courtiers, "now we have found her! What a wonderful power for such a small beast to have! I am sure we have heard her before!"

"No; that is a cow mooing!" said the little kitchenmaid. "We are still a long way off!"

Then the frogs began to croak in the marsh. "Splendid!" said the Chinese chaplain. "Now we hear her; it sounds like a little church-bell!"

"No, no; those are frogs!" said the little kitchenmaid. "But I think we shall soon hear her now!"

Then the Nightingale began to sing.

"There she is!" cried the little girl. "Listen! She is sitting there!" And she pointed to a little dark-grey bird up in the branches.

"Is it possible!" said the First Lord. "I should never have thought it! How ordinary she looks! She must surely have lost her feathers because she sees so many distinguished men round her!"

"Little Nightingale," called out the little kitchenmaid, "our Gracious Emperor wants you to sing before him!"

"With the greatest of pleasure!" said the Nightingale; and she sang so gloriously that it was a pleasure to listen.

"It sounds like glass bells!" said the First Lord. "And look how her little throat works! It is wonderful that we have never heard her before! She will be a great success at Court."

"Shall I sing once more for the Emperor?" asked the Nightingale, thinking that the Emperor was there.

"My esteemed little Nightingale," said the First Lord, "I have the great pleasure to invite you to Court this evening, where His Gracious Imperial Highness will be enchanted with your charming song!"

"It sounds best in the green wood," said the Nightingale; but still, she came gladly when she heard that the Emperor wished it. At the Palace everything was splendidly prepared. The porcelain walls and floors glittered in the light of many thousand gold lamps; the most gorgeous flowers which tinkled out well were placed in the corridors. There was such a hurrying and draught that all the bells jingled so much that one could not hear oneself speak. In the center of the great hall where the Emperor sat was a golden perch, on which the Nightingale sat. The whole Court was there, and the little kitchenmaid was allowed to stand behind the door, now that she was a Court-cook. Everyone was dressed in his best, and everyone was looking towards the little grey bird to whom the Emperor nodded.

The Nightingale sang so gloriously that the tears came into the Emperor's eyes and ran down his cheeks. Then the Nightingale sang even more beautifully; it went straight to all hearts. The Emperor was so delighted that he said she should wear his gold slipper round her neck. But the Nightingale thanked him, and said she had had

The Present from
the Emperor of Japan

enough reward already. "I have seen tears in the Emperor's eyes—
that is a great reward. An Emperor's tears have such power!" Then
she sang again with her gloriously sweet voice.

"That is the most charming coquetry I have ever seen!" said all the
ladies round. And they all took to holding water in their mouths
that they might gurgle whenever anyone spoke to them. Then they
thought themselves nightingales. Yes, the lackeys and chambermaids
announced that they were pleased; which means a great deal, for
they are the most difficult people of all to satisfy. In short, the
Nightingale was a real success.

She had to stay at Court now; she had her own cage, and permission to walk out twice in the day and once at night.

She was given twelve servants, who each held a silken string
which was fastened round her leg. There was little pleasure in flying
about like this.

The whole town was talking about the wonderful bird, and when two people met each other one would say "Nightin," and the other "Gale," and then they would both sigh and understand one another. Yes, and eleven grocer's children were called after her, but not one of them could sing a note.

One day the Emperor received a large parcel on which was written "The Nightingale."

"Here is another new book about our famous bird!" said the Emperor.

But it was not a book, but a little mechanical toy, which lay in a box—an artificial nightingale which was like the real one, only that it was set all over with diamonds, rubies, and sapphires. When it was wound up, it could sing the piece the real bird sang, and moved its tail up and down, and glittered with silver and gold. Round its neck was a little collar on which was written, "The Nightingale of the Emperor of Japan is nothing compared to that of the Emperor of China."

"This is magnificent!" they all said, and the man who had brought the clockwork bird received on the spot the title of "Bringer of the Imperial First Nightingale."

"Now they must sing together; what a duet we shall have!"

And so they sang together, but their voices did not blend, for the real Nightingale sang in her way and the clockwork bird sang waltzes.

"It is not its fault!" said the bandmaster; "it keeps very good time and is quite after my style!"

Then the artificial bird had to sing alone. It gave just as much pleasure as the real one, and then it was so much prettier to look at; it sparkled like bracelets and necklaces. Three-and-thirty times it sang the same piece without being tired. People would like to have heard it again, but the Emperor thought that the living Nightingale should sing now—but where was she? No one had noticed that she had flown out of the open window away to her green woods.

"What *shall* we do!" said the Emperor.

And all the Court scolded, and said that the Nightingale was very ungrateful. "But we have still the best bird!" they said and the artificial bird had to sing again, and that was the thirty-fourth time they had heard the same piece. But they did not yet know it by heart; it was much too difficult. And the bandmaster praised the bird tremendously; yes, he assured them it was better than a real nightingale, not only because of its beautiful plumage and diamonds, but inside as well. "For see, my Lords and Ladies and your Imperial Majesty, with the real Nightingale one can never tell what will come out, but all is known about the artificial bird! You can explain it, you can open it and show people where the waltzes lie, how they go, and how one follows the other!"

"That's just what we think!" said everyone; and the bandmaster received permission to show the bird to the people the next Sunday. They should hear it sing, commanded the Emperor. And they heard it, and they were as pleased as if they had been intoxicated with tea, after the Chinese fashion, and they all said "Oh!" and held up their forefingers and nodded time. But the poor fishermen who had heard the real Nightingale said: "This one sings well enough, the tunes glide out; but there is something wanting—I don't know what!"

The real Nightingale was banished from the kingdom.

The artificial bird was put on silken cushions by the Emperor's bed, all the presents which it received, gold and precious stones, lay round it, and it was given the title of Imperial Night-singer, First from the left. For the Emperor counted that side as the more distinguished, being the side on which the heart is; the Emperor's heart is also on the left.

And the bandmaster wrote a work of twenty-five volumes about the artificial bird. It was so learned, long, and so full of the hardest Chinese words that everyone said they had read it and understood it; for once they had been very stupid about a book, and had been trampled under foot in consequence. So a whole year passed. The Emperor, the Court, and all the Chinese knew every note of the artificial bird's song by heart. But they liked it all the better for this; they could even sing with it, and they did. The street boys sang "Tra-la-la-la-la," and the Emperor sang too sometimes. It was indeed delightful.

But one evening, when the artificial bird was singing its best, and the Emperor lay in bed listening to it, something in the bird went crack. Something snapped! Whir-r-r! all the wheels ran down and then the music ceased. The Emperor sprang up, and had his physician summoned, but what could *he* do! Then the clockmaker came, and, after a great deal of talking and examining, he put the bird somewhat in order, but he said that it must be very seldom used as the works were nearly worn out, and it was impossible to put in new ones. Here was a calamity! Only once a year was the artificial bird allowed to sing, and even that was almost too much for it. But then the bandmaster made a little speech full of hard words, saying that it was just as good as before. And so, of course, it *was* just as good as before. So five years passed, and then a great sorrow came to the nation. The Chinese look upon their Emperor as everything, and now he was ill, and not likely to live it was said.

Already a new Emperor had been chosen, and the people stood outside in the street and asked the First Lord how the old Emperor was. "P!" said he, and shook his head.

Cold and pale lay the Emperor in his splendid great bed; the whole Court believed him dead, and one after the other left him to pay their respects to the new Emperor. Everywhere in the halls and corridors cloth was laid down so that no footstep could be heard, and everything was still—very, very still. And nothing came to break the silence.

The Emperor longed for something to come and relieve the monotony of this deathlike stillness. If only someone would speak to him! If only someone would sing to him. Music would carry his thoughts away, and would break the spell lying on him. The moon was streaming in at the open window; but that, too, was silent, quite silent.

"Music! music!" cried the Emperor. "You little bright golden bird, sing! do sing! I gave you gold and jewels; I have hung my gold slipper round your neck with my own hand—sing! do sing!" But the bird was silent. There was no one to wind it up, and so it could not sing. And all was silent, so terribly silent!

All at once there came in at the window the most glorious burst of song. It was the little living Nightingale, who, sitting outside on a bough, had heard the need of her Emperor and had come to sing to him of comfort and hope. And as she sang the blood flowed quicker and quicker in the Emperor's weak limbs, and life began to return.

"Thank you, thank you!" said the Emperor. "You divine little bird! I know you. I chased you from my kingdom, and you have given me life again! How can I reward you?"

"You have done that already!" said the Nightingale. "I brought tears to your eyes the first time I sang. I shall never forget that. They are jewels that rejoice a singer's heart. But now sleep and get strong again; I will sing you a lullaby." And the Emperor fell into a deep, calm sleep as she sang.

The sun was shining through the window when he awoke, strong and well. None of his servants had come back yet, for they thought he was dead. But the Nightingale sat and sang to him.

"You must always stay with me!" said the Emperor. "You shall sing whenever you like, and I will break the artificial bird into a thousand pieces."

"Don't do that!" said the Nightingale. "He did his work as long as he could. Keep him as you have done! I cannot build my nest in the Palace and live here; but let me come whenever I like. I will sit

in the evening on the bough outside the window, and I will sing you something that will make you feel happy and grateful. I will sing of joy, and of sorrow; I will sing of the evil and the good which lies hidden from you. The little singing-bird flies all around, to the poor fisherman's hut, to the farmer's cottage, to all those who are far away from you and your Court. I love your heart more than your crown, though that has about it a brightness as of something holy. Now I will sing to you again; but you must promise me one thing—"

"Anything!" said the Emperor, standing up in his Imperial robes, which he had himself put on, and fastening on his sword richly embossed with gold.

"One thing I beg of you! Don't tell anyone that you have a little bird who tells you everything. It will be much better not to!" Then the Nightingale flew away.

The servants came in to look at their dead Emperor.

The Emperor said, "Good-morning!"

HANS CHRISTIAN ANDERSEN

DONKEY SKIN

THERE WAS once upon a time a king who was so much beloved by his subjects that he thought himself the happiest monarch in the whole world, and he had everything his heart could desire. His palace was filled with the rarest of curiosities, and his gardens with the sweetest flowers, while in the marble stalls of his stables stood a row of milk-white Arabs, with big brown eyes.

Strangers who had heard of the marvels which the king had collected, and made long journeys to see them, were, however, surprised to find the most splendid stall of all occupied by a donkey, with particularly large and drooping ears. It was a very fine donkey; but still, as far as they could tell, nothing so very remarkable as to account for the care with which it was lodged; and they went away wondering, for they could not know that every night, when it was asleep, bushels of gold pieces tumbled out of its ears, which were picked up each morning by the attendants.

After many years of prosperity a sudden blow fell upon the king in the death of his wife, whom he loved dearly. But before she died, the queen, who had always thought first of his happiness, gathered all her strength, and said to him:

"Promise me one thing: you must marry again, I know, for the good of your people, as well as of yourself. But do not set about it in a hurry. Wait until you have found a woman more beautiful and better formed than myself."

"Oh, do not speak to me of marrying," sobbed the king; "rather let me die with you!" But the queen only smiled faintly, and turned over on her pillow and died.

For some months the king's grief was great; then gradually he began to forget a little, and, besides, his counselors were always urging him to seek another wife. At first he refused to listen to them, but by-and-by he allowed himself to be persuaded to think of it,

The King's Pet Donkey

only stipulating that the bride should be more beautiful and attractive than the late queen, according to the promise he had made her.

Overjoyed at having obtained what they wanted, the counselors sent envoys far and wide to get portraits of all the most famous beauties of every country. The artists were very busy and did their best, but, alas! nobody could even pretend that any of the ladies could compare for a moment with the late queen.

At length, one day, when he had turned away discouraged from a fresh collection of pictures, the king's eyes fell on his adopted daughter, who had lived in the palace since she was a baby, and he saw that, if a woman existed on the whole earth more lovely than the queen, this was she! He at once made known what his wishes were, but the young girl, who was not at all ambitious, and had not the faintest desire to marry him, was filled with dismay, and begged for time to think about it. That night, when everyone was asleep, she started in a little car drawn by a big sheep, and went to consult her fairy godmother.

"I know what you have come to tell me," said the fairy, when the maiden stepped out of the car; "and if you don't wish to marry him, I will show you how to avoid it. Ask him to give you a dress that exactly matches the sky. It will be impossible for him to get one, so you will be quite safe." The girl thanked the fairy and returned home again.

The next morning, when her father (as she had always called him) came to see her, she told him that she could give him no answer until he had presented her with a dress the color of the sky. The king, overjoyed at this answer, sent for all the choicest weavers and dressmakers in the kingdom, and commanded them to make a robe the color of the sky without an instant's delay, or he would cut off their heads at once. Dreadfully frightened at this threat, they all began to dye and cut and sew, and in two days they brought back the dress, which looked as if it had been cut straight out of the heavens! The poor girl was thunderstruck, and did not know what to do; so in the night she harnessed her sheep again, and went in search of her godmother.

"The king is cleverer than I thought," said the fairy; "but tell him you must have a dress of moonbeams."

And the next day, when the king summoned her into his presence, the girl told him what she wanted.

"Madam, I can refuse you nothing," said he; and he ordered the dress to be ready in twenty-four hours, or every man should be hanged.

They set to work with all their might, and by dawn next day, the dress of moonbeams was laid across her bed. The girl, though she could not help admiring its beauty, began to cry, till the fairy, who heard her, came to her help.

"Well, I could not have believed it of him!" said she; "but ask for a dress of sunshine, and I shall be surprised indeed if he manages that!"

The goddaughter did not feel much faith in the fairy after her two previous failures; but not knowing what else to do, she told her father what she was bid.

The Fairy, The Princess & The Donkey's Skin

The king made no difficulties about it, and even gave his finest rubies and diamonds to ornament the dress, which was so dazzling, when finished, that it could not be looked at save through smoked glasses!

When the princess saw it, she pretended that the sight hurt her eyes, and retired to her room, where she found the fairy awaiting her, very much ashamed of herself.

"There is only one thing to be done now," cried she; "you must demand the skin of the ass he sets such store by. It is from that donkey he obtains all his vast riches, and I am sure he will never give it to you."

The princess was not so certain; however, she went to the king, and told him she could never marry him till he had given her the ass's skin.

The king was both astonished and grieved at this new request, but did not hesitate an instant. The ass was sacrificed, and the skin laid at the feet of the princess.

The poor girl, seeing no escape from the fate she dreaded, wept afresh, and tore her hair; when, suddenly, the fairy stood before her.

"Take heart," she said, "all will now go well! Wrap yourself in this skin, and leave the palace and go as far as you can. I will look after you. Your dresses and your jewels shall follow you underground, and if you strike the earth whenever you need anything, you will have it at once. But go quickly: you have no time to lose."

So the princess clothed herself in the ass's skin, and slipped from the palace without being seen by anyone.

Directly she was missed there was a great hue and cry, and every corner, possible and impossible, was searched. Then the king sent out parties along all the roads, but the fairy threw her invisible mantle over the girl when they approached, and none of them could see her.

The princess walked on a long, long way, trying to find some one who would take her in, and let her work for them; but though the cottagers, whose houses she passed, gave her food from charity, the ass's skin was so dirty they would not allow her to enter their houses. For her flight had been so hurried she had had no time to clean it.

Tired and disheartened at her ill-fortune, she was wandering, one day, past the gate of a farmyard, situated just outside the walls of a large town, when she heard a voice calling to her. She turned and saw the farmer's wife standing among her turkeys, and making signs to her to come in.

"I want a girl to wash the dishes and feed the turkeys, and clean out the pig-sty," said the woman, "and, to judge by your dirty clothes, you would not be too fine for the work."

The girl accepted her offer with joy, and she was at once set to work in a corner of the kitchen, where all the farm servants came and made fun of her, and the ass's skin in which she was wrapped. But by-and-by they got so used to the sight of it that it ceased to amuse them, and she worked so hard and so well, that her mistress grew quite fond of her. And she was so clever at keeping sheep and herding turkeys that you would have thought she had done nothing else during her whole life!

One day she was sitting on the banks of a stream bewailing her wretched lot, when she suddenly caught sight of herself in the water. Her hair and part of her face was quite concealed by the ass's head, which was drawn right over like a hood, and the filthy matted skin covered her whole body. It was the first time she had seen herself as other people saw her, and she was filled with shame at the spectacle. Then she threw off her disguise and jumped into the water, plunging in again and again, till she shone like ivory. When it was time to go back to the farm, she was forced to put on the skin which disguised her, and now seemed more dirty than ever; but, as she did so, she comforted herself with the thought that tomorrow was a holiday, and that she would be able for a few hours to forget that she was a farm girl, and be a princess once more.

So, at break of day, she stamped on the ground, as the fairy had told her, and instantly the dress like the sky lay across her tiny bed. Her room was so small that there was no place for the train of her dress to spread itself out, but she pinned it up carefully when she combed her beautiful hair and piled it up on the top of her head, as she had always worn it. When she had done, she was so pleased with herself that she determined never to let a chance pass of putting on her splendid clothes, even if she had to wear them in the fields, with no one to admire her but the sheep and turkeys.

Now the farm was a royal farm, and, one holiday, when "Donkey Skin" (as they had nicknamed the princess) had locked the door of her room and clothed herself in her dress of sunshine, the king's son rode through the gate, and asked if he might come and rest himself a little after hunting. Some food and milk were set before him in the garden, and when he felt rested he got up, and began to explore the house, which was famous throughout the whole kingdom for its age and beauty. He opened one door after the other, admiring the old rooms, when he came to a handle that would not turn. He stooped and peeped through the keyhole to see what was inside, and was greatly astonished at beholding a beautiful girl, clad in a dress so dazzling that he could hardly look at it.

The dark gallery seemed darker than ever as he turned away, but he went back to the kitchen and inquired who slept in the room at the end of the passage. The scullery maid, they told him, whom everybody laughed at, and called "Donkey Skin;" and though he perceived there was some strange mystery about this, he saw quite clearly there was nothing to be gained by asking any more questions. So he rode back to the palace, his head filled with the vision he had seen through the keyhole.

All night long he tossed about, and awoke the next morning in a high fever. The queen, who had no other child, and lived in a state of perpetual anxiety about this one, at once gave him up for lost, and indeed his sudden illness puzzled the greatest doctors, who tried the usual remedies in vain. At last they told the queen that some secret sorrow must be at the bottom of all this, and she threw herself on her knees beside her son's bed, and implored him to confide his trouble to her. If it was ambition to be king, his father would gladly resign the cares of the crown, and suffer him to reign in his stead; or, if it was love, everything should be sacrificed to get for him the wife he desired, even if she were daughter of a king with whom the country was at war at present!

"Madam," replied the prince, whose weakness would hardly allow him to speak, "do not think me so unnatural as to wish to deprive my father of his crown. As long as he lives I shall remain the most faithful of his subjects! And as to the princesses you speak of, I have seen none that I should care for as a wife, though I would always obey your wishes, whatever it might cost me."

"Ah! my son," cried she, "we will do anything in the world to save your life—and ours too, for if you die, we shall die also."

"Well, then," replied the prince, "I will tell you the only thing that will cure me—a cake made by the hand of 'Donkey Skin.'"

"Donkey Skin?" exclaimed the queen, who thought her son had gone mad; "and who or what is that?"

"Madam," answered one of the attendants present, who had been with the prince at the farm, "'Donkey Skin' is, next to the wolf, the most disgusting creature on the face of the earth. She is a girl who wears a black, greasy skin, and lives at your farmer's as hen-wife."

"Never mind," said the queen; "my son seems to have eaten some of her pastry. It is the whim of a sick man, no doubt; but send at once and let her bake a cake."

The attendant bowed and ordered a page to ride with the message.

Now it is by no means certain that "Donkey Skin" had not caught a glimpse of the prince, either when his eyes looked through the keyhole, or else from her little window, which was over the road. But whether she had actually seen him or only heard him spoken of, directly she received the queen's command, she flung off the dirty skin, washed herself from head to foot, and put on a skirt and bodice of shining silver. Then, locking herself into her room, she took the richest cream, the finest flour, and the freshest eggs on the farm, and set about making her cake.

As she was stirring the mixture in the saucepan a ring that she sometimes wore in secret slipped from her finger and fell into the dough. Perhaps "Donkey Skin" saw it, or perhaps she did not; but, any way, she went on stirring, and soon the cake was ready to be put in the oven. When it was nice and brown she took off her dress and put on her dirty skin, and gave the cake to the page, asking at the same time for news of the prince. But the page turned his head aside, and would not even condescend to answer.

The page rode like the wind, and as soon as he arrived at the palace he snatched up a silver tray and hastened to present the cake to the prince. The sick man began to eat it so fast that the doctors thought he would choke; and, indeed, he very nearly did, for the ring was in one of the bits which he broke off, though he managed to extract it from his mouth without anyone seeing him.

The moment the prince was left alone he drew the ring from under his pillow and kissed it a thousand times. Then he set his mind to find how he was to see the owner—for even he did not dare to confess that he had only beheld "Donkey Skin" through a key-hole, lest they should laugh at this sudden passion. All this worry brought back the fever, which the arrival of the cake had diminished for the time; and the doctors, not knowing what else to say, informed the queen that her son was simply dying of love. The queen, stricken with horror, rushed into the king's presence with the news, and together they hastened to their son's bedside.

"My boy, my dear boy!" cried the king, "who is it you want to marry? We will give her to you for a bride; even if she is the humblest of our slaves. What is there in the whole world that we would not do for you?"

The prince, moved to tears at these words, drew the ring, which was an emerald of the purest water, from under his pillow.

"Ah, dear father and mother, let this be a proof that she whom I love is no peasant girl. The finger which that ring fits has never been thickened by hard work. But be her condition what it may, I will marry no other."

The king and queen examined the tiny ring very closely, and

agreed, with their son, that the wearer could be no mere farm girl. Then the king went out and ordered heralds and trumpeters to go through the town, summoning every maiden to the palace. And she whom the ring fitted would some day be queen.

First came all the princesses, then all the duchesses' daughters, and so on, in proper order. But not one of them could slip the ring over the tip of her finger, to the great joy of the prince, whom excitement was fast curing. At last, when the high-born damsels had failed, the shopgirls and chambermaids took their turn; but with no better fortune.

"Call in the scullions and shepherdesses," commanded the prince; but the sight of their fat, red fingers satisfied everybody.

"There is not a woman left, your Highness," said the chamberlain; but the prince waved him aside.

"Have you sent for "Donkey Skin," who made me the cake?" asked he, and the courtiers began to laugh, and replied that they would not have dared to introduce so dirty a creature into the palace.

"Let some one go for her at once," ordered the king. "I commanded the presence of every maiden, high or low, and I meant it."

The princess had heard the trumpets and the proclamations, and knew quite well that her ring was at the bottom of it all. She, too, had fallen in love with the prince in the brief glimpse she had had of him, and trembled with fear lest someone else's finger might be as small as her own. When, therefore, the messenger from the palace rode up to the gate, she was nearly beside herself with delight. Hoping all the time for such a summons, she had dressed herself with great care, putting on the garment of moonlight, whose skirt was scattered over with emeralds. But when they began calling to her to come down, she hastily covered herself with her donkey-skin and announced she was ready to present herself before his Highness. She was taken straight into the hall, where the prince was awaiting her, but at the sight of the donkey-skin his heart sank. Had he been mistaken after all?

"Are you the girl," he said, turning his eyes away as he spoke, "are you the girl who has a room in the furthest corner of the inner court of the farmhouse?"

"Yes, my lord, I am," answered she.

"Hold out your hand then," continued the prince, feeling that he must keep his word, whatever the cost, and, to the astonishment of every one present, a little hand, white and delicate, came from beneath the black and dirty skin. The ring slipped on with the utmost ease, and, as it did so, the skin fell to the ground, disclosing

The Donkey-skin falls off.

a figure of such beauty that the prince, weak as he was, fell on his knees before her, while the king and queen joined their prayers to his. Indeed, their welcome was so warm, and their caresses so bewildering, that the princess hardly knew how to find words to reply, when the ceiling of the hall opened, and the fairy godmother appeared, seated in a car made entirely of white lilac. In a few words she explained the history of the princess, and how she came to be there, and, without losing a moment, preparations of the most magnificent kind were made for the wedding.

The kings of every country in the earth were invited, including, of course, the princess's adopted father (who by this time had married a widow), and not one refused.

But what a strange assembly it was! Each monarch traveled in the way he thought most impressive; and some came borne in litters, others had carriages of every shape and kind, while the rest were mounted on elephants, tigers, and even upon eagles. So splendid a wedding had never been seen before; and when it was over the king announced that it was to be followed by a coronation, for he and the queen were tired of reigning, and the young couple must take their place. The rejoicings lasted for three whole months, then the new sovereigns settled down to govern their kingdom, and made themselves so much beloved by their subjects, that when they died, a hundred years later, each man mourned them as his own father and mother.

CHARLES PERRAULT

JACK AND THE BEANSTALK

Jack Sells the Cow

ONCE UPON a time there was a poor widow who lived in a little cottage with her only son Jack.

Jack was a giddy, thoughtless boy, but very kind-hearted and affectionate. There had been a hard winter, and after it the poor woman had suffered from fever and ague. Jack did no work as yet, and by degrees they grew dreadfully poor. The widow saw that there was no means of keeping Jack and herself from starvation but by selling her cow; so one morning she said to her son, "I am too weak to go myself, Jack, so you must take the cow to market for me, and sell her."

Jack liked going to market to sell the cow very much; but as he was on the way, he met a butcher who had some beautiful beans in his hand. Jack stopped to look at them, and the butcher told the boy that they were of great value, and persuaded the silly lad to sell the cow for these beans.

When he brought them home to his mother instead of the money she expected for her nice cow, she was very vexed and shed many tears, scolding Jack for his folly. He was very sorry, and mother and son went to bed very sadly that night; their last hope seemed gone.

At daybreak Jack rose and went out into the garden.

"At least," he thought, "I will sow the wonderful beans. Mother says that they are just common scarlet-runners, and nothing else; but I may as well sow them."

So he took a piece of stick, and made some holes in the ground, and put in the beans.

That day they had very little dinner, and went sadly to bed, knowing that for the next day there would be none and Jack, unable to sleep from grief and vexation, got up at day-dawn and went out into the garden.

What was his amazement to find that the beans had grown up in the night, and climbed up and up till they covered the high cliff that sheltered the cottage, and disappeared above it! The stalks had twined and twisted themselves together till they formed quite a ladder.

"It would be easy to climb it," thought Jack.

And, having thought of the experiment, he at once resolved to carry it out, for Jack was a good climber. However, after his late mistake about the cow, he thought he had better consult his mother first.

Wonderful Growth of the Beanstalk

So Jack called his mother, and they both gazed in silent wonder at the Beanstalk, which was not only of great height, but was thick enough to bear Jack's weight.

"I wonder where it ends," said Jack to his mother; "I think I will climb up and see."

His mother wished him not to venture up this strange ladder, but Jack coaxed her to give her consent to the attempt, for he was certain there must be something wonderful in the Beanstalk; so at last she yielded to his wishes.

Jack instantly began to climb, and went up and up on the ladder-like bean till everything he had left behind him—the cottage, the village, and even the tall church tower—looked quite little, and still he could not see the top of the Beanstalk.

Jack felt a little tired, and thought for a moment that he would go back again; but he was a very persevering boy, and he knew that the way to succeed in anything is not to give up. So after resting for a moment he went on.

After climbing higher and higher, till he grew afraid to look down for fear he should be giddy, Jack at last reached the top of the Beanstalk, and found himself in a beautiful country, finely wooded, with beautiful meadows covered with sheep. A crystal stream ran through the pastures; not far from the place where he had got off the Beanstalk stood a fine, strong castle.

Jack wondered very much that he had never heard of or seen this castle before; but when he reflected on the subject, he saw that it was as much separated from the village by the perpendicular rock on which it stood as if it were in another land.

While Jack was standing looking at the castle, a very strange-looking woman came out of the wood, and advanced towards him.

She wore a pointed cap of quilted red satin turned up with

ermine, her hair streamed loose over her shoulders, and she walked with a staff. Jack took off his cap and made her a bow.

"If you please, ma'am," said he, "is this your house?"

"No," said the old lady. "Listen, and I will tell you the story of that castle.

"Once upon a time there was a noble knight, who lived in this castle, which is on the borders of Fairyland. He had a fair and beloved wife and several lovely children: and as his neighbors, the little people, were very friendly towards him, they bestowed on him many excellent and precious gifts.

"Rumor whispered of these treasures; and a monstrous giant, who lived at no great distance, and who was a very wicked being, resolved to obtain possession of them.

"So he bribed a false servant to let him inside the castle, when the knight was in bed and asleep, and he killed him as he lay. Then he went to the part of the castle which was the nursery, and also killed all the poor little ones he found there.

"Happily for her, the lady was not to be found. She had gone with her infant son, who was only two or three months old, to visit her old nurse, who lived in the valley; and she had been detained all night there by a storm.

"The next morning, as soon as it was light, one of the servants at the castle, who had managed to escape, came to tell the poor lady of the sad fate of her husband and her pretty babes. She could scarcely believe him at first, and was eager at once to go back and share the fate of her dear ones; but the old nurse, with many tears, besought her to remember that she had still a child, and that it was her duty to preserve her life for the sake of the poor innocent.

"The lady yielded to this reasoning, and consented to remain at her nurse's house as the best place of concealment; for the servant told her that the giant had vowed, if he could find her, he would kill both her and her baby. Years rolled on. The old nurse died, leaving her cottage and the few articles of furniture it contained to her poor lady, who dwelt in it, working as a peasant for her daily bread. Her spinning-wheel and the milk of a cow, which she had purchased with the little money she had with her, sufficed for the scanty subsistence of herself and her little son. There was a nice little garden attached to the cottage, in which they cultivated peas, beans, and cabbages, and the lady was not ashamed to go out at harvest time, and glean in the fields to supply her little son's wants.

"Jack, that poor lady is your mother. This castle was once your father's, and must again be yours."

Jack uttered a cry of surprise.

"My mother! oh, madam, what ought I to do? My poor father! My dear mother!"

"Your duty requires you to win it back for your mother. But the task is a very difficult one, and full of peril, Jack. Have you courage to undertake it?"

"I fear nothing when I am doing right," said Jack.

"Then," said the lady in the red cap, "you are one of those who slay giants. You must get into the castle, and if possible possess yourself of a hen that lays golden eggs, and a harp that talks. Remember, all the giant possesses is really yours." As she ceased speaking, the lady of the red hat suddenly disappeared, and of course Jack knew she was a fairy.

Jack determined at once to attempt the adventure; so he advanced, and blew the horn which hung at the castle portal. The door was opened in a minute or two by a frightful giantess, with one great eye in the middle of her forehead.

As soon as Jack saw her he turned to run away, but she caught him, and dragged him into the castle.

"Ho, ho!" she laughed terribly. "You didn't expect to see *me* here, that is clear! No, I shan't let you go again. I am weary of my life. I am so overworked, and I don't see why I should not have a page as well as other ladies. And you shall be my boy. You shall clean the knives, and black the boots, and make the fires, and help me generally when the giant is out. When he is at home I must hide you, for he has eaten up all my pages hitherto, and you would be a dainty morsel, my little lad."

While she spoke she dragged Jack right into the castle. The poor boy was very much frightened, as I am sure you and I would have been in his place. But he remembered that fear disgraces a man; so he struggled to be brave and make the best of things.

"I am quite ready to help you, and do all I can to serve you, madam," he said, "only I beg you will be good enough to hide me from your husband, for I should not like to be eaten at all."

"That's a good boy," said the Giantess, nodding her head; "it is lucky for you that you did not scream out when you saw me, as the other boys who have been here did, for if you had done so my husband would have awakened and have eaten you, as he did them, for breakfast. Come here, child; go into my wardrobe: he never ventures to open *that*; you will be safe there."

And she opened a huge wardrobe which stood in the great hall, and shut him into it. But the keyhole was so large that it admitted plenty of air, and he could see everything that took place through

it. By-and-by he heard a heavy tramp on the stairs, like the lumbering along of a great cannon, and then a voice like thunder cried out:

> "Fe, fa, fi-fo-fum,
> I smell the breath of an Englishman.
> Let him be alive or let him be dead,
> I'll grind his bones to make my bread."

"Wife," cried the Giant, "there is a man in the castle. Let me have him for breakfast."

"You are grown old and stupid," cried the lady in her loud tones. "It is only a nice fresh steak off an elephant, that I have cooked for you, which you smell. There, sit down and make a good breakfast."

And she placed a huge dish before him of savory steaming meat, which greatly pleased him, and made him forget his idea of an Englishman being in the castle. When he had breakfasted he went out for a walk; and then the Giantess opened the door, and made Jack come out to help her. He helped her all day. She fed him well, and when evening came put him back in the wardrobe.

The Hen That Lays Golden Eggs

The Giant came in to supper. Jack watched him through the keyhole, and was amazed to see him pick a wolf's bone, and put half a fowl at a time into his capacious mouth.

When the supper was ended he bade his wife bring him his hen that laid the golden eggs.

"It lays as well as it did when it belonged to that paltry knight," he said; "indeed I think the eggs are heavier than ever."

The Giantess went away, and soon returned with a little brown hen, which she placed on the table before her husband. "And now, my dear," she said, "I am going for a walk, if you don't want me any longer."

"Go," said the Giant; "I shall be glad to have a nap by-and-by."

Then he took up the brown hen and said to her:

"Lay!" And she instantly laid a golden egg.

"Lay!" said the Giant again. And she laid another.

"Lay!" he repeated the third time. And again a golden egg lay on the table.

Now Jack was sure this hen was that of which the fairy had spoken.

By-and-by the Giant put the hen down on the floor, and soon after went fast asleep, snoring so loud that it sounded like thunder.

Directly Jack perceived that the Giant was fast asleep, he pushed open the door of the wardrobe and crept out; very softly he stole across the room, and, picking up the hen, made haste to quit the apartment. He knew the way to the kitchen, the door of which he found was left ajar; he opened it, shut and locked it after him, and flew back to the Beanstalk, which he descended as fast as his feet would move.

When his mother saw him enter the house she wept for joy, for she had feared that the fairies had carried him away, or that the

Giant had found him. But Jack put the brown hen down before her, and told her how he had been in the Giant's castle, and all his adventures. She was very glad to see the hen, which would make them rich once more.

The Money Bags

Jack made another journey up the Beanstalk to the Giant's castle one day while his mother had gone to market; but first he dyed his hair and disguised himself. The old woman did not know him again, and dragged him in as she had done before, to help her to do the work; but she heard her husband coming, and hid him in the wardrobe, not thinking that it was the same boy who had stolen the hen. She bade him stay quite still there, or the Giant would eat him.

Then the Giant came in saying:

> "Fe, fa, fi-fo-fum,
> I smell the breath of an Englishman.
> Let him be alive or let him be dead,
> I'll grind his bones to make my bread."

"Nonsense!" said the wife, "it is only a roasted bullock that I thought would be a tit-bit for your supper; sit down and I will bring it up at once." The Giant sat down, and soon his wife brought up a roasted bullock on a large dish, and they began their supper. Jack was amazed to see them pick the bones of the bullock as if it had been a lark. As soon as they had finished their meal, the Giantess rose and said:

"Now, my dear, with your leave I am going up to my room to finish the story I am reading. If you want me call for me."

"First," answered the Giant, "bring me my money bags, that I may count my golden pieces before I sleep." The Giantess obeyed. She went and soon returned with two large bags over her shoulders, which she put down by her husband.

"There," she said; "that is all that is left of the knight's money. When you have spent it you must go and take another baron's castle."

"That he shan't, if I can help it," thought Jack.

The Giant, when his wife was gone, took out heaps and heaps of golden pieces, and counted them, and put them in piles, till he was tired of the amusement. Then he swept them all back into their bags, and leaning back in his chair fell fast asleep, snoring so loud that no other sound was audible.

Jack stole softly out of the wardrobe, and taking up the bags of money (which were his very own, because the Giant had stolen them from his father), he ran off, and with great difficulty descending the Beanstalk, laid the bags of gold on his mother's table. She had just returned from town, and was crying at not finding Jack.

"There, mother, I have brought you the gold that my father lost."

"Oh, Jack! you are a very good boy, but I wish you would not risk your precious life in the Giant's castle. Tell me how you came to go there again."

And Jack told her all about it.

Jack's mother was very glad to get the money, but she did not like him to run any risk for her.

But after a time Jack made up his mind to go again to the Giant's castle.

The Talking Harp

So he climbed the Beanstalk once more, and blew the horn at the Giant's gate. The Giantess soon opened the door; she was very stupid, and did not know him again, but she stopped a minute before she took him in. She feared another robbery; but Jack's fresh face looked so innocent that she could not resist him, and so she bade him come in, and again hid him away in the wardrobe.

By-and-by the Giant came home, and as soon as he had crossed the threshold he roared out:

> "Fe, fa, fi-fo-fum,
> I smell the breath of an Englishman.
> Let him be alive or let him be dead,
> I'll grind his bones to make my bread."

"You stupid old Giant," said his wife, "you only smell a nice sheep, which I have grilled for your dinner."

And the Giant sat down, and his wife brought up a whole sheep for his dinner. When he had eaten it all up, he said:

"Now bring me my harp, and I will have a little music while you take your walk."

The Giantess obeyed, and returned with a beautiful harp. The framework was all sparkling with diamonds and rubies, and the strings were all of gold.

"This is one of the nicest things I took from the knight," said the Giant. "I am very fond of music, and my harp is a faithful servant."

So he drew the harp towards him, and said:
"Play!"
And the harp played a very soft, sad air.
"Play something merrier!" said the Giant.
And the harp played a merry tune.
"Now play me a lullaby," roared the Giant; and the harp played a sweet lullaby, to the sound of which its master fell asleep.

Then Jack stole softly out of the wardrobe, and went into the huge kitchen to see if the Giantess had gone out; he found no one there, so he went to the door and opened it softly, for he thought he could not do so with the harp in his hand.

Then he entered the Giant's room and seized the harp and ran away with it; but as he jumped over the threshold the harp called out:

"MASTER! MASTER!"

And the Giant woke up.

With a tremendous roar he sprang from his seat, and in two strides had reached the door.

But Jack was very nimble. He fled like lightning with the harp, talking to it as he went (for he saw it was a fairy), and telling it he was the son of its old master, the knight.

Still the Giant came on so fast that he was quite close to poor Jack, and had stretched out his great hand to catch him. But, luckily, just at that moment he stepped upon a loose stone, stumbled, and fell flat on the ground, where he lay at his full length.

This accident gave Jack time to get on the Beanstalk and hasten down it; but just as he reached their own garden he beheld the Giant descending after him.

"Mother! mother!" cried Jack, "make haste and give me the axe."

His mother ran to him with a hatchet in her hand, and Jack with one tremendous blow cut through all the Beanstalks except one.

"Now, mother, stand out of the way!" said he.

The Giant Breaks His Neck

Jack's mother shrank back, and it was well she did so, for just as the Giant took hold of the last branch of the Beanstalk, Jack cut the stem quite through and darted from the spot.

Down came the Giant with a terrible crash, and as he fell on his head, he broke his neck, and lay dead at the feet of the woman he had so much injured.

Before Jack and his mother had recovered from their alarm and agitation, a beautiful lady stood before them.

"Jack," said she, "you have acted like a brave knight's son, and deserve to have your inheritance restored to you. Dig a grave and bury the Giant, and then go and kill the Giantess."

"But," said Jack, "I could not kill anyone unless I were fighting with him; and I could not draw my sword upon a woman. Moreover, the Giantess was very kind to me."

The Fairy smiled on Jack.

"I am very much pleased with your generous feeling," she said. "Nevertheless, return to the castle, and act as you will find needful."

Jack asked the Fairy if she would show him the way to the castle, as the Beanstalk was now down. She told him that she would drive him there in her chariot, which was drawn by two peacocks. Jack thanked her, and sat down in the chariot with her.

The Fairy drove him a long distance round, till they reached a village which lay at the bottom of the hill. Here they found a number of miscrable-looking men assembled. The Fairy stopped her carriage and addressed them:

"My friends," said she, "the cruel giant who oppressed you and ate up all your flocks and herds is dead, and this young gentleman was the means of your being delivered from him, and is the son of your kind old master, the knight."

The men gave a loud cheer at these words, and pressed forward to say that they would serve Jack as faithfully as they had served his father. The Fairy bade them follow her to the castle, and they marched thither in a body, and Jack blew the horn and demanded admittance.

The old Giantess saw them coming from the turret loop-hole. She was very much frightened, for she guessed that something had happened to her husband; and as she came downstairs very fast she caught her foot in her dress, and fell from the top to the bottom and broke her neck.

When the people outside found that the door was not opened to them, they took crowbars and forced the portal. Nobody was to be seen, but on leaving the hall they found the body of the Giantess at the foot of the stairs.

Thus Jack took possession of the castle. The Fairy went and brought his mother to him, with the hen and the harp. He had the Giantess buried, and endeavored as much as lay in his power to do right to those whom the Giant had robbed.

Before her departure for fairyland, the Fairy explained to Jack that she had sent the butcher to meet him with the beans, in order to try what sort of lad he was.

If you had looked at the gigantic Beanstalk and only stupidly wondered about it," she said, "I should have left you where misfortune had placed you, only restoring her cow to your mother. But you showed an inquiring mind, and great courage and enterprise, therefore you deserve to rise; and when you mounted the Beanstalk you climbed the Ladder of Fortune."

She then took her leave of Jack and his mother.

BENJAMIN TABART

THE GOOSE-GIRL

ONCE UPON a time an old queen, whose husband had been dead for many years, had a beautiful daughter. When she grew up she was betrothed to a prince who lived a great way off. Now, when the time drew near for her to be married and to depart into a foreign kingdom, her old mother gave her much costly baggage, and many ornaments, gold and silver, trinkets and knickknacks, and, in fact, everything that belonged to a royal trousseau, for she loved her daughter very dearly. She gave her a waiting-maid also, who was to ride with her and hand her over to the bridegroom, and she provided each of them with a horse for the journey. Now the Princess's horse was called Falada, and could speak.

When the hour for departure drew near the old mother went to her bedroom, and taking a small knife she cut her fingers till they bled; then she held a white rag under them, and letting three drops of blood fall into it, she gave it to her daughter, and said: "Dear child, take great care of this rag: it may be of use to you on the journey."

So they took a sad farewell of each other, and the Princess stuck the rag in front of her dress, mounted her horse, and set forth on the journey to her bridegroom's kingdom. After they had ridden for about an hour the Princess began to feel very thirsty, and said to her waiting-maid: "Pray get down and fetch me some water in my golden cup out of yonder stream: I would like a drink." "If you're thirsty," said the maid, "dismount yourself, and lie down by the water and drink; I don't mean to be your servant any longer." The Princess was so thirsty that she got down, bent over the stream, and drank, for she wasn't allowed to drink out of the golden goblet. As she drank she murmured: "Oh! heaven, what am I to do?" and the three drops of blood replied:

> "If your mother only knew,
> Her heart would surely break in two."

But the Princess was meek, and said nothing about her maid's rude behavior, and quietly mounted her horse again. They rode on their way for several miles, but the day was hot, and the sun's rays smote fiercely on them, so that the Princess was soon overcome by thirst again. And as they passed a brook she called once more to her waiting-maid: "Pray get down and give me a drink from my golden cup," for she had long ago forgotten her maid's rude words. But the waiting-maid replied, more haughtily even than before: "If you want a drink, you can dismount and get it; I don't mean to be your servant." Then the Princess was compelled by her thirst to get down, and bending over the flowing water she cried and said: "Oh! heaven, what am I to do?" and the three drops of blood replied:

> "If your mother only knew,
> Her heart would surely break in two."

And as she drank thus, and leaned right over the water, the rag containing the three drops of blood fell from her bosom and floated down the stream, and she in her anxiety never even noticed her loss. But the waiting-maid had observed it with delight, as she knew it gave her power over the bride, for in losing the drops of blood the Princess had become weak and powerless. When she wished to get on her horse Falada again, the waiting-maid called out: "I mean to ride Falada: you must mount my beast"; and this too she had to submit to. Then the waiting-maid commanded her harshly to take off her royal robes, and to put on her common ones, and finally she made her swear by heaven not to say a word about the matter when they reached the palace; and if she hadn't taken this oath she would have been killed on the spot. But Falada observed everything, and laid it all to heart.

The waiting-maid now mounted Falada, and the real bride the worse horse, and so they continued their journey till at length they arrived at the palace yard. There was great rejoicing over the arrival, and the Prince sprang forward to meet them, and taking the waiting-maid for his bride, he lifted her down from her horse and led her upstairs to the royal chamber. In the meantime the real Princess was left standing below in the courtyard. The old King, who was looking out of his window, beheld her in this plight, and it struck him how sweet and gentle, even beautiful, she looked. He went at once to the royal chamber, and asked the bride who it was she had brought with her and had left thus standing in the court below. "Oh!" replied the bride, "I brought her with me to keep me company on the journey; give the girl something to do, that she mayn't be idle." But the old King had no work for her, and couldn't think of anything; so he said, "I've a small boy who looks after the geese, she'd better help him." The youth's name was Curdken, and the real bride was made to assist him in herding geese.

Soon after this the false bride said to the Prince: "Dearest husband, I pray you grant me a favor." He answered: "that I will." "Then let the slaughterer cut off the head of the horse I rode here upon, because it behaved very badly on the journey." But the truth was she was afraid lest the horse should speak and tell how she had treated the Princess. She carried her point, and the faithful Falada was doomed to die. When the news came to the ears of the real Princess she went to the slaughterer, and secretly promised him a piece of gold if he would do something for her. There was in the town a large dark gate, through which she had to pass night and morning with the geese; would he "kindly hang up Falada's head there, that she might see it once again?" The slaughterer said he would do as she desired, chopped off the head, and nailed it firmly over the gateway.

Early next morning, as she and Curdken were driving their flock through the gate, she said as she passed under:

> "Oh! Falada, 'tis you hang there";

and the head replied:

> "'Tis you; pass under, Princess fair:
> If your mother only knew,
> Her heart would surely break in two."

Then she left the tower and drove the geese into a field. And when they had reached the common where the geese fed she sat down and unloosed her hair, which was of pure gold. Curdken loved to see it glitter in the sun, and wanted much to pull some hair out. Then she spoke:

> "Wind, wind, gently sway,
> Blow Curdken's hat away;
> Let him chase o'er field and wold
> Till my locks of ruddy gold,
> Now astray and hanging down,
> Be combed and plaited in a crown."

Then a gust of wind blew Curdken's hat away, and he had to chase it over hill and dale. When he returned from the pursuit she had finished her combing and curling, and his chance of getting any hair was gone. Curdken was very angry, and wouldn't speak to her. So they herded the geese till evening and then went home.

The next morning, as they passed under the gate, the girl said:

> "Oh! Falada, 'tis you hang there;"

and the head replied:

"'Tis you; pass under, Princess fair:
If your mother only knew,
Her heart would surely break in two."

Then she went on her way till she came to the common, where she sat down and began to comb out her hair; then Curdken ran up to her and wanted to grasp some of the hair from her head, but she called out hastily:

> "Wind, wind, gently sway,
> Blow Curdken's hat away;
> Let him chase o'er field and wold
> Till my locks of ruddy gold,
> Now astray and hanging down,
> Be combed and plaited in a crown."

Then a puff of wind came and blew Curdken's hat far away, so that he had to run after it; and when he returned she had long finished putting up her golden locks, and he couldn't get any hair; so they watched the geese till it was dark.

But that evening when they got home Curdken went to the old King, and said: "I refuse to herd geese any longer with that girl." "For what reason?" asked the old King. "Because she does nothing but annoy me all day long," replied Curdken; and he proceeded to relate all her iniquities, and said: "Every morning as we drive the flock through the dark gate she says to a horse's head that hangs on the wall:

> "Oh! Falada, 'tis you hang there";

and the head replies:

> "'Tis you; pass under, Princess fair:
> If your mother only knew,
> Her heart would surely break in two."

And Curdken went on to tell what passed on the common where the geese fed, and how he had always to chase his hat.

The old King bade him go and drive forth his flock as usual next day; and when morning came he himself took up his position behind the dark gate, and heard how the goose-girl greeted Falada. Then he followed her through the field, and hid himself behind a bush on the common. He soon saw with his own eyes how the goose-boy and the goose-girl looked after the geese, and how after a time the maiden sat down and loosed her hair, that glittered like gold, and repeated:

"Wind, wind, gently sway,
Blow Curdken's hat away;
Let him chase o'er field and wold
Till my locks of ruddy gold
Now astray and hanging down,
Be combed and plaited in a crown."

Then a gust of wind came and blew Curdken's hat away, so that
he had to fly over hill and dale after it, and the girl in the meantime
quietly combed and plaited her hair: all this the old King observed,
and returned to the palace without anyone having noticed him. In
the evening when the goose-girl came home he called her aside, and
asked her why she behaved as she did. "I mayn't tell you why; how
dare I confide my woes to anyone? for I swore not to by heaven,
otherwise I should have lost my life." The old King begged her to
tell him all, and left her no peace, but he could get nothing out of
her. At last he said: "Well, if you won't tell me, confide your trouble
to the iron stove there," and he went away. Then she crept to the
stove, and began to sob and cry and to pour out her poor little heart,
and said: "Here I sit, deserted by all the world, I who am a king's
daughter, and a false waiting-maid has forced me to take off my own

clothes, and has taken my place with my bridegroom, while I have to fulfill the lowly office of goose-girl.

> "If my mother only knew,
> Her heart would surely break in two."

But the old King stood outside at the stove chimney, and listened to her words. Then he entered the room again, and bidding her leave the stove, he ordered royal apparel to be put on her, in which she looked amazingly lovely. Then he summoned his son, and revealed to him that he had got the false bride, who was nothing but a waiting-maid, while the real one, in the guise of the ex-goose-girl, was standing at his side. The young King rejoiced from his heart when he saw her beauty and learnt how good she was, and a great banquet was prepared, to which everyone was bidden. The bridegroom sat at the head of the table, the Princess on one side of him and the waiting-maid on the other; but she was so dazzled that she did not recognize the Princess in her glittering garments. Now when they had eaten and drunk, and were merry, the old King asked the waiting-maid to solve a knotty point for him. "What," said he, "should be done to a certain person who has deceived everyone?" and he proceeded to relate the whole story, ending up with, "Now what sentence should be passed?" Then the false bride answered: "She deserves to be put stark naked into a barrel lined with sharp nails, which should be dragged by two white horses up and down the street till she is dead."

"You are the person," said the King, "and you have passed sentence on yourself; and even so it shall be done to you." And when the sentence had been carried out the young King was married to his real bride, and both reigned over the kingdom in peace and happiness.

THE BROTHERS GRIMM

THE UGLY DUCKLING

IT WAS summer in the land of Denmark, and though for most of the year the country looks flat and ugly, it was beautiful now. The wheat was yellow, the oats were green, the hay was dry and delicious to roll in, and from the old ruined house which nobody lived in, down to the edge of the canal, was a forest of great burdocks, so tall that a whole family of children might have dwelt in them and never have been found out.

It was under these burdocks that a duck had built herself a warm nest, and was now sitting all day on six pretty eggs. Five of them were white, but the sixth, which was larger than the others, was of an ugly grey color. The duck was always puzzled about that egg, and how it came to be so different from the rest. Other birds might have thought that when the duck went down in the morning and evening to the water to stretch her legs in a good swim, some lazy mother might have been on the watch, and have popped her egg into the nest. But ducks are not clever at all, and are not quick at counting, so this duck did not worry herself about the matter, but just took care that the big egg should be as warm as the rest.

This was the first set of eggs that the duck had ever laid, and, to begin with, she was very pleased and proud, and laughed at the other mothers, who were always neglecting their duties to gossip with each other or to take little extra swims besides the two in the morning and evening that were necessary for health. But at length she grew tired of sitting there all day. "Surely eggs take longer hatching than they did," she said to herself; and she pined for a little amusement also. Still, she knew that if she left her eggs and the ducklings in them to die none of her friends would ever speak to her again; so there she stayed, only getting off the eggs several times a day to see if the shells were cracking—which may have been the very reason why they did not crack sooner.

She had looked at the eggs at least a hundred and fifty times, when, to her joy, she saw a tiny crack on two of them, and scrambling back to the nest she drew the eggs closer the one to the other, and never moved for the whole of that day. Next morning she was rewarded by noticing cracks in the whole five eggs, and by midday two little yellow heads were poking out from the shells. This encouraged her so much that, after breaking the shells with her bill, so that the little creatures could get free of them, she sat steadily for a whole night upon the nest, and before the sun arose the five white eggs were empty, and five pairs of eyes were gazing out upon the green world.

Now the duck had been carefully brought up, and did not like dirt, and, besides, broken shells are not at all comfortable things to sit or walk upon; so she pushed the rest out over the side, and felt delighted to have some company to talk to till the big egg hatched. But day after day went on, and the big egg showed no signs of cracking, and the duck grew more and more impatient, and began to wish to consult her husband, who never came.

"I can't think what is the matter with it," the duck grumbled to her neighbor who had called in to pay her a visit. "Why I could have hatched two broods in the time that this one has taken!"

"Let me look at it," said the old neighbor. "Ah, I thought so; it is a turkey's egg. Once, when I was young, they tricked me to sitting on a brood of turkey's eggs myself, and when they were hatched the creatures were so stupid that nothing would make them learn to swim. I have no patience when I think of it."

"Well, I will give it another chance," sighed the duck, "and if it does not come out of its shell in another twenty-four hours, I will just leave it alone and teach the rest of them to swim properly and to find their own food. I really can't be expected to do two things at once." And with a fluff of her feathers she pushed the egg into the middle of the nest.

All through the next day she sat on, giving up even her morning bath for fear that a blast of cold might strike the big egg. In the evening, when she ventured to peep, she thought she saw a tiny crack in the upper part of the shell. Filled with hope, she went back to her duties, though she could hardly sleep all night for excitement. When she woke with the first steaks of light she felt something stirring under her. Yes, there it was at last; and as she moved, a big awkward bird tumbled head foremost on the ground.

There was no denying it was ugly, even the mother was forced to admit that to herself, though she only said it was "large" and "strong." "You won't need any teaching when you are once in the water," she told him, with a glance of surprise at the dull brown which covered his back, and at his long naked neck. And indeed he did not, though he was not half so pretty to look at as the little yellow balls that followed her.

When they returned they found the old neighbor on the bank waiting for them to take them into the duckyard. "No, it is not a young turkey, certainly," whispered she in confidence to the mother, "for though it is lean and skinny, and has no color to speak of, yet there is something rather distinguished about it, and it holds its head up well."

"It is very kind of you to say so," answered the mother, who by this time had some secret doubts of its loveliness. "Of course, when you see it by itself it is all right, though it is different, somehow, from the others. But one cannot expect *all* one's children to be beautiful!"

By this time they had reached the center of the yard, where a very old duck was sitting, who was treated with great respect by all the fowls present.

"You must go up and bow low before her," whispered the mother to her children, nodding her head in the direction of the old lady, "and keep your legs well apart, as you see me do. No well-bred duckling turns in its toes. It is a sign of common parents."

The little ducks tried hard to make their small fat bodies copy the movements of their mother, and the old lady was quite pleased with them; but the rest of the ducks looked on discontentedly, and said to each other:

"Oh, dear me, here are ever so many more! The yard is full already; and did you *ever* see anything quite as ugly as that great tall creature? He is a disgrace to any brood. I shall go and chase him out!" So saying she put up her feathers, and running to the big duckling bit his neck.

The duckling gave a loud quack; it was the first time he had felt any pain, and at the sound his mother turned quickly.

"Leave him alone," she said fiercely, "or I will send for his father. He was not troubling *you*."

"No; but he is so ugly and awkward no one can put up with him," answered the stranger. And though the duckling did not understand the meaning of the words, he felt he was being blamed, and became more uncomfortable still when the old Spanish duck who ruled the fowlyard struck in:

"It certainly *is* a great pity he is so different from these beautiful darlings. If he could only be hatched over again!"

The poor little fellow drooped his head, and did not know where to look, but was comforted when his mother answered:

"He may not be quite as handsome as the others, but he swims better, and is very strong; I am sure he will make his way in the world as well as anybody."

"Well, you must feel quite at home here," said the old duck waddling off. And so they did, all except the duckling, who was snapped at by everyone when they thought his mother was not looking. Even the turkey-cock, who was so big, never passed him without mocking words, and his brothers and sisters, who would not have noticed any difference unless it had been put into their heads, soon became as rude and unkind as the rest.

At last he could bear it no longer, and one day he fancied he saw signs of his mother turning against him too; so that night, when the ducks and hens were still asleep, he stole away through an open door, and under cover of the burdock leaves scrambled on by the bank of the canal, till he reached a wide grassy moor, full of soft marshy places where the reeds grew. Here he lay down, but he was too tired and too frightened to fall asleep, and with the earliest peep of the sun the reeds began to rustle, and he saw that he had blundered into a colony of wild ducks. But as he could not run away again he stood up and bowed politely.

"You *are* ugly," said the wild ducks, when they had looked him well over; "but, however, it is no business of ours, unless you wish to marry one of our daughters, and that we should not allow." And the duckling answered that he had no idea of marrying anybody, and wanted nothing but to be left alone after his long journey.

So for two whole days he lay quietly among the reeds, eating such food as he could find, and drinking the water of the moorland pool, till he felt himself quite strong again. He wished he might stay were he was forever, he was so comfortable and happy, away from everyone, with nobody to bite him and tell him how ugly he was.

He was thinking these thoughts, when two young ganders caught sight of him as they were having their evening splash among the reeds, looking for their supper.

"We are getting tired of this moor," they said, "and tomorrow we think of trying another, where the lakes are larger and the feeding better. Will you come with us?"

"Is it nicer than this?" asked the duckling doubtfully. And the words were hardly out of his mouth, when "Pif! paf!" and the two new-comers were stretched dead beside him.

At the sound of the gun the wild ducks in the rushes flew into the air, and for a few minutes the firing continued.

Luckily for himself the duckling could not fly, and he floundered along through the water till he could hide himself amidst some tall ferns which grew in a hollow. But before he got there he met a huge creature on four legs, which he afterwards knew to be a dog, who stood and gazed at him with a long red tongue hanging out of his mouth. The duckling grew cold with terror, and tried to hide his head beneath his little wings; but the dog snuffed at him and passed on, and he was able to reach his place of shelter.

"I am too ugly even for a dog to eat," said he to himself. "Well, that is a great mercy." And he curled himself up in the soft grass till the shots died away in the distance.

When all had been quiet for a long time, and there were only stars to see him, he crept out and looked about him.

He would never go near a pool again, *never*, thought he; and seeing that the moor stretched far away in the opposite direction from which he had come, he marched bravely on till he got to a small cottage, which seemed too tumbledown for the stones to hold together many hours longer. Even the door only hung upon one hinge, and as the only light in the room sprang from a tiny fire, the duckling edged himself cautiously in, and lay down under a chair close to the broken door, from which he could get out if necessary. But no one seemed to see him or smell him; so he spent the rest of the night in peace.

Now in the cottage dwelt an old woman, her cat, and a hen; and it was really they, and not *she*, who were masters of the house. The old woman, who passed all her days in spinning yarn, which she sold at the nearest town, loved both the cat and the hen as her own children, and never contradicted them in any way; so it was their grace, and not hers, that the duckling would have to gain.

It was only next morning, when it grew light, that they noticed their visitor, who stood trembling before them, with his eye on the door ready to escape at any moment. They did not, however, appear very fierce, and the duckling became less afraid as they approached him.

"Can you lay eggs?" asked the hen. And the duckling answered meekly:

"No; I don't know how." Upon which the hen turned her back, and the cat came forward.

"Can you ruffle your fur when you are angry, or purr when you

are pleased?" said she. And again the duckling had to admit that he
could do nothing but swim, which did not seem of much use to
anybody.

So the cat and the hen went straight off to the old woman, who
was still in bed.

"Such a useless creature has taken refuge here," they said. "It calls
itself a duckling; but it can neither lay eggs nor purr! What had we
better do with it?"

"Keep it, to be sure!" replied the old woman briskly. "It is all
nonsense about it not laying eggs. Anyway, we will let it stay here
for a bit, and see what happens."

So the duckling remained for three weeks, and shared the food of
the cat and the hen; but nothing in the way of eggs happened at all.
Then the sun came out, and the air grew soft, and the duckling grew
tired of being in a hut, and wanted with all his might to have a swim.
And one morning he got so restless that even his friends noticed it.

"What is the matter?" asked the hen; and the duckling told her.

"I am so longing for the water again. You can't think how delicious it is to put your head under the water and dive straight to the
bottom."

"I don't think *I* should enjoy it," replied the hen doubtfully. "And
I don't think the cat would like it either." And the cat, when asked,
agreed there was nothing she would hate so much.

"I can't stay here any longer, I *must* get to the water," repeated the
duck. And the cat and the hen, who felt hurt and offended, answered
shortly:

"Very well then, go."

The duckling would have liked to say good-bye, and thank them
for their kindness, as he was polite by nature; but they had both
turned their backs on him, so he went out of the rickety door feeling
rather sad. But, in spite of himself, he could not help a thrill of joy
when he was out in the air and water once more, and cared little for
the rude glances of the creatures he met. For a while he was quite
happy and content; but soon the winter came on, and snow began
to fall, and everything to grow very wet and uncomfortable. And
the duckling soon found that it is one thing to enjoy being in the
water, and quite another to like being damp on land.

The sun was setting one day, like a great scarlet globe, and the
river, to the duckling's vast bewilderment, was getting hard and slippery, when he heard a sound of whirring wings, and high up in the
air a flock of swans were flying. They were as white as snow which
had fallen during the night, and their long necks with yellow bills

were stretched southwards, for they were going—they did not quite
know whither—but to a land where the sun shone all day. Oh, if he
only could have gone with them! But that was not possible, of
course; and besides, what sort of companion could an ugly thing like
him be to those beautiful beings? So he walked sadly down to a
sheltered pool and dived to the very bottom, and tried to think it
was the greatest happiness he could dream of. But, all the same, he
knew it wasn't!

And every morning it grew colder and colder, and the duckling
had hard work to keep himself warm. Indeed, it would be truer to
say that he never was warm at all; and at last, after one bitter night,
his legs moved so slowly that the ice crept closer and closer, and
when the morning light broke he was caught fast, as in a trap; and
soon his senses went from him.

A few hours more and the poor duckling's life had been ended.
But, by good fortune, a man was crossing the river on his way to his
work, and saw in a moment what had happened. He had on thick
wooden shoes, and he went and stamped so hard on the ice that it
broke, and then he picked up the duckling and tucked him under
his sheepskin coat, where his frozen bones began to thaw a little.

Instead of going on his work, the man turned back and took the
bird to his children, who gave him a warm mess to eat and put him
in a box by the fire, and when they came back from school he was
much more comfortable than he had been since he had left the old
woman's cottage. They were kind little children, and wanted to play
with him; but, alas! the poor fellow had never played in his life, and
thought they wanted to tease him, and flew straight into the milk-
pan, and then into the butter-dish, and from that into the meal-
barrel, and at last, terrified at the noise and confusion, right out of
the door, and hid himself in the snow amongst the bushes at the back
of the house.

He never could tell afterwards exactly how he had spent the rest
of the winter. He only knew that he was very miserable and that he
never had enough to eat. But by-and-by things grew better. The
earth became softer, the sun hotter, the birds sang, and the flowers
once more appeared in the grass. When he stood up, he felt different, somehow, from what he had done before he fell asleep among
the reeds to which he had wandered after he had escaped from the
peasant's hut. His body seemed larger, and his wings stronger.
Something pink looked at him from the side of a hill. He thought
he would fly towards it and see what it was.

Oh, how glorious it felt to be rushing through the air, wheeling first one way and then the other! He had never thought that flying could be like that! The duckling was almost sorry when he drew near the pink cloud and found it was made up of apple blossoms growing beside a cottage whose garden ran down to the banks of the canal. He fluttered slowly to the ground and paused for a few minutes under a thicket of syringas, and while he was gazing about him, there walked slowly past a flock of the same beautiful birds he had seen so many months ago. Fascinated, he watched them one by one step into the canal, and float quietly upon the waters as if they were part of them.

"I will follow them," said the duckling to himself; "ugly though I am, I would rather be killed by them than suffer all I have suffered from cold and hunger, and from the ducks and fowls who should have treated me kindly." And flying quickly down to the water, he swam after them as fast as he could.

It did not take him long to reach them, for they had stopped to rest in a green pool shaded by a tree whose branches swept the water. And directly they saw him coming some of the younger ones swam out to meet him with cries of welcome, which again the duckling hardly understood. He approached them glad, yet trembling, and turning to one of the older birds, who by this time had left the shade of the tree, he said:

"If I am to die, I would rather you should kill me. I don't know why I was ever hatched, for I am too ugly to live." And as he spoke, he bowed his head and looked down into the water.

Reflected in the still pool he saw many white shapes, with long necks and golden bills, and, without thinking, he looked for the dull grey body and the awkward skinny neck. But no such thing was there. Instead, he beheld beneath him a beautiful white swan!

"The new one is the best of all," said the children when they came down to feed the swans with biscuit and cake before going to bed. "His feathers are whiter and his beak more golden than the rest." And when he heard that, the duckling thought that it was worthwhile having undergone all the persecution and loneliness that he had passed through, as otherwise he would never have known what it was to be really happy.

HANS CHRISTIAN ANDERSEN

TOADS AND DIAMONDS

THERE WAS once upon a time a widow who had two daughters. The eldest was so much like her in the face and humor that whoever looked upon the daughter saw the mother. They were both so disagreeable and so proud that there was no living with them.

The youngest, who was the very picture of her father for courtesy and sweetness of temper, was withal one of the most beautiful girls ever seen. As people naturally love their own likeness, this mother even doted on her eldest daughter and at the same time had a horrible aversion for the youngest—she made her eat in the kitchen and work continually.

Among other things, this poor child was forced twice a day to draw water above a mile and a-half off the house, and bring home a pitcher full of it. One day, as she was at this fountain, there came to her a poor woman, who begged of her to let her drink.

"Oh! ay, with all my heart, Goody," said this pretty little girl; and rinsing immediately the pitcher, she took up some water from the clearest place of the fountain, and gave it to her, holding up the pitcher all the while, that she might drink the easier.

The good woman, having drunk, said to her:

"You are so very pretty, my dear, so good and so mannerly, that I cannot help giving you a gift." For this was a fairy, who had taken the form of a poor country woman, to see how far the civility and good manners of this pretty girl would go. "I will give you for a gift," continued the Fairy, "that, at every word you speak, there shall come out of your mouth either a flower or a jewel."

When this pretty girl came home her mother scolded her for staying so long at the fountain.

"I beg your pardon, mamma," said the poor girl, "for not making more haste."

And in speaking these words there came out of her mouth two roses, two pearls, and two diamonds.

"What is it I see there?" said the mother, quite astonished. "I think I see pearls and diamonds come out of the girl's mouth! How happens this, child?"

This was the first time she had ever called her child.

The poor creature told her frankly all the matter, not without dropping out infinite numbers of diamonds.

"In good faith," cried the mother, "I must send my child thither. Come hither, Fanny; look what comes out of thy sister's mouth when she speaks. Wouldst not thou be glad, my dear, to have the same gift given thee? Thou hast nothing else to do but go and draw water out of the fountain, and when a certain poor woman asks you to let her drink, to give it to her very civilly."

"It would be a very fine sight indeed," said this ill-bred minx, "to see me go draw water."

"You shall go, hussy!" said the mother; "and this minute."

So away she went, but grumbling all the way, taking with her the best silver tankard in the house.

She was no sooner at the fountain than she saw coming out of the wood a lady most gloriously dressed, who came up to her, and asked to drink. This was, you must know, the very fairy who appeared to her sister, but now had taken the air and dress of a princess, to see how far this girl's rudeness would go.

"Am I come hither," said the proud, saucy one, "to serve you with water, pray? I suppose the silver tankard was brought purely for your ladyship, was it? However, you may drink out of it, if you have a fancy."

"You are not over and above mannerly," answered the Fairy, without putting herself in a passion. "Well, then, since you have so little breeding, and are so disobliging, I give you for a gift that at every word you speak there shall come out of your mouth a snake or a toad."

So soon as her mother saw her coming she cried out:

"Well, daughter?"

"Well, mother?" answered the pert hussy, throwing out of her mouth two vipers and two toads.

"Oh! mercy," cried the mother; "what is it I see? Oh! it is that wretch her sister who has occasioned all this; but she shall pay for it"; and immediately she ran to beat her. The poor child fled away from her, and went to hide herself in the forest, not far from thence.

The King's son, then on his return from hunting, met her, and seeing her so very pretty, asked her what she did there alone and why she cried.

"Alas! sir, my mamma has turned me out of doors."

The King's son, who saw five or six pearls and as many diamonds come out of her mouth, desired her to tell him how that happened. She thereupon told him the whole story; and so the King's son fell in love with her, and, considering himself that such a gift was worth more than any marriage portion, conducted her to the palace of the King his father, and there married her.

As for the sister, she made herself so much hated that her own mother turned her off; and the miserable wretch, having wandered about a good while without finding anybody to take her in, went to a corner of the wood, and there died.

CHARLES PERRAULT

SNOW-WHITE AND ROSE-RED

A POOR widow once lived in a little cottage with a garden in front of it, in which grew two rose trees, one bearing white roses and the other red. She had two children, who were just like the two rose trees; one was called Snow-White and the other Rose-Red, and they were the sweetest and best children in the world, always diligent and always cheerful; but Snow-White was quieter and more gentle than Rose-Red. Rose-Red loved to run about the fields and meadows, and to pick flowers and catch butterflies; but Snow-White sat at home with her mother and helped her in the household, or read aloud to her when there was no work to do. The two children loved each other so dearly that they always walked about hand-in-hand whenever they went out together, and when Snow-White said, "We will never desert each other," Rose-Red answered: "No, not as long as we live"; and the mother added: "Whatever one gets she shall share with the other." They often roamed about in the woods gathering berries and no beast offered to hurt them; on the contrary, they came up to them in the most confiding manner; the little hare would eat a cabbage leaf from their hands, the deer grazed beside them, the stag would bound past them merrily, and the birds remained on the branches and sang to them with all their might. No evil ever befell them; if they tarried late in the wood and night overtook them, they lay down together on the moss and slept till morning, and their mother knew they were quite safe, and never felt anxious about them. Once, when they had slept all night in the wood and had been wakened by the morning sun, they perceived a beautiful child in a shining white robe sitting close to their resting-place. The figure got up, looked at them kindly, but said nothing, and vanished into the wood. And when they looked round about them they became aware that they had slept quite close to a precipice, over which they would certainly have fallen had they gone on a few steps further in the darkness. And when they told their mother of their adventure, she said what they had seen must have been the angel that guards good children.

Snow-White and Rose-Red kept their mother's cottage so beautifully clean and neat that it was a pleasure to go into it. In summer Rose-Red looked after the house, and every morning before her mother awoke she placed a bunch of flowers before the bed, from each tree a rose. In winter Snow-White lit the fire and put on the kettle, which was made of brass, but so beautifully polished that it shone like gold. In the evening when the snowflakes fell their mother said: "Snow-White, go and close the shutters"; and they drew round the fire, while the mother put on her spectacles and read aloud from a big book and the two girls listened and sat and span. Beside them on the ground lay a little lamb, and behind them perched a little white dove with its head tucked under its wings.

One evening as they sat thus cozily together someone knocked at the door as though he desired admittance. The mother said: "Rose-Red, open the door quickly; it must be some traveler seeking shelter." Rose-Red hastened to unbar the door, and thought she saw a poor man standing in the darkness outside; but it was no such thing, only a bear, who poked his thick black head through the door. Rose-Red screamed aloud and sprang back in terror, the lamb began to bleat, the dove flapped its wings, and Snow-White ran and hid behind her mother's bed. But the bear began to speak, and said: "Don't be afraid: I won't hurt you. I am half frozen, and only wish to warm myself a little." "My poor bear," said the mother, "lie down by the fire, only take care you don't burn your fur." Then she called out: "Snow-White and Rose-Red, come out; the bear will do you no harm; he is a good, honest creature." So they both came out of their hiding-places, and gradually the lamb and dove drew near too, and they all forgot their fear. The bear asked the children to beat the snow a little out of his fur, and they fetched a brush and scrubbed him till he was dry. Then the beast stretched himself in front of the fire, and growled quite happily and comfortably. The children soon grew quite at their ease with him, and led their helpless guest a fearful life. They tugged his fur with their hands, put their small feet on his back, and rolled him about here and there, or took a hazel wand and beat him with it; and if he growled they only laughed. The bear submitted to everything with the best possible good-nature, only when they went too far he cried: "Oh! children, spare my life!

"Snow-White and Rose-Red,
Don't beat your lover dead."

When it was time to retire for the night, and the others went to bed, the mother said to the bear: "You can lie there on the hearth, in heaven's name; it will be shelter for you from the cold and wet." As soon as day dawned the children let him out, and he trotted over the snow into the wood. From this time on the bear came every evening at the same hour, and lay down by the hearth and let the children play what pranks they liked with him; and they got so accustomed to him that the door was never shut till their black friend had made his appearance.

When spring came, and all outside was green, the bear said one morning to Snow-White: "Now I must go away, and not return again the whole summer." "Where are you going to, dear bear?" asked Snow-White. "I must go to the wood and protect my treasure from the wicked dwarfs. In winter, when the earth is frozen hard, they are obliged to remain underground, for they can't work their way through; but now, when the sun has thawed and warmed the ground, they break through and come up above to spy the land and steal what they can; what once falls into their hands and into their caves is not easily brought back to light." Snow-White was quite sad over their friend's departure, and when she unbarred the door for him, the bear, stepping out, caught a piece of his fur in the door-knocker, and Snow-White thought she caught sight of glittering gold beneath it, but she couldn't be certain of it; and the bear ran hastily away, and soon disappeared behind the trees.

A short time after this the mother sent the children into the wood to collect fagots. They came in their wanderings upon a big tree which lay felled on the ground, and on the trunk among the long grass they noticed something jumping up and down, but what it was they couldn't distinguish. When they approached nearer they perceived a dwarf with a wizened face and a beard a yard long. The end of the beard was jammed into a cleft of the tree, and the little man sprang about like a dog on a chain, and didn't seem to know what he was to do. He glared at the girls with his fiery red eyes, and screamed out: "What are you standing there for? Can't you come and help me?" "What were you doing, little man?" asked Rose-Red. "You stupid, inquisitive goose!" replied the dwarf; "I wanted to split the tree, in order to get little chips of wood for our kitchen fire; those thick logs that serve to make fires for coarse, greedy people like yourselves quite burn up all the little food we need. I had successfully driven in the wedge, and all was going well, but the cursed wood was so slippery that it suddenly sprang out, and the tree closed up so rapidly that I had no time to take my beautiful white beard out, so here I am stuck fast, and I can't get away; and you silly,

smooth-faced, milk-and-water girls just stand and laugh! Ugh! what wretches you are!"

The children did all in their power, but they couldn't get the beard out; it was wedged in far too firmly. "I will run and fetch somebody," said Rose-Red. "Crazy blockheads!" snapped the dwarf; "what's the good of calling anyone else? You're already two too many for me. Does nothing better occur to you than that?" "Don't be so impatient," said Snow-White, "I'll see you get help"; and taking her scissors out of her pocket she cut off the end of his beard. As soon as the dwarf felt himself free he seized a bag full of gold which was hidden among the roots of the tree, lifted it up, and muttered aloud: "Curse these rude wretches, cutting off a piece of my splendid beard!" With these words he swung the bag over his back, and disappeared without as much as looking at the children again.

Shortly after this Snow-White and Rose-Red went out to get a dish of fish. As they approached the stream they saw something which looked like an enormous grasshopper springing toward the water as if it were going to jump in. They ran forward and recognized their old friend the dwarf. "Where are you going to?" asked Rose-Red; "you're surely not going to jump into the water?" "I'm not such a fool," screamed the dwarf. "Don't you see that cursed fish is trying to drag me in?" The little man had been sitting on the bank fishing, when unfortunately the wind had entangled his beard in the line; and when immediately afterwards a big fish bit, the feeble little creature had no strength to pull it out; the fish had the upper fin, and dragged the dwarf toward him. He clung on with all his might to every rush and blade of grass, but it didn't help him much; he had to follow every movement of the fish, and was in great danger of being drawn into the water. The girls came up just at the right moment, held him firm, and did all they could to disentangle his beard from the line; but in vain, beard and line were in a hopeless muddle. Nothing remained but to produce the scissors and cut the beard, by which a small part of it was sacrificed.

When the dwarf perceived what they were about he yelled to them: "Do you call that manners, you toad-stools! to disfigure a fellow's face? It wasn't enough that you shortened my beard before, but you must now needs cut off the best bit of it. I can't appear like this before my own people. I wish you'd been at Jericho first." Then he fetched a sack of pearls that lay among the rushes, and without saying another word he dragged it away and disappeared behind a stone.

It happened that soon after this the mother sent the two girls to the town to buy needles, thread, laces, and ribbons. Their road led

over a heath where huge boulders of rock lay scattered here and
there. While trudging along they saw a big bird hovering in the air,
circling slowly above them, but always descending lower, till at last
it settled on a rock not far from them. Immediately afterwards they
heard a sharp, piercing cry. They ran forward, and saw with horror
that the eagle had pounced on their old friend the dwarf, and was
about to carry him off. The tender-hearted children seized hold of
the little man, and struggled so long with the bird that at last he let
go his prey. When the dwarf had recovered from the first shock he
screamed in his screeching voice: "Couldn't you have treated me
more carefully? You have torn my thin little coat all to shreds, useless, awkward hussies that you are!" Then he took a bag of precious
stones and vanished under the rocks into his cave. The girls were
accustomed to his ingratitude, and went on their way and did their
business in town. On their way home, as they were again passing the
heath, they surprised the dwarf pouring out his precious stones on
an open space, for he had thought no one would pass by at so late an
hour. The evening sun shone on the glittering stones, and they
glanced and gleamed so beautifully that the children stood still and
gazed on them. "What are you standing there gaping for?" screamed
the dwarf, and his ashen-gray face became scarlet with rage. He was
about to go off with these angry words when a sudden growl was
heard, and a black bear trotted out of the wood. The dwarf jumped
up in great fright, but he hadn't time to reach his place of retreat,
for the bear was already close to him. Then he cried in terror: "Dear
Mr. Bear, spare me! I'll give you all my treasure. Look at those
beautiful precious stones lying there. Spare my life! what pleasure
would you get from a poor feeble little fellow like me? You won't
feel me between your teeth. There, lay hold of these two wicked
girls, they will be a tender morsel for you, as fat as young quails; eat
them up, for heaven's sake." But the bear, paying no attention to his
words, gave the evil little creature one blow with his paw, and he
never moved again.

The girls had run away, but the bear called after them: "Snow-
White and Rose-Red, don't be afraid; wait, and I'll come with
you." Then they recognized his voice and stood still, and when the
bear was quite close to them his skin suddenly fell off, and a beautiful man stood beside them, all dressed in gold. "I am a king's son,"
he said, "and have been doomed by that unholy little dwarf, who
had stolen my treasure, to roam about the woods as a wild bear till
his death should set me free. Now he has got his well-merited
punishment."

Snow-White married him, and Rose-Red his brother, and they divided the great treasure the dwarf had collected in his cave between them. The old mother lived for many years peacefully with her children; and she carried the two rose trees with her, and they stood in front of her window, and every year they bore the finest red and white roses.

THE BROTHERS GRIMM

THE STORY OF THE EMPEROR'S
NEW CLOTHES

MANY YEARS ago there lived an Emperor who was so fond of new clothes that he spent all his money on them in order to be beautifully dressed. He did not care about his soldiers, he did not care about the theater; he only liked to go out walking to show off his new clothes. He had a coat for every hour of the day; and just as they say of a king, "He is in the council-chamber," they always said here, "The Emperor is in the wardrobe."

In the great city in which he lived there was always something going on; every day many strangers came there. One day two impostors arrived who gave themselves out as weavers, and said that they knew how to manufacture the most beautiful cloth imaginable. Not only were the texture and pattern uncommonly beautiful, but the clothes which were made of the stuff possessed this wonderful property that they were invisible to anyone who was not fit for his office, or who was unpardonably stupid.

"Those must indeed be splendid clothes," thought the Emperor. "If I had them on I could find out which men in my kingdom are unfit for the offices they hold; I could distinguish the wise from the stupid! Yes, this cloth must be woven for me at once." And he gave both the impostors much money, so that they might begin their work.

They placed two weaving-looms, and began to do as if they were working, but they had not the least thing on the looms. They also demanded the finest silk and the best gold, which they put in their pockets, and worked at the empty looms till late into the night.

"I should like very much to know how far they have got on with the cloth," thought the Emperor. But he remembered when he thought about it that whoever was stupid or not fit for his office would not be able to see it. Now he certainly believed that he had nothing to fear for himself, but he wanted first to send somebody else in order to see how he stood with regard to his office. Everybody in the whole town knew what a wonderful power the cloth had, and they were all curious to see how bad or how stupid their neighbor was.

"I will send my old and honored minister to the weavers," thought the Emperor. "He can judge best what the cloth is like, for he has intellect, and no one understands his office better than he."

Now the good old minister went into the hall where the two impostors sat working at the empty weaving-looms. "Dear me!" thought the old minister, opening his eyes wide, "I can see nothing!" But he did not say so.

Both the impostors begged him to be so kind as to step closer, and asked him if it were not a beautiful texture and lovely colors. They pointed to the empty loom, and the poor old minister went forward rubbing his eyes; but he could see nothing, for there was nothing there.

"Dear, dear!" thought he, "can I be stupid? I have never thought that, and nobody must know it! Can I be not fit for my office? No, I must certainly not say that I cannot see the cloth!"

"Have you nothing to say about it?" asked one of the men who was weaving.

"Oh, it is lovely, most lovely!" answered the old minister, looking through his spectacles. "What a texture! What colors! Yes, I will tell the Emperor that it pleases me very much."

"Now we are delighted at that," said both the weavers, and thereupon they named the colors and explained the make of the texture.

The old minister paid great attention, so that he could tell the same to the Emperor when he came back to him, which he did.

The impostors now wanted more money, more silk, and more gold to use in their weaving. They put it all in their own pockets, and there came no threads on the loom, but they went on as they had done before, working at the empty loom. The Emperor soon sent another worthy statesman to see how the weaving was getting on, and whether the cloth would soon be finished. It was the same with him as the first one; he looked and looked, but because there was nothing on the empty loom he could see nothing.

"Is it not a beautiful piece of cloth?" asked the two impostors, and they pointed to and described the splendid material which was not there.

"Stupid I am not!" thought the man, "so it must be my good office for which I am not fitted. It is strange, certainly, but no one must be allowed to notice it." And so he praised the cloth which he did not see, and expressed to them his delight at the beautiful colors and the splendid texture. "Yes, it is quite beautiful," he said to the Emperor.

Everybody in the town was talking of the magnificent cloth.

Now the Emperor wanted to see it himself while it was still on the loom. With a great crowd of select followers, amongst whom were both the worthy statesmen who had already been there before, he went to the cunning impostors, who were now weaving with all their might, but without fiber or thread.

"Is it not splendid!" said both the old statesmen who had already been there. "See, your Majesty, what a texture! What colors!" And then they pointed to the empty loom, for they believed that the others could see the cloth quite well.

"What!" thought the Emperor, "I can see nothing! This is indeed horrible! Am I stupid? Am I not fit to be Emperor? That were the most dreadful thing that could happen to me. Oh, it is very beautiful," he said. "It has my gracious approval." And then he nodded pleasantly, and examined the empty loom, for he would not say that he could see nothing.

His whole Court round him looked and looked, and saw no more than the others; but they said like the Emperor, "Oh! it is beautiful!" And they advised him to wear these new and magnificent clothes for the first time at the great procession which was soon to take place. "Splendid! Lovely! Most beautiful!" went from mouth to mouth; everyone seemed delighted over them, and the Emperor gave to the impostors the title of Court weavers to the Emperor.

Throughout the whole of the night before the morning on which the procession was to take place, the impostors were up and were working by the light of over sixteen candles. The people could see that they were very busy making the Emperor's new clothes ready. They pretended they were taking the cloth from the loom, cut with huge scissors in the air, sewed with needles without thread, and then said at last, "Now the clothes are finished!"

The Emperor came himself with his most distinguished knights, and each impostor held up his arm just as if he were holding something, and said, "See! here are the breeches! Here is the coat! Here the cloak!" and so on.

"Spun clothes are so comfortable that one would imagine one had nothing on at all; but that is the beauty of it!"

"Yes," said all the knights, but they could see nothing, for there was nothing there.

"Will it please your Majesty graciously to take off your clothes,"

said the impostors, "then we will put on the new clothes, here before the mirror."

The Emperor took off all his clothes, and the impostors placed themselves before him as if they were putting on each part of his new clothes which was ready, and the Emperor turned and bent himself in front of the mirror.

"How beautifully they fit! How well they sit!" said everybody. "What material! What colors! It is a gorgeous suit!"

"They are waiting outside with the canopy which your Majesty is wont to have borne over you in the procession," announced the Master of the Ceremonies.

"Look, I am ready," said the Emperor. "Doesn't it sit well!" And he turned himself again to the mirror to see if his finery was on all right.

The chamberlains who were used to carry the train put their

hands near the floor as if they were lifting up the train; then they did as if they were holding something in the air. They would not have it noticed that they could see nothing.

So the Emperor went along in the procession under the splendid canopy, and all the people in the streets and at the windows said, "How matchless are the Emperor's new clothes! That train fastened to his dress, how beautifully it hangs!"

No one wished it to be noticed that he could see nothing, for then he would have been unfit for his office, or else very stupid. None of the Emperor's clothes had met with such approval as these had.

"But he has nothing on!" said a little child at last.

"Just listen to the innocent child!" said the father, and each one whispered to his neighbor what the child had said.

"But he has nothing on!" the whole of the people called out at last.

This struck the Emperor, for it seemed to him as if they were right; but he thought to himself, "I must go on with the procession now. And the chamberlains walked along still more uprightly, holding up the train which was not there at all.

HANS CHRISTIAN ANDERSEN

THE FIR-TREE

THERE WAS once a pretty little fir-tree in a wood. It was in a capital position, for it could get sun, and there was enough air, and all around grew many tall companions, both pines and firs. The little fir-tree's greatest desire was to grow up. It did not heed the warm sun and the fresh air, or notice the little peasant children who ran about chattering when they came out to gather wild strawberries and raspberries. Often they found a whole basketful and strung strawberries on a straw; they would sit down by the little fir-tree and say, "What a pretty little one this is!" The tree did not like that at all.

By the next year it had grown a whole ring taller, and the year after that another ring more, for you can always tell a fir-tree's age from its rings.

"Oh! if I were only a great tree like the others!" sighed the little fir-tree, "then I could stretch out my branches far and wide and look out into the great world! The birds would build their nests in my branches, and when the wind blew I would bow to it politely just like the others!" It took no pleasure in the sunshine, nor in the birds, nor in the rose-colored clouds that sailed over it at dawn and at sunset. Then the winter came, and the snow lay white and sparkling all around, and a hare would come and spring right over the little fir-tree, which annoyed it very much. But when two more winters had passed the fir-tree was so tall that the hare had to run round it. "Ah! to grow and grow, and become great and old! that is the only pleasure in life," thought the tree. In the autumn the woodcutters used to come and hew some of the tallest trees; this happened every year, and the young fir-tree would shiver as the magnificent trees fell crashing and crackling to the ground, their branches hewn off, and the great trunks left bare, so that they were almost unrecognizable. But then they were laid on wagons and dragged out of the wood by horses. "Where are they going? What will happen to them?"

In spring, when the swallows and storks came, the fir-tree asked them, "Do you know where they were taken? Have you met them?"

The swallows knew nothing of them, but the stork nodded his head thoughtfully, saying, "I think I know. I met many new ships as I flew from Egypt; there were splendid masts on the ships. I'll wager those were they! They had the scent of fir-trees. Ah! those are grand, grand!"

"Oh! if I were only big enough to sail away over the sea too! What sort of thing is the sea? what does it look like?"

"Oh! it would take much too long to tell you all that," said the stork, and off he went.

"Rejoice in your youth," said the sunbeams, "rejoice in the sweet growing time, in the young life within you."

And the wind kissed it and the dew wept tears over it, but the fir-tree did not understand.

Towards Christmas-time quite little trees were cut down, some not as big as the young fir-tree, or just the same age, and now it had no peace or rest for longing to be away. These little trees, which were chosen for their beauty, kept all their branches; they were put in carts and drawn out of the wood by horses.

"Whither are those going?" asked the fir-tree; "they are no bigger than I, and one there was much smaller even! Why do they keep their branches? Where are they taken to?"

"We know! we know!" twittered the sparrows. "Down there in the city we have peeped in at the windows, we know where they go! They attain to the greatest splendor and magnificence you can imagine! We have looked in at the windows and seen them planted in the middle of the warm room and adorned with the most beautiful things—golden apples, sweet-meats, toys and hundreds of candles."

"And then?" asked the fir-tree, trembling in every limb with eagerness, "and then? what happens then?"

"Oh, we haven't seen anything more than that. That was simply matchless!"

"Am I too destined to the same brilliant career?" wondered the fir-tree excitedly. "That is even better than sailing over the sea! I am sick with longing. If it were only Christmas! Now I am tall and grown-up like those which were taken away last year. Ah, if I were only in the cart! If I were only in the warm room with all the splendor and magnificence! And then? Then comes something better, something still more beautiful, else why should they dress us up? There must be something greater, something grander to come—but what? Oh! I am pining away! I really don't know what's the matter with me!"

"Rejoice in us," said the air and sunshine, "rejoice in your fresh youth in the free air!"

But it took no notice, and just grew and grew; there it stood fresh and green in winter and summer, and all who saw it said, "What a beautiful tree!" And at Christmas-time it was the first to be cut down. The axe went deep into the pith; the tree fell to the ground with a groan; it felt bruised and faint. It could not think of happiness, it was sad at leaving its home, the spot where it had sprung up; it knew, too, that it would never see again its dear old companions, or the little shrubs and flowers, perhaps not even the birds. Altogether the parting was not pleasant.

When the tree came to itself again it was packed in a yard with other trees, and a man was saying, "this is a splendid one, we shall only want this."

Then came two footmen in livery and carried the fir-tree to a large and beautiful room. There were pictures hanging on the walls, and near the Dutch stove stood great Chinese vases with lions on their lids; there were armchairs, silk-covered sofas, big tables laden with picture-books and toys, worth hundreds of pounds—at least, so the children said. The fir-tree was placed in a great tub filled with sand, but no one could see that it was a tub, for it was all hung with greenery and stood on a gay carpet. How the tree trembled! What was coming now? On its branches they hung little nets cut out of colored paper, each full of sugarplums; gilt apples and nuts hung down as if they were growing, over a hundred red, blue, and white tapers were fastened among the branches. Dolls as life—like as human beings—the fir-tree had never seen any before were suspended among the green, and right up at the top was fixed a gold tinsel star; it was gorgeous, quite unusually gorgeous!

"Tonight," they all said, "tonight it will be lighted!"

"Ah!" thought the tree, "if it were only evening! Then the tapers would soon be lighted. What will happen then? I wonder whether the trees will come from the wood to see me, or if the sparrows will fly against the window panes? Am I to stand here decked out thus through winter and summer?"

It was not a bad guess, but the fir-tree had real bark-ache from sheer longing, and bark-ache in trees is just as bad as headache in human beings.

Now the tapers were lighted. What a glitter! What splendor! The tree quivered in all its branches so much, that one of the candles caught the green, and singed it. "Take care!" cried the young ladies, and they extinguished it.

Now the tree did not even dare to quiver. It was really terrible! It was so afraid of losing any of its ornaments, and it was quite bewildered by all the radiance.

And then the folding doors were opened, and a crowd of children rushed in, as though they wanted to knock down the whole tree, whilst the older people followed soberly. The children stood quite silent, but only for a moment, and then they shouted again, and danced round the tree, and snatched off one present after another.

"What are they doing?" thought the tree. "What is going to happen?" And the tapers burnt low on the branches, and were put out one by one, and then the children were given permission to plunder the tree. They rushed at it so that all its boughs creaked; if it had not been fastened by the gold star at the top to the ceiling, it would have been overthrown.

The children danced about with their splendid toys, and no one looked at the tree, except the old nurse, who came and peeped amongst the boughs, just to see if a fig or an apple had been forgotten.

"A story! a story!" cried the children, and dragged a little stout man to the tree; he sat down beneath it, saying, "Here we are in the greenwood, and the tree will be delighted to listen! But I am only going to tell one story. Shall it be Henny Penny or Humpty Dumpty who fell downstairs, and yet gained great honor and married a princess?"

"Henny Penny!" cried some; "Humpty Dumpty!" cried others; there was a perfect babel of voices! Only the fir-tree kept silent, and thought, "Am I not to be in it? Am I to have nothing to do with it?"

But it had already been in it, and played out its part. And the man told them about Humpty Dumpty who fell downstairs and married a princess. The children clapped their hands and cried, "Another! another!" They wanted the story of Henny Penny also, but they only got Humpty Dumpty. The fir-tree stood quite astonished and thoughtful; the birds in the wood had never related anything like that. "Humpty Dumpty fell downstairs and yet married a princess! yes, that is the way of the world!" thought the tree, and was sure it must be true, because such a nice man had told the story. "Well, who knows? Perhaps I shall fall downstairs and marry a princess." And it rejoiced to think that next day it would be decked out again with candles, toys, glittering ornaments, and fruits. "Tomorrow I shall quiver again with excitement. I shall enjoy to the full all my splendor. Tomorrow I shall hear Humpty Dumpty again, and perhaps Henny Penny too." And the tree stood silent and lost in thought all through the night.

Next morning the servants came in. "Now the dressing up will begin again," thought the tree. But they dragged it out of the room, and up the stairs to the lumber-room, and put it in a dark corner, where no ray of light could penetrate. "What does this mean?" thought the tree. "What am I to do here? What is there for me to hear?" And it leant against the wall, and thought and thought. And there was time enough for that, for days and nights went by, and no one came; at last when some one did come, it was only to put some great boxes into the corner. Now the tree was quite covered; it seemed as if it had been quite forgotten.

"Now it is winter out-doors," thought the fir-tree. "The ground is hard and covered with snow, they can't plant me yet, and that is why I am staying here under cover till the spring comes. How thoughtful they are! Only I wish it were not so terribly dark and lonely here; not even a little hare! It was so nice out in the wood, when the snow lay all around, and the hare leapt past me; yes, even when he leapt over me: but I didn't like it then. It's so dreadfully lonely up here."

"Squeak, squeak!" said a little mouse, stealing out, followed by a second. They sniffed at the fir-tree, and then crept between its boughs. "It's frightfully cold," said the little mice. "How nice it is to be here! Don't you think so too, you old fir-tree?"

"I'm not at all old," said the tree; "there are many much older than I am."

"Where do you come from?" asked the mice, "and what do you know?" They were extremely inquisitive. "Do tell us about the most beautiful place in the world. Is that where you come from? Have you been in the storeroom, where cheeses lie on the shelves, and hams hang from the ceiling, where one dances on tallow candles, and where one goes in thin and comes out fat?"

"I know nothing about that," said the tree. "But I know the wood, where the sun shines, and the birds sing." And then it told them all about its young days, and the little mice had never heard anything like that before, and they listened with all their ears, and said: "Oh, how much you have seen! How lucky you have been!"

"I?" said the fir-tree, and then it thought over what it had told them. "Yes, on the whole those were very happy times." But then it went on to tell them about Christmas Eve, when it had been adorned with sweet-meats and tapers.

"Oh!" said the little mice, "how lucky you have been, you old fir-tree!"

"I'm not at all old," said the tree. "I only came from the wood this winter. I am only a little backward, perhaps, in my growth."

"How beautifully you tell stories!" said the little mice. And next evening they came with four others, who wanted to hear the tree's story, and it told still more, for it remembered everything so clearly and thought: "Those were happy times! But they may come again. Humpty Dumpty fell downstairs, and yet he married a princess; perhaps I shall also marry a princess!" And then it thought of a pretty little birch-tree that grew out in the wood, and seemed to the fir-tree a real princess, and a very beautiful one too.

"Who is Humpty Dumpty?" asked the little mice.

And then the tree told the whole story; it could remember every single word, and the little mice were ready to leap on to the topmost branch out of sheer joy! Next night many more mice came, and on Sunday even two rats; but they did not care about the story, and that troubled the little mice, for now they thought less of it too.

"Is that the only story you know?" asked the rats.

"The only one," answered the tree. "I heard that on my happiest evening, but I did not realize then how happy I was."

"That's a very poor story. Don't you know one about bacon or tallow candles? a storeroom story?"

"No," said the tree.

"Then we are much obliged to you," said the rats, and they went back to their friends.

At last the little mice went off also, and the tree said, sighing: "Really it was very pleasant when the lively little mice sat round and listened whilst I told them stories. But now that's over too. But now I will think of the time when I shall be brought out again, to keep up my spirits."

But when did that happen? Well, it was one morning when they came to tidy up the lumber-room; the boxes were set aside, and the tree brought out; they threw it really rather roughly on the floor, but a servant dragged it off at once downstairs, where there was daylight once more.

"Now life begins again!" thought the tree. It felt the fresh air, the first rays of the sun, and there it was out in the yard! Everything passed so quickly; the tree quite forgot to notice itself, there was so much to look at all around. The yard opened on a garden full of flowers; the roses were so fresh and sweet, hanging over a little trellis, the lime-trees were in blossom, and the swallows flew about, saying: "Quirre-virre-vil, my husband has come home;" but it was not the fir-tree they meant.

"Now I shall live," thought the tree joyfully, stretching out its branches wide; but, alas! they were all withered and yellow; and it was lying in a corner among weeds and nettles. The golden star was still on its highest bough, and it glittered in the bright sunlight. In the yard some of the merry children were playing, who had danced so gaily round the tree at Christmas. One of the little ones ran up, and tore off the gold star.

"Look what was left on the ugly old fir-tree!" he cried, and stamped on the boughs so that they cracked under his feet.

And the tree looked at all the splendor and freshness of the flowers in the garden, and then looked at itself, and wished that it had been left lying in the dark corner of the lumber-room; it thought of its fresh youth in the wood, of the merry Christmas Eve, and of the little mice who had listened so happily to the story of Humpty Dumpty.

"Too late! Too late!" thought the old tree. "If only I had enjoyed myself whilst I could. Now all is over and gone."

And a servant came and cut the tree into small pieces, there was quite a bundle of them; they flickered brightly under the great copper in the brew-house; the tree sighed deeply, and each sigh was like a pistol-shot; so the children who were playing there ran up, and sat in front of the fire, gazing at it, and crying, "Piff! puff! bang!" But for each report, which was really a sigh, the tree was thinking of a summer's day in the wood, or of a winter's night out there, when the stars were shining; it thought of Christmas Eve, and of Humpty Dumpty, which was the only story it had heard, or could tell, and then the tree had burnt away.

The children played on in the garden, and the youngest had the golden star on his breast, which the tree had worn on the happiest evening of its life; and now that was past—and the tree had passed away—and the story too, all ended and done with.

And that's the way with all stories!

Here our Danish author ends. This is what people call *sentiment*, and I hope you enjoy it!

HANS CHRISTIAN ANDERSEN

EAST OF THE SUN AND
WEST OF THE MOON

ONCE UPON a time there was a poor husbandman who had many children and little to give them in the way either of food or clothing. They were all pretty, but the prettiest of all was the youngest daughter, who was so beautiful that there were no bounds to her beauty.

So once—it was late on a Thursday evening in autumn, and wild weather outside, terribly dark, and raining so heavily and blowing so hard that the walls of the cottage shook again—they were all sitting together by the fireside, each of them busy with something or other, when suddenly someone rapped three times against the window-pane. The man went out to see what could be the matter, and when he got out there stood a great big white bear.

"Good-evening to you," said the White Bear.

"Good-evening," said the man.

"Will you give me your youngest daughter?" said the White Bear; "if you will, you shall be as rich as you are now poor."

Truly the man would have had no objection to be rich, but he thought to himself: "I must first ask my daughter about this," so he went in and told them that there was a great white bear outside who had faithfully promised to make them all rich if he might but have the youngest daughter.

She said no, and would not hear of it; so the man went out again, and settled with the White Bear that he should come again next Thursday evening, and get her answer. Then the man persuaded her, and talked so much to her about the wealth that they would have, and what a good thing it would be for herself, that at last she made up her mind to go, and washed and mended all her rags, made herself as smart as she could, and held herself in readiness to set out. Little enough had she to take away with her.

Next Thursday evening the White Bear came to fetch her. She

seated herself on his back with her bundle, and thus they departed.
When they had gone a great part of the way, the White Bear said:
"Are you afraid?"

"No, that I am not," said she.

"Keep tight hold of my fur, and then there is no danger," said he.

And thus she rode far, far away, until they came to a great mountain. Then the White Bear knocked on it, and a door opened, and they went into a castle where there were many brilliantly lighted rooms which shone with gold and silver, likewise a large hall in which there was a well-spread table, and it was so magnificent that it would be hard to make anyone understand how splendid it was. The White Bear gave her a silver bell, and told her that when she needed anything she had but to ring this bell, and what she wanted would appear. So after she had eaten, and night was drawing near, she grew sleepy after her journey, and thought she would like to go to bed. She rang the bell, and scarcely had she touched it before she found herself in a chamber where a bed stood ready made for her, which was as pretty as anyone could wish to sleep in. It had pillows of silk, and curtains of silk fringed with gold, and everything that was in the room was of gold or silver; but when she had lain down and put out the light a man came and lay down beside her, and behold it was the White Bear, who cast off the form of a beast during the night. She never saw him, however, for he always came after she had put out her light, and went away before daylight appeared.

So all went well and happily for a time, but then she began to be very sad and sorrowful, for all day long she had to go about alone; and she did so wish to go home to her father and mother and brothers and sisters. Then the White Bear asked what it was that she wanted, and she told him that it was so dull there in the mountain, and that she had to go about all alone, and that in her parents' house at home there were all her brothers and sisters, and it was because she could not go to them that she was so sorrowful.

"There might be a cure for that," said the White Bear, "if you would but promise me never to talk with your mother alone, but only when the others are there too; for she will take hold of your hand," he said, "and will want to lead you into a room to talk with you alone; but that you must by no means do, or you will bring great misery on both of us."

So one Sunday the White Bear came and said that they could now set out to see her father and mother, and they journeyed thither, she sitting on his back, and they went a long, long way, and it took a long, long time; but at last they came to a large white farmhouse, and her brothers and sisters were running about outside it, playing, and it was so pretty that it was a pleasure to look at it.

"Your parents dwell here now," said the White Bear; "but do not forget what I said to you, or you will do much harm both to yourself and me."

"No, indeed," said she, "I shall never forget;" and as soon as she was at home the White Bear turned round and went back again.

There were such rejoicings when she went in to her parents that it seemed as if they would never come to an end. Everyone thought that he could never be sufficiently grateful to her for all she had done for them all. Now they had everything that they wanted, and everything was as good as it could be. They all asked her how she was getting on where she was. All was well with her too, she said; and she had everything that she could want. What other answers she gave I cannot say, but I am pretty sure that they did not learn much from her. But in the afternoon, after they had dined at midday, all happened just as the White Bear had said. Her mother wanted to talk with her alone in her own chamber. But she remembered what the White Bear had said, and would on no account go. "What we have to say can be said at any time," she answered. But somehow or other her mother at last persuaded her, and she was forced to tell the whole story. So she told how every night a man came and lay down beside her when the lights were all put out, and how she never saw him, because he always went away before it grew light in the morning, and how she continually went about in sadness, thinking how happy she would be if she could but see him, and how all day long she had to go about alone, and it was so dull and solitary. "Oh!" cried the mother, in horror, "you are very likely sleeping with a troll! But I will teach you a way to see him. You shall have a bit of one of my candles, which you can take away with you hidden in your breast. Look at him with that when he is asleep, but take care not to let any tallow drop upon him."

So she took the candle, and hid it in her breast, and when evening drew near the White Bear came to fetch her away. When they had gone some distance on their way, the White Bear asked her if everything had not happened just as he had foretold, and she could not but own that it had. "Then, if you have done what your mother wished," said he, "you have brought great misery on both of us." "No," she said, "I have not done anything at all." So when she had reached home and had gone to bed it was just the same as it had been before, and a man came and lay down beside her, and late at night, when she could hear that he was sleeping, she got up and kindled a light, lit her candle, let her light shine on him, and saw him, and he was the handsomest prince that eyes had ever beheld, and she loved him so much that it seemed to her that she must die if she did not kiss him that very moment. So she did kiss him; but while she was doing it she let three drops of hot tallow fall upon his shirt, and he awoke. "What have you done now?" said he; "you have brought misery on both of us. If you had but held out for the space of one year I should have been free. I have a stepmother who has bewitched me so that I am a white bear by day and a man by night; but now all is at an end between you and me, and I must leave you, and go to her. She lives in a castle which lies east of the sun and west of the moon, and there too is a princess with a nose which is three ells long, and she now is the one whom I must marry."

She wept and lamented, but all in vain, for go he must. Then she asked him if she could not go with him. But no, that could not be. "Can you tell me the way then, and I will seek you—that I may surely be allowed to do!"

"Yes, you may do that," said he; "but there is no way thither. It lies east of the sun and west of the moon, and never would you find your way there."

When she awoke in the morning both the Prince and the castle were gone, and she was lying on a small green patch in the midst of a dark, thick wood. By her side lay the self-same bundle of rags which she had brought with her from her own home. So when she had rubbed the sleep out of her eyes, and wept till she was weary, she set out on her way, and thus she walked for many and many a long day, until at last she came to a great mountain. Outside it an aged woman was sitting, playing with a golden apple. The girl asked her if she knew the way to the Prince who lived with his stepmother in the castle which lay east of the sun and west of the moon, and who was to marry a princess with a nose which was three ells long. "How do you happen to know about him?" inquired the old woman; "maybe you are she who ought to have had him." "Yes, indeed, I am," she said. "So it is you, then?" said the old woman; "I know nothing about him but that he dwells in a castle which is east of the sun and west of the moon. You will be a long time in getting to it, if ever you get to it at all; but you shall have the loan of my horse, and then you can ride on it to an old woman who is a neighbor of mine: perhaps she can tell you about him. When you have got there you must just strike the horse beneath the left ear and bid it go home again; but you may take the golden apple with you."

So the girl seated herself on the horse, and rode for a long, long way, and at last she came to the mountain, where an aged woman was sitting outside with a gold carding-comb. The girl asked her if she knew the way to the castle which lay east of the sun and west of the moon; but she said what the first old woman had said: "I know nothing about it, but that it is east of the sun and west of the moon, and that you will be a long time in getting to it, if ever you get there at all; but you shall have the loan of my horse to an old woman who lives the nearest to me: perhaps she may know where the castle is, and when you have got to her you may just strike the horse beneath the left ear and bid it go home again." Then she gave her the gold carding-comb, for it might, perhaps, be of use to her, she said.

So the girl seated herself on the horse, and rode a wearisome long way onwards again, and after a very long time she came to a great mountain, where an aged woman was sitting, spinning at a golden spinning-wheel. Of this woman, too, she inquired if she knew the way to the Prince, and where to find the castle which lay east of the sun and west of the moon. But it was only the same thing once again. "Maybe it was you who should have had the Prince," said the old woman. "Yes, indeed, I should have been the one," said the girl. But this old crone knew the way no better than the others—it was east of the sun and west of the moon, she knew that, "and you will be a long time in getting to it, if ever you get to it at all," she said; "but you may have the loan of my horse, and I think you had better ride to the East Wind, and ask him: perhaps he may know where the castle is, and will blow you thither. But when you have got to him you must just strike the horse beneath the left ear, and he will come home again." And then she gave her the golden spinning-wheel, saying: "Perhaps you may find that you have a use for it."

The girl had to ride for a great many days, and for a long and wearisome time, before she got there; but at last she did arrive, and then she asked the East Wind if he could tell her the way to the Prince who dwelt east of the sun and west of the moon. "Well," said the East Wind, "I have heard tell of the Prince, and of his castle, but I do not know the way to it, for I have never blown so far; but, if you like, I will go with you to my brother the West Wind: he may know that, for he is much stronger than I am. You may sit on my back, and then I can carry you there." So she seated herself on his back, and they did go so swiftly! When they got there, the East Wind went in and said that the girl whom he had brought was the one who ought to have had the Prince up at the castle which lay east of the sun and west of the moon, and that now she was traveling about to find him again, so he had come there with her, and would like to hear if the West Wind knew whereabout the castle was. "No," said the West Wind; "so far as that have I never blown; but if you like I will go with you to the South Wind, for he is much stronger than either of us, and he has roamed far and wide, and perhaps he can tell you what you want to know. You may seat yourself on my back, and then I will carry you to him."

So she did this, and journeyed to the South Wind, neither was she very long on the way. When they had got there, the West Wind asked him if he could tell her the way to the castle that lay east of the sun and west of the moon, for she was the girl who ought to marry the Prince who lived there. "Oh, indeed!" said the South Wind, "is that she? Well," said he, "I have wandered about a great deal in my time, and in all kinds of places, but I have never blown so far as that. If you like, however, I will go with you to my brother, the North Wind; he is the oldest and strongest of all of us, and if he does not know where it is no one in the whole world will be able to tell you. You may sit upon my back, and then I will carry you there." So she seated herself on his back, and off he went from his house in great haste, and they were not long on the way. When they came near the North Wind's dwelling, he was so wild and frantic that they felt cold gusts a long while before they got there. "What do you want?" he roared out from afar, and they froze as they heard. Said the South Wind: "It is I, and this is she who should have had the Prince who lives in the castle which lies east of the sun and west of the moon. And now she wishes to ask you if you have ever been there, and can tell her the way, for she would gladly find him again."

"Yes," said the North Wind, "I know where it is. I once blew an aspen leaf there, but I was so tired that for many days afterward I was not able to blow at all. However, if you really are anxious to go there, and are not afraid to go with me, I will take you on my back, and try if I can blow you there."

"Get there I must," said she; "and if there is any way of going I will; and I have no fear, no matter how fast you go."

"Very well then," said the North Wind; "but you must sleep here tonight, for if we are ever to get there we must have the day before us."

The North Wind woke her betimes next morning, and puffed himself up, and made himself so big and so strong that it was frightful to see him, and away they went, high up through the air, as if they would not stop until they had reached the very end of the

world. Down below there was such a storm! It blew down woods and houses, and when they were above the sea the ships were wrecked by hundreds. And thus they tore on and on, and a long time went by, and then yet more time passed, and still they were above the sea, and the North Wind grew tired, and more tired, and at last so utterly weary that he was scarcely able to blow any longer, and he sank and sank, lower and lower, until at last he went so low that the waves dashed against the heels of the poor girl he was carrying. "Art thou afraid?" said the North Wind. "I have no fear," said she; and it was true. But they were not very, very far from land, and there was just enough strength left in the North Wind to enable him to throw her on to the shore, immediately under the windows of a castle which lay east of the sun and west of the moon; but then he was so weary and worn out that he was forced to rest for several days before he could go to his own home again.

Next morning she sat down beneath the walls of the castle to play with the golden apple, and the first person she saw was the maiden with the long nose, who was to have the Prince. "How much do you want for that gold apple of yours, girl?" said she, opening the window. "It can't be bought either for gold or money," answered the girl. "If it cannot be bought either for gold or money, what will buy it? You may say what you please," said the Princess.

"Well, if I may go to the Prince who is here, and be with him tonight, you shall have it," said the girl who had come with the North Wind. "You may do that," said the Princess, for she had made up her mind what she would do. So the Princess got the golden apple, but when the girl went up to the Prince's apartment that night he was asleep, for the Princess had so contrived it. The poor girl called to him, and shook him, and between whiles she wept; but she could not wake him. In the morning, as soon as day dawned, in came the Princess with the long nose, and drove her out again. In the daytime she sat down once more beneath the windows of the castle, and began to card with her golden carding-comb; and then all happened as it had happened before. The Princess asked her what she wanted for it, and she replied that it was not for sale, either for gold or money, but that if she could get leave to go to the Prince, and be with him during the night, she should have it. But when she went up to the Prince's room he was again asleep, and, let her call him, or shake him, or weep as she would, he still slept on, and she could not put any life in him. When daylight came in the morning, the Princess with the long nose came too, and once more drove her away. When day had quite come, the girl seated herself under the castle windows, to spin with her golden spinning-wheel, and the Princess with the long nose wanted to have that also. So she opened the window, and asked what she would take for it. The girl said what she had said on each of the former occasions—that it was not for sale either for gold or for money, but if she could get leave to go to the Prince who lived there, and be with him during the night, she should have it.

"Yes," said the Princess, "I will gladly consent to that."

But in that place there were some Christian folk who had been carried off, and they had been sitting in the chamber which was next to that of the Prince, and had heard how a woman had been in there who had wept and called on him two nights running, and they told the Prince of this. So that evening, when the Princess came once more with her sleeping-drink, he pretended to drink, but threw it away behind him, for he suspected that it was a sleeping-drink. So, when the girl went into the Prince's room this time he was awake, and she had to tell him how she had come there. "You have come just in time," said the Prince, "for I should have been married tomorrow; but I will not have the long-nosed Princess, and you alone can save me. I will say that I want to see what my bride can do, and bid her wash the shirt which has the three drops of tallow on it. This she will consent to do, for she does not know that it is you who let them fall on it; but no one can wash them out but one born of Christian folk: it cannot be done by one of a pack of trolls; and then I will say that no one shall ever be my bride but the woman who can do this, and I know that you can." There was great joy and

gladness between them all that night, but the next day, when the wedding was to take place, the Prince said, "I must see what my bride can do." "That you may do," said the stepmother.

"I have a fine shirt which I want to wear as my wedding shirt, but three drops of tallow have got upon it which I want to have washed off, and I have vowed to marry no one but the woman who is able to do it. If she cannot do that, she is not worth having."

Well, that was a very small matter, they thought, and agreed to do it. The Princess with the long nose began to wash as well as she could, but, the more she washed and rubbed, the larger the spots grew. "Ah! you can't wash at all," said the old troll-hag, who was her mother. "Give it to me." But she too had not had the shirt very long in her hands before it looked worse still, and, the more she washed it and rubbed it, the larger and blacker grew the spots.

So the other trolls had to come and wash, but, the more they did, the blacker and uglier grew the shirt, until at length it was as black as if it had been up the chimney. "Oh," cried the Prince, "not one

of you is good for anything at all! There is a beggar-girl sitting outside the window, and I'll be bound that she can wash better than any
of you! Come in, you girl there!" he cried. So she came in. "Can
you wash this shirt clean?" he cried. "Oh! I don't know," she said;
"but I will try." And no sooner had she taken the shirt and dipped
it in the water than it was white as driven snow, and even whiter
than that. "I will marry you," said the Prince.

Then the old troll-hag flew into such a rage that she burst, and
the Princess with the long nose and all the little trolls must have
burst too, for they have never been heard of since. The Prince and
his bride set free all the Christian folk who were imprisoned there,
and took away with them all the gold and silver that they could
carry, and moved far away from the castle which lay east of the sun
and west of the moon.

PETER CHRISTEN ASBJORNSEN AND JORGEN MOE

THE PRINCESS ON THE GLASS HILL

ONCE UPON a time there was a man who had a meadow which lay on the side of a mountain, and in the meadow there was a barn in which he stored hay. But there had not been much hay in the barn for the last two years, for every St. John's eve, when the grass was in the height of its vigor, it was all eaten clean up, just as if a whole flock of sheep had gnawed it down to the ground during the night. This happened once, and it happened twice, but then the man got tired of losing his crop, and said to his sons—he had three of them, and the third was called Cinderlad—that one of them must go and sleep in the barn on St. John's night, for it was absurd to let the grass be eaten up again, blade and stalk, as it had been the last two years, and the one who went to watch must keep a sharp look-out, the man said.

The eldest was quite willing to go to the meadow; he would watch the grass, he said, and he would do it so well that neither man, nor beast, nor even the devil himself should have any of it. So when evening came he went to the barn, and lay down to sleep, but when night was drawing near there was such a rumbling and such an earthquake that the walls and roof shook again, and the lad jumped up and took to his heels as fast as he could, and never even looked back, and the barn remained empty that year just as it had been for the last two.

Next St. John's eve the man again said that he could not go on in this way, losing all the grass in the outlying field year after year, and that one of his sons must just go there and watch it, and watch well too. So the next oldest son was willing to show what he could do. He went to the barn and lay down to sleep, as his brother had done; but when night was drawing near there was a great rumbling, and then an earthquake, which was even worse than that on the former St. John's night, and when the youth heard it he was terrified, and went off, running as if for a wager.

The year after, it was Cinderlad's turn, but when he made ready

185

to go the others laughed at him, and mocked him. "Well, you are just the right one to watch the hay, you who have never learned anything but how to sit among the ashes and bake yourself!" said they. Cinderlad, however, did not trouble himself about what they said, but when evening drew near rambled away to the outlying field. When he got there he went into the barn and lay down, but in about an hour's time the rumbling and creaking began, and it was frightful to hear it. "Well, if it gets no worse than that, I can manage to stand it," thought Cinderlad. In a little time the creaking began again, and the earth quaked so that all the hay flew about the boy. "Oh! if it gets no worse than that I can manage to stand it," thought Cinderlad. But then came a third rumbling, and a third earthquake, so violent that the boy thought the walls and roof had fallen down, but when that was over everything suddenly grew as still as death around him. "I am pretty sure that it will come again," thought Cinderlad; but no, it did not. Everything was quiet, and everything stayed quiet, and when he had lain still a short time he heard something that sounded as if a horse were standing chewing just outside the barn door. He stole away to the door, which was ajar, to see what was there, and a horse was standing eating. It was so big, and fat, and fine a horse that Cinderlad had never seen one like it before, and a saddle and bridle lay upon it, and a complete suit of armor for a knight, and everything was of copper, and so bright that it shone again. "Ha, ha! it is thou who eatest up our hay then," thought the boy; "but I will stop that." So he made haste, and took out his steel for striking fire, and threw it over the horse, and then it had no power to stir from the spot, and became so tame that the boy could do what he liked with it. So he mounted it and rode away to a place which no one knew of but himself, and there he tied it up. When he went home again his brothers laughed and asked how he had got on.

"You didn't lie long in the barn, if even you have been so far as the field!" said they.

"I lay in the barn till the sun rose, but I saw nothing and heard nothing, not I," said the boy. "God knows what there was to make you two so frightened."

"Well, we shall soon see whether you have watched the meadow or not," answered the brothers, but when they got there the grass was all standing just as long and as thick as it had been the night before.

The next St. John's eve it was the same thing once again: neither of the two brothers dared to go to the outlying field to watch the crop, but Cinderlad went, and everything happened exactly the same as on the previous St. John's eve: first there was a rumbling and

an earthquake, and then there was another, and then a third: but all three earthquakes were much, very much more violent than they had been the year before. Then everything became still as death again, and the boy heard something chewing outside the barn door, so he stole as softly as he could to the door, which was slightly ajar, and again there was a horse standing close by the wall of the house, eating and chewing, and it was far larger and fatter than the first horse, and it had a saddle on its back, and a bridle was on it too, and a full suit of armor for a knight, all of bright silver, and as beautiful as anyone could wish to see. "Ho, ho!" thought the boy, "is it thou who eatest up our hay in the night? but I will put a stop to that." So he took out his steel for striking fire, and threw it over the horse's mane, and the beast stood there as quiet as a lamb. Then the boy rode this horse, too, away to the place where he kept the other, and then went home again.

"I suppose you will tell us that you have watched well again this time," said the brothers.

"Well, so I have," said Cinderlad. So they went there again, and there the grass was, standing as high and as thick as it had been before, but that did not make them any kinder to Cinderlad.

When the third St. John's night came neither of the two elder brothers dared to lie in the outlying barn to watch the grass, for they had been so heartily frightened the night that they had slept there that they could not get over it, but Cinderlad dared to go, and everything happened just the same as on the two former nights. There were three earthquakes, each worse than the other, and the last flung the boy from one wall of the barn to the other, but then everything suddenly became still as death. When he had lain quietly a short time, he heard something chewing outside the barn door; then he once more stole to the door, which was slightly ajar, and behold, a horse was standing just outside it, which was much larger and fatter than the two others he had caught. "Ho, ho! it is thou, then, who art eating up our hay this time," thought the boy; "but I will put a stop to that." So he pulled out his steel for striking fire, and threw it over the horse, and it stood as still as if it had been nailed to the field, and the boy could do just what he liked with it. Then he mounted it and rode away to the place where he had the two others, and then he went home again. Then the two brothers mocked him just as they had done before, and told him that they could see that he must have watched the grass very carefully that night, for he looked just as if he were walking in his sleep; but Cinderlad did not trouble himself about that, but just bade them go to the field and see. They did go, and this time too the grass was standing, looking as fine and as thick as ever.

The King of the country in which Cinderlad's father dwelt had a daughter whom he would give to no one who could not ride up to the top of the glass hill, for there was a high, high hill of glass, slippery as ice, and it was close to the King's palace. Upon the very top of this the King's daughter was to sit with three gold apples in her lap, and the man who could ride up and take the three golden apples should marry her, and have half the kingdom. The King had this proclaimed in every church in the whole kingdom, and in many other kingdoms too. The Princess was very beautiful, and all who saw her fell violently in love with her, even in spite of themselves. So it is needless to say that all the princes and knights were eager to win her, and half the kingdom besides, and that for this cause they came riding thither from the very end of the world, dressed so splendidly that their raiments gleamed in the sunshine, and riding on horses which seemed to dance as they went, and there was not one of these princes who did not think that he was sure to win the Princess.

When the day appointed by the King had come, there was such a host of knights and princes under the glass hill that they seemed to swarm, and everyone who could walk or even creep was there too, to see who won the King's daughter. Cinderlad's two brothers were there too, but they would not hear of letting him go with them, for he was so dirty and black with sleeping and grubbing among the ashes that they said everyone would laugh at them if they were seen in the company of such an oaf.

"Well, then, I will go all alone by myself," said Cinderlad.

When the two brothers got to the glass hill, all the princes and knights were trying to ride up it, and their horses were in a foam; but it was all in vain, for no sooner did the horses set foot upon the hill than down they slipped, and there was not one which could get even so much as a couple of yards up. Nor was that strange, for the hill was as smooth as a glass window-pane, and as steep as the side of a house. But they were all eager to win the King's daughter and half the kingdom, so they rode and they slipped, and thus it went on. At length all the horses were so tired that they could do no more, and so hot that the foam dropped from them and the riders were forced to give up the attempt. The King was just thinking that he would cause it to be proclaimed that the riding should begin afresh on the following day, when perhaps it might go better, when suddenly a knight came riding up on so fine a horse that no one had ever seen the like of it before, and the knight had armor of copper, and his bridle was of copper too, and all his accoutrements were so bright that they shone again. The other knights all called out to him that he might just as well spare himself the trouble of trying to ride up the glass hill, for it was of no use to try; but he did not heed them, and rode straight off to it, and went up as if it were nothing at all. Thus he rode for a long way—it may have been a third part of the way up—but when he had got so far he turned his horse round and rode down again. But the Princess thought that she had never yet seen so handsome a knight, and while he was riding up she was sitting thinking: "Oh! how I hope he may be able to come up to the top!" And when she saw that he was turning his horse back she threw one of the golden apples down after him, and it rolled into his shoe. But when he had come down from off the hill he rode away, and that so fast that no one knew what had become of him.

So all the princes and knights were bidden to present themselves before the King that night, so that he who had ridden so far up the glass hill might show the golden apple which the King's daughter had thrown down. But no one had anything to show. One knight presented himself after the other, and none could show the apple.

At night, too, Cinderlad's brothers came home again and had a long story to tell about riding up the glass hill. At first, they said, there was not one who was able to get even so much as one step up, but then came a knight who had armor of copper, and a bridle of copper, and his armor and trappings were so bright that they shone to a great distance, and it was something like a sight to see him riding. He rode one-third of the way up the glass hill, and he could easily have ridden the whole of it if he had liked; but he had turned back, for he had made up his mind that that was enough for once. "Oh! I should have liked to see him too, that I should," said Cinderlad, who was as usual sitting by the chimney among the cinders. "You, indeed!" said the brothers, "you look as if you were fit to be among such great lords, nasty beast that you are to sit there!"

Next day the brothers were for setting out again, and this time too Cinderlad begged them to let him go with them and see who rode; but no, they said he was not fit to do that, for he was much too ugly and dirty. "Well, well, then I will go all alone by myself," said Cinderlad. So the brothers went to the glass hill, and all the princes and knights began to ride again, and this time they had taken care to roughen the shoes of their horses; but that did not help them: they rode and they slipped as they had done the day before, and not one of them could get even so far as a yard up the hill. When they had tired out their horses, so that they could do no more, they again had to stop altogether. But just as the King was thinking that it would be well to proclaim that the riding should take place next day for the last time, so that they might have one more chance, he suddenly bethought himself that it would be well to wait a little longer to see if the knight in copper armor would come on this day too. But nothing was to be seen of him. Just as they were still looking for him, however, came a knight riding on a steed that was much, much finer than that which the knight in copper armor had ridden, and this knight had silver armor and a silver saddle and bridle, and all were so bright that they shone and glistened when he was a long way off. Again the other knights called to him, and said that he might just as well give up the attempt to ride up the glass hill, for it was useless to try; but the knight paid no heed to that, but rode straight away to the glass hill, and went still farther up than the knight in copper armor had gone; but when he had ridden two-thirds of the way up he turned his horse round, and rode down again. The Princess liked this knight still better than she had liked the other, and sat longing that he might be able to get up above, and when she saw him turning back she threw the second apple after him, and it rolled into his shoe, and as soon as he had got down the glass hill he rode away so fast that no one could see what had become of him.

In the evening, when everyone was to appear before the King and Princess, in order that he who had the golden apple might show it,

one knight went in after the other, but none of them had a golden apple to show.

At night the two brothers went home as they had done the night before, and told how things had gone, and how everyone had ridden, but no one had been able to get up the hill. "But last of all," they said, "came one in silver armor, and he had a silver bridle on his horse, and a silver saddle, and oh, but he could ride! He took his horse two-thirds of the way up the hill, but then he turned back. He was a fine fellow," said the brothers, "and the Princess threw the second golden apple to him!"

"Oh, how I should have liked to see him too!" said Cinderlad.

"Oh, indeed! He was a little brighter than the ashes that you sit grubbing among, you dirty black creature!" said the brothers.

On the third day everything went just as on the former days.

Cinderlad wanted to go with them to look at the riding, but the two brothers would not have him in their company, and when they got to the glass hill there was no one who could ride even so far as a yard up it, and everyone waited for the knight in silver armor, but he was neither to be seen nor heard of. At last, after a long time, came a knight riding upon a horse that was such a fine one, its equal had never yet been seen. The knight had golden armor, and the horse a golden saddle and bridle, and these were all so bright that they shone and dazzled everyone, even while the knight was still at a great distance. The other princes and knights were not able even to call to tell him how useless it was to try to ascend the hill, so amazed were they at sight of his magnificence. He rode straight away to the glass hill, and galloped up it as if it were no hill at all, so that the Princess had not even time to wish that he might get up the whole way. As soon as he had ridden to the top, he took the third golden apple from

the lap of the Princess and then turned his horse about and rode down again, and vanished from their sight before anyone was able to say a word to him.

When the two brothers came home again at night they had much to tell of how the riding had gone off that day, and at last they told about the knight in the golden armor too. "He was a fine fellow, that was! Such another splendid knight is not to be found on earth!" said the brothers.

"Oh, how I should have liked to see him too!" said Cinderlad.

"Well, he shone nearly as brightly as the coal-heaps that thou art always lying raking among, dirty black creature that thou art!" said the brothers.

Next day all the knights and princes were to appear before the King and Princess—it had been too late for them to do it the night before—in order that he who had the golden apple might produce it. They all went in turn, first princes, and then knights, but none of them had a golden apple.

"But somebody must have it," said the King, "for with our own eyes we all saw a man ride up and take it." So he commanded that everyone in the kingdom should come to the palace, and see if he could show the apple. And one after the other they all came, but no one had the golden apple, and after a long, long time Cinderlad's two brothers came likewise. They were the last of all, so the King inquired of them if there was no one else in the kingdom left to come.

"Oh! yes, we have a brother," said the two, "but he never got the golden apple! He never left the cinder-heap on any of the three days."

"Never mind that," said the King; "as everyone else has come to the palace, let him come too."

So Cinderlad was forced to go to the King's palace.

"Hast thou the golden apple?" asked the King.

"Yes, here is the first, and here is the second, and here is the third, too," said Cinderlad, and he took all three apples out of his pocket, and with that drew off his sooty rags, and appeared there before them in his bright golden armor, which gleamed as he stood.

"Thou shalt have my daughter, and the half of my kingdom, and thou hast well earned both!" said the King. So there was a wedding, and Cinderlad got the King's daughter, and everyone made merry at the wedding, for all of them could make merry, though they could not ride up the glass hill, and if they have not left off their merry-making they must be at it still.

PETER CHRISTEN ASBJORNSEN AND JORGEN MOE

THE TINDER-BOX

A SOLDIER came marching along the high road—left, right! left, right! He had his knapsack on his back and a sword by his side, for he had been to the wars and was now returning home.

An old Witch met him on the road. She was very ugly to look at: her under-lip hung down to her breast.

"Good evening, Soldier!" she said. "What a fine sword and knapsack you have! You are something like a soldier! You ought to have as much money as you would like to carry!"

"Thank you, old Witch," said the Soldier.

"Do you see that great tree there?" said the Witch, pointing to a tree beside them. "It is hollow within. You must climb up to the top, and then you will see a hole through which you can let yourself down into the tree. I will tie a rope round your waist, so that I may be able to pull you up again when you call."

"What shall I do down there?" asked the Soldier.

"Get money!" answered the Witch. "Listen! When you reach the bottom of the tree you will find yourself in a large hall; it is light there, for there are more than three hundred lamps burning. Then you will see three doors, which you can open—the keys are in the locks. If you go into the first room, you will see a great chest in the middle of the floor with a dog sitting upon it; he has eyes as large as saucers, but you needn't trouble about him. I will give you my blue-check apron, which you must spread out on the floor, and then go back quickly and fetch the dog and set him upon it; open the chest and take as much money as you like. It is copper there. If you would rather have silver, you must go into the next room, where there is a dog with eyes as large as mill-wheels. But don't take any notice of him; just set him upon my apron, and help yourself to the money. If you prefer gold, you can get that too, if you go into the third room, and as much as you like to carry. But the dog that

194

guards the chest there has eyes as large as the Round Tower at Copenhagen! He is a savage dog, I can tell you; but you needn't be afraid of him either. Only, put him on my apron and he won't touch you, and you can take out of the chest as much gold as you like!"

"Come, this is not bad!" said the Soldier. "But what am I to give you, old Witch; for surely you are not going to do this for nothing?"

"Yes, I am!" replied the Witch. "Not a single farthing will I take! For me you shall bring nothing but an old tinder-box which my grandmother forgot last time she was down there."

"Well, tie the rope round my waist!" said the Soldier.

"Here it is," said the Witch, "and here is my blue-check apron."

Then the Soldier climbed up the tree, let himself down through the hole, and found himself standing, as the Witch had said, underground in the large hall, where the three hundred lamps were burning.

Well, he opened the first door. Ugh! there sat the dog with eyes as big as saucers glaring at him.

"You are a fine fellow!" said the Soldier, and put him on the Witch's apron, took as much copper as his pockets could hold; then he shut the chest, put the dog on it again, and went into the second room. Sure enough there sat the dog with eyes as large as mill-wheels.

"You had better not look at me so hard!" said the Soldier. "Your eyes will come out of their sockets!"

And then he set the dog on the apron. When he saw all the silver in the chest, he threw away the copper he had taken, and filled his pockets and knapsack with nothing but silver.

Then he went into the third room. Horrors! the dog there had two eyes, each as large as the Round Tower at Copenhagen, spinning round in his head like wheels.

"Good evening!" said the Soldier and saluted, for he had never seen a dog like this before. But when he had examined him more closely, he thought to himself: "Now then, I've had enough of this!" and put him down on the floor, and opened the chest. Heavens! what a heap of gold there was! With all that he could buy up the whole town, and all the sugar pigs, all the tin soldiers, whips and rocking-horses in the whole world. Now he threw away all the silver with which he had filled his pockets and knapsack, and filled them with gold instead—yes, all his pockets, his knapsack, cap and boots even, so that he could hardly walk. Now he was rich indeed. He put the dog back upon the chest, shut the door, and then called up through the tree:

"Now pull me up again, old Witch!"

"Have you got the tinder-box also?" asked the Witch.

The Soldier fills his Knapsack
with Money

"Botheration!" said the Soldier, "I had clean forgotten it!" And then he went back and fetched it.

The Witch pulled him up, and there he stood again on the high road, with pockets, knapsack, cap and boots filled with gold.

"What do you want to do with the tinder-box?" asked the Soldier.

"That doesn't matter to you," replied the Witch. "You have got your money, give me my tinder-box."

"We'll see!" said the Soldier. "Tell me at once what you want to do with it, or I will draw my sword, and cut off your head!"

"No!" screamed the Witch.

The Soldier immediately cut off her head. That was the end of her! But he tied up all his gold in her apron, slung it like a bundle over his shoulder, put the tinder-box in his pocket, and set out towards the town.

It was a splendid town! He turned into the finest inn, ordered the best chamber and his favorite dinner; for now that he had so much money he was really rich.

It certainly occurred to the servant who had to clean his boots that they were astonishingly old boots for such a rich lord. But that was because he had not yet bought new ones; next day he appeared in respectable boots and fine clothes. Now, instead of a common soldier he had become a noble lord, and the people told him about all the grand doings of the town and the King, and what a beautiful Princess his daughter was.

"How can one get to see her?" asked the Soldier.

"She is never to be seen at all!" they told him; "she lives in a great copper castle, surrounded by many walls and towers! No one except the King may go in or out, for it is prophesied that she will marry a common soldier, and the King cannot submit to that."

"I should very much like to see her," thought the Soldier; but he could not get permission.

Now he lived very gaily, went to the theatre, drove in the King's garden, and gave the poor a great deal of money, which was very nice of him; he had experienced in former times how hard it is not to have a farthing in the world. Now he was rich, wore fine clothes, and made many friends, who all said that he was an excellent man, a real nobleman. And the Soldier liked that. But as he was always spending money, and never made any more, at last the day came when he had nothing left but two shillings, and he had to leave the beautiful rooms in which he had been living, and go into a little attic under the roof, and clean his own boots, and mend them with a darning-needle. None of his friends came to visit him there, for there were too many stairs to climb.

It was a dark evening, and he could not even buy a light. But all at once it flashed across him that there was a little end of tinder in the tinder-box, which he had taken from the hollow tree into which the Witch had helped him down. He found the box with the tinder in it; but just as he was kindling a light, and had struck a spark out of the tinder-box, the door burst open, and the dog with eyes as large as saucers, which he had seen down in the tree, stood before him and said:

"What does my lord command?"

"What's the meaning of this?" exclaimed the Soldier. "This is a pretty kind of tinder-box, if I can get whatever I want like this. Get me money!" he cried to the dog, and hey, presto! he was off and back again, holding a great purse full of money in his mouth.

Now the Soldier knew what a capital tinder-box this was. If he rubbed once, the dog that sat on the chest of copper appeared; if he rubbed twice, there came the dog that watched over the silver chest; and if he rubbed three times, the one that guarded the gold

The DOG BRings in The Princess

appeared. Now, the Soldier went down again to his beautiful rooms, and appeared once more in splendid clothes. All his friends immediately recognized him again, and paid him great court.

One day he thought to himself: "It is very strange that no one can get to see the Princess. They all say she is very pretty, but what's the use of that if she has to sit forever in the great copper castle with all the towers? Can I not manage to see her somehow? Where is my tinder-box?" and so he struck a spark, and, presto! there came the dog with eyes as large as saucers.

"It is the middle of the night, I know," said the Soldier; "but I should very much like to see the Princess for a moment."

The dog was already outside the door, and before the Soldier could look round, in he came with the Princess. She was lying asleep on the dog's back, and was so beautiful that anyone could see she was a real Princess. The Soldier really could not refrain from kissing her—he was such a thorough Soldier. Then the dog ran back with the Princess. But when it was morning, and the King and Queen were drinking tea, the Princess said that the night before she had had such a strange dream about a dog and a Soldier: she had ridden on the dog's back, and the Soldier had kissed her.

"That is certainly a fine story," said the Queen. But the next night one of the ladies-in-waiting was to watch at the Princess's bed, to see if it was only a dream, or if it had actually happened.

The Soldier had an overpowering longing to see the Princess again, and so the dog came in the middle of the night and fetched her, running as fast as he could. But the lady-in-waiting slipped on India-rubber shoes and followed them. When she saw them disappear into a large house, she thought to herself: "Now I know where it is; "and made a great cross on the door with a piece of chalk. Then she went home and lay down, and the dog came back also, with the Princess. But when he saw that a cross had been made on the door of the house where the Soldier lived, he took a piece of chalk also, and made crosses on all the doors in the town; and that was very clever, for now the lady-in-waiting could not find the right house, as there were crosses on all the doors.

Early next morning the King, Queen, ladies-in-waiting, and officers came out to see where the Princess had been.

"There it is!" said the King, when he saw the first door with a cross on it.

"No, there it is, my dear!" said the Queen, when she likewise saw a door with a cross.

"But here is one, and there is another!" they all exclaimed; wherever they looked there was a cross on the door. Then they realized that the sign would not help them at all.

But the Queen was an extremely clever woman, who could do a great deal more than just drive in a coach. She took her great golden scissors, cut up a piece of silk, and made a pretty little bag of it. This she filled with the finest buckwheat grains, and tied it round the Princess' neck; this done, she cut a little hole in the bag, so that the grains would strew the whole road wherever the Princess went.

In the night the dog came again, took the Princess on his back and ran away with her to the Soldier, who was very much in love with her, and would have liked to have been a Prince, so that he might have had her for his wife.

The dog did not notice how the grains were strewn right from the castle to the Soldier's window, where he ran up the wall with the Princess.

In the morning the King and the Queen saw plainly where their daughter had been, and they took the Soldier and put him into prison.

There he sat. Oh, how dark and dull it was there! And they told him: "Tomorrow you are to be hanged." Hearing that did not exactly cheer him, and he had left his tinder-box in the inn.

Next morning he could see through the iron grating in front of his little window how the people were hurrying out of the town to

' He was skipping along so merrily '

see him hanged. He heard the drums and saw the soldiers marching; all the people were running to and fro. Just below his window was a shoemaker's apprentice, with leather apron and shoes; he was skipping along so merrily that one of his shoes flew off and fell against the wall, just where the Soldier was sitting peeping through the iron grating.

"Oh, shoemaker's boy, you needn't be in such a hurry!" said the Soldier to him. "There's nothing going on till I arrive. But if you will run back to the house where I lived, and fetch me my tinder-box,

I will give you four shillings. But you must put your best foot foremost."

The shoemaker's boy was very willing to earn four shillings, and fetched the tinder-box, gave it to the Soldier, and—yes—now you shall hear.

Outside the town a great scaffold had been erected, and all round were standing the soldiers, and hundreds of thousands of people. The King and Queen were sitting on a magnificent throne opposite the judges and the whole council.

The Soldier was already standing on the top of the ladder; but when they wanted to put the rope round his neck, he said that the fulfillment of one innocent request was always granted to a poor criminal before he underwent his punishment. He would so much like to smoke a small pipe of tobacco; it would be his last pipe in this world.

The King could not refuse him this, and so he took out his tinder-box, and rubbed it once, twice, three times. And lo, and behold! there stood all three dogs—the one with eyes as large as saucers, the second with eyes as large as mill-wheels, and the third with eyes each as large as the Round Tower of Copenhagen.

"Help me now, so that I may not be hanged!" cried the Soldier. And thereupon the dogs fell upon the judges and the whole council, seized some by the legs, others by the nose, and threw them so high into the air that they fell and were smashed into pieces.

"I won't stand this!" said the King; but the largest dog seized him too, and the Queen as well, and threw them up after the others. This frightened the soldiers, and all the people cried: "Good Soldier, you shall be our King, and marry the beautiful Princess!"

Then they put the Soldier into the King's coach, and the three dogs danced in front, crying "Hurrah!" And the boys whistled and the soldiers presented arms.

The Princess came out of the copper castle, and became Queen; and that pleased her very much.

The wedding festivities lasted for eight days, and the dogs sat at table and made eyes at everyone.

HANS CHRISTIAN ANDERSEN

THE STORY OF THE FISHERMAN
AND HIS WIFE

THERE WAS once a fisherman and his wife who lived together in a little hut close to the sea, and the fisherman used to go down every day to fish; and he would fish and fish. So he used to sit with his rod and gaze into the shining water; and he would gaze and gaze.

Now, once the line was pulled deep under the water, and when he hauled it up he hauled a large flounder with it. The flounder said to him, "Listen, fisherman. I pray you to let me go; I am not a real flounder, I am an enchanted Prince. What good will it do you if you kill me—I shall not taste nice? Put me back into the water and let me swim away."

"Well," said the man, "you need not make so much noise about it; I am sure I had much better let a flounder that can talk swim away." With these words he put him back again into the shining water, and the flounder sank to the bottom, leaving a long streak of blood behind. Then the fisherman got up, and went home to his wife in the hut.

"Husband," said his wife, "have you caught nothing today?"

"No," said the man. "I caught a flounder who said he was an enchanted prince, so I let him swim away again."

"Did you wish nothing from him?" said his wife.

"No," said the man; "what should I have wished from him?"

"Ah!" said the woman, "it's dreadful to have to live all one's life in this hut that is so small and dirty; you ought to have wished for a cottage. Go now and call him; say to him that we choose to have a cottage, and he will certainly give it you."

"Alas!" said the man, "why should I go down there again?"

"Why," said his wife, "you caught him, and then let him go again, so he is sure to give you what you ask. Go down quickly."

The man did not like going at all, but as his wife was not to be persuaded, he went down to the sea.

When he came there the sea was quite green and yellow, and was no longer shining. So he stood on the shore and said:

> "Once a prince, but changed you be
> Into a flounder in the sea.
> Come! for my wife, Ilsebel,
> Wishes what I dare not tell."

Then the flounder came swimming up and said, "Well, what does she want?"

"Alas!" said the man, "my wife says I ought to have kept you and wished something from you. She does not want to live any longer in the hut; she would like a cottage."

"Go home, then," said the flounder; "she has it."

So the man went home, and there was his wife no longer in the hut, but in its place was a beautiful cottage, and his wife was sitting in front of the door on a bench. She took him by the hand and said to him, "Come inside, and see if this is not much better." They went in, and inside the cottage was a tiny hall, and a beautiful sitting-room, and a bedroom in which stood a bed, a kitchen and a dining-room all furnished with the best of everything, and fitted up with every kind of tin and copper utensil. And outside was a little yard in

which were chickens and ducks, and also a little garden with vegetables and fruit trees.

"See," said the wife, "isn't this nice?"

"Yes," answered her husband; "here we shall remain and live very
happily."

"We will think about that," said his wife.

With these words they had their supper and went to bed. All went
well for a week or a fortnight, then the wife said:

"Listen, husband; the cottage is much too small, and so is the yard
and the garden; the flounder might just as well have sent us a larger
house. I should like to live in a great stone castle. Go down to the
flounder, and tell him to send us a castle."

"Ah, wife!" said the fisherman, "the cottage is quite good enough;
why do we choose to live in a castle?"

"Why?" said the wife. "You go down; the flounder can quite well
do that."

"No, wife," said the man; "the flounder gave us the cottage. I do
not like to go to him again; he might take it amiss."

"Go," said his wife. "He can certainly give it us, and ought to do
so willingly. Go at once."

The fisherman's heart was very heavy, and he did not like going.
He said to himself, "It is not right." Still, he went down.

When he came to the sea, the water was all violet and dark-blue, and
dull and thick, and no longer green and yellow, but it was still smooth.

So he stood there and said:

> "Once a prince, but changed you be
> Into a flounder in the sea.
> Come! for my wife, Ilsebel,
> Wishes what I dare not tell."

"What does she want now?" said the flounder.

"Ah!" said the fisherman, half-ashamed, "she wants to live in a
great stone castle."

"Go home; she is standing before the door," said the flounder.

The fisherman went home and thought he would find no house.
When he came near, there stood a great stone palace, and his wife
was standing on the steps, about to enter. She took him by the hand
and said, "Come inside."

Then he went with her, and inside the castle was a large hall with
a marble floor, and there were heaps of servants who threw open the
great doors, and the walls were covered with beautiful tapestry, and

in the apartments were gilded chairs and tables, and crystal chandeliers hung from the ceiling, and all the rooms were beautifully carpeted. The best of food and drink also was set before them when they wished to dine. And outside the house was a large courtyard with horse and cow stables and a coach-house—all fine buildings; and a splendid garden with most beautiful flowers and fruit, and in a park quite a league long were deer and roe and hares, and everything one could wish for.

"Now," said the wife, "isn't this beautiful?"

"Yes, indeed," said the fisherman. "Now we will stay here and live in this beautiful castle, and be very happy."

"We will consider the matter," said his wife, and they went to bed.

The next morning the wife woke up first at daybreak, and looked out of the bed at the beautiful country stretched before her. Her husband was still sleeping, so she dug her elbows into his side and said:

"Husband, get up and look out of the window. Could we not become the king of all this land? Go down to the flounder and tell him we choose to be king."

"Ah, wife!" replied her husband, "why should we be king? I don't want to be king."

"Well," said his wife, "if you don't want to be king, *I* will be king. Go down to the flounder; *I* will be king."

"Alas! wife," said the fisherman, "why do you want to be king? I can't ask him that."

"And why not?" said his wife. "Go down at once. I must be king."

So the fisherman went, though much vexed that his wife wanted to be king. "It is not right! It is not right," he thought. He did not wish to go, yet he went.

When he came to the sea, the water was a dark-grey color, and it was heaving against the shore. So he stood and said:

> "Once a prince, but changed you be
> Into a flounder in the sea.
> Come! for my wife, Ilsebel,
> Wishes what I dare not tell."

"What does she want now?" asked the flounder.

"Alas!" said the fisherman, "she wants to be king."

"Go home; she is that already," said the flounder.

The fisherman went home, and when he came near the palace he saw that it had become much larger, and that it had great towers and splendid ornamental carving on it. A sentinel was standing before the gate, and there were numbers of soldiers with kettledrums and trumpets. And when he went into the palace, he found everything was of pure marble and gold, and the curtains of damask with tassels of gold. Then the doors of the hall flew open, and there stood the whole Court round his wife, who was sitting on a high throne of gold and diamonds; she wore a great golden crown, and had a scepter of gold and precious stones in her hand, and by her on either side stood six pages in a row, each one a head taller than the other. Then he went before her and said:

"Ah, wife! are you king now?"

"Yes," said his wife; "now I am king."

He stood looking at her, and when he had looked for some time, he said:

"Let that be enough, wife, now that you are king! Now we have nothing more to wish for."

"Nay, husband," said his wife restlessly, "my wishing powers are boundless; I cannot restrain them any longer. Go down to the flounder; king I am, now I must be emperor."

"Alas! wife," said the fisherman, "why do you want to be emperor?"

"Husband," said she, "go to the flounder; I *will* be emperor."

"Ah, wife," he said, "he cannot make you emperor; I don't like to ask him that. There is only one emperor in the kingdom. Indeed and indeed he cannot make you emperor."

"What!" said his wife. "I am king, and you are my husband. Will you go at once? Go! If he can make king he can make emperor, and emperor I must and will be. Go!"

So he had to go. But as he went, he felt quite frightened, and he thought to himself, "this can't be right; to be emperor is too ambitious; the flounder will be tired out at last."

Thinking this he came to the shore. The sea was quite black and thick, and it was breaking high on the beach; the foam was flying about, and the wind was blowing; everything looked bleak. The fisherman was chilled with fear. He stood and said:

> "Once a prince, but changed you be
> Into a flounder in the sea.
> Come! for my wife, Ilsebel,
> Wishes what I dare not tell."

"What does she want now?" asked the flounder.

"Alas! flounder," he said, "my wife wants to be emperor."

"Go home," said the flounder; "she is that already."

So the fisherman went home, and when he came there he saw the whole castle was made of polished marble, ornamented with alabaster statues and gold. Before the gate soldiers were marching, blowing trumpets and beating drums. Inside the palace were walking barons, counts, and dukes, acting as servants; they opened the door, which was of beaten gold. And when he entered, he saw his wife upon a throne which was made out of a single block of gold, and which was quite six cubits high. She had on a great golden crown which was three yards high and set with brilliants and sparkling gems. In one hand she held a scepter, and in the other the imperial globe, and on either side of her stood two rows of halberdiers, each smaller than the other, from a seven-foot giant to the tiniest little dwarf no higher than my little finger. Many princes and dukes were standing before her. The fisherman went up to her quietly and said:

"Wife, are you emperor now?"

"Yes," she said, "I am emperor."

He stood looking at her magnificence, and when he had watched her for some time, said:

"Ah, wife, let that be enough, now that you are emperor."

"Husband," said she, "why are you standing there? I am emperor now, and I want to be pope too; go down to the flounder."

"Alas! wife," said the fisherman, "what more do you want? You cannot be pope; there is only one pope in Christendom, and he cannot make you that."

"Husband," she said, "I *will* be pope. Go down quickly; I must be pope today."

"No, wife," said the fisherman; "I can't ask him that. It is not right; it is too much. The flounder cannot make you pope."

"Husband, what nonsense!" said his wife. "If he can make emperor, he can make pope too. Go down this instant; I am emperor and you are my husband. Will you be off at once?"

So he was frightened and went out; but he felt quite faint, and trembled and shook, and his knees and legs began to give way under him. The wind was blowing fiercely across the land, and the clouds flying across the sky looked as gloomy as if it were night; the leaves were being blown from the trees; the water was foaming and seething and dashing upon the shore, and in the distance he saw the ships in great distress, dancing and tossing on the waves. Still the sky was very blue in the middle, although at the sides it was an angry red as in a great storm. So he stood shuddering in anxiety, and said:

"Once a prince, but changed you be
Into a flounder in the sea.
Come! for my wife, Ilsebel,
Wishes what I dare not tell."

"Well, what does she want now?" asked the flounder.

"Alas!" said the fisherman, "she wants to be pope."

"Go home, then; she is that already," said the flounder.

Then he went home, and when he came there he saw, as it were, a large church surrounded by palaces. He pushed his way through the people. The interior was lit up with thousands and thousands of candles, and his wife was dressed in cloth of gold and was sitting on a much higher throne, and she wore three great golden crowns. Round her were numbers of Church dignitaries, and on either side were standing two rows of tapers, the largest of them as tall as a steeple, and the smallest as tiny as a Christmas-tree candle. All the emperors and kings were on their knees before her, and were kissing her foot.

"Wife," said the fisherman looking at her, "are you pope now?"

"Yes," said she; "I am pope."

So he stood staring at her, and it was as if he were looking at the bright sun. When he had watched her for some time he said:

"Ah, wife, let it be enough now that you are pope."

But she sat as straight as a tree, and did not move or bend the least bit. He said again:

"Wife, be content now that you are pope. You cannot become anything more."

"We will think about that," said his wife.

With these words they went to bed. But the woman was not content; her greed would not allow her to sleep, and she kept on thinking and thinking what she could still become. The fisherman slept well and soundly, for he had done a great deal that day, but his wife could not sleep at all, and turned from one side to another the whole night long, and thought, till she could think no longer, what more she could become. Then the sun began to rise, and when she saw the red dawn she went to the end of the bed and looked at it, and as she was watching the sun rise, out of the window, she thought, "Ha! could I not make the sun and man rise?"

"Husband," said she, poking him in the ribs with her elbows, "wake up. Go down to the flounder; I will be a god."

The fisherman was still half asleep, yet he was so frightened that

he fell out of bed. He thought he had not heard aright, and opened his eyes wide and said:

"What did you say, wife?"

"Husband," she said, "if I cannot make the sun and man rise when I appear I cannot rest. I shall never have a quiet moment till I can make the sun and man rise."

He looked at her in horror, and a shudder ran over him.

"Go down at once; I will be a god."

"Alas! wife," said the fisherman, falling on his knees before her, "the flounder cannot do that. Emperor and pope he can make you. I implore you, be content and remain pope."

Then she flew into a passion, her hair hung wildly about her face, she pushed him with her foot and screamed:

"I am not contented, and I shall not be contented! Will you go?"

So he hurried on his clothes as fast as possible, and ran away as if he were mad.

But the storm was raging so fiercely that he could scarcely stand. Houses and trees were being blown down, the mountains were being shaken, and pieces of rock were rolling in the sea. The sky was as black as ink, it was thundering and lightening, and the sea was tossing in great waves as high as church towers and mountains, and each had a white crest of foam.

So he shouted, not able to hear his own voice:

> "Once a prince, but changed you be
> Into a flounder in the sea.
> Come! for my wife, Ilsebel,
> Wishes what I dare not tell."

"Well, what does she want now?" asked the flounder.

"Alas!" said he, "she wants to be a god."

"Go home, then; she is sitting again in the hut."

And there they are sitting to this day.

THE BROTHERS GRIMM

THE MASTER CAT; OR,
PUSS IN BOOTS

THERE WAS a miller who left no more estate to the three sons he had than his mill, his ass, and his cat. The partition was soon made. Neither scrivener nor attorney was sent for. They would soon have eaten up all the poor patrimony. The eldest had the mill, the second the ass, and the youngest nothing but the cat. The poor young fellow was quite comfortless at having so poor a lot.

"My brothers," said he, "may get their living handsomely enough by joining their stocks together; but for my part, when I have eaten up my cat, and made me a muff of his skin, I must die of hunger."

The Cat, who heard all this, but made as if he did not, said to him with a grave and serious air:

"Do not thus afflict yourself, my good master. You have nothing else to do but to give me a bag and get a pair of boots made for me that I may scamper through the dirt and the brambles, and you shall see that you have not so bad a portion in me as you imagine."

The Cat's master did not build very much upon what he said; he had, however, often seen him play a great many cunning tricks to catch rats and mice, as when he used to hang by the heels, or hide himself in the meal, and make as if he were dead; so that he did not altogether despair of his affording him some help in his miserable condition. When the Cat had what he asked for he booted himself very gallantly, and putting his bag about his neck, he held the strings of it in his two forepaws and went into a warren where was great abundance of rabbits. He put bran and sow-thistle into his bag, and stretching out at length, as if he had been dead, he waited for some young rabbits, not yet acquainted with the deceits of the world, to come and rummage his bag for what he had put into it.

Scarce was he lain down but he had what he wanted: a rash and foolish young rabbit jumped into his bag, and Monsieur Puss,

immediately drawing close the strings, took and killed him without pity. Proud of his prey, he went with it to the palace and asked to speak with his majesty. He was shown upstairs into the King's apartment, and, making a low reverence, said to him:

"I have brought you, sir, a rabbit of the warren, which my noble lord the Marquis of Carabas" (for that was the title which Puss was pleased to give his master) "has commanded me to present to your majesty from him."

"Tell thy master," said the king, "that I thank him and that he does me a great deal of pleasure."

Another time he went and hid himself among some standing corn, holding still his bag open; and, when a brace of partridges ran into it he drew the strings and so caught them both. He went and made a present of these to the king, as he had done before of the rabbit which he took in the warren. The king, in like manner, received the partridges with great pleasure, and ordered him some money, to drink.

The Cat continued for two or three months thus to carry his

Majesty, from time to time, game of his master's taking. One day in particular, when he knew for certain that he was to take the air along the riverside, with his daughter, the most beautiful princess in the world, he said to his master:

"If you will follow my advice your fortune is made. You have nothing else to do but go and wash yourself in the river, in that part I shall show you, and leave the rest to me."

The Marquis of Carabas did what the Cat advised him to, without knowing why or wherefore. While he was washing the King passed by, and the Cat began to cry out:

"Help! help! My Lord Marquis of Carabas is going to be drowned."

At this noise the King put his head out of the coach-window, and, finding it was the Cat who had so often brought him such good game, he commanded his guards to run immediately to the assistance of his Lordship the Marquis of Carabas. While they were drawing the poor Marquis out of the river, the Cat came up to the coach and told the King that, while his master was washing, there came by some rogues, who went off with his clothes, though he had cried out: "Thieves! thieves!" several times, as loud as he could.

This cunning Cat had hidden them under a great stone. The King immediately commanded the officers of his wardrobe to run and fetch one of his best suits for the Lord Marquis of Carabas.

The King caressed him after a very extraordinary manner, and as the fine clothes he had given him extremely set off his good mien (for he was well made and very handsome in his person), the King's daughter took a secret inclination to him, and the Marquis of Carabas had no sooner cast two or three respectful and somewhat tender glances but she fell in love with him to distraction. The King would needs have him come into the coach and take part of the airing. The Cat, quite overjoyed to see his project begin to succeed, marched on before, and, meeting with some countrymen, who were mowing a meadow, he said to them:

"Good people, you who are mowing, if you do not tell the King that the meadow you mow belongs to my Lord Marquis of Carabas, you shall be chopped as small as herbs for the pot."

The King did not fail asking of the mowers to whom the meadow they were mowing belonged.

"To my Lord Marquis of Carabas," answered they altogether, for the Cat's threats had made them terribly afraid.

"You see, sir," said the Marquis, "this is a meadow which never fails to yield a plentiful harvest every year."

The Master Cat, who went still on before, met with some reapers, and said to them:

"Good people, you who are reaping, if you do not tell the King that all this corn belongs to the Marquis of Carabas, you shall be chopped as small as herbs for the pot."

The King, who passed by a moment after, would needs know to whom all that corn, which he then saw, did belong.

"To my Lord Marquis of Carabas," replied the reapers, and the King was very well pleased with it, as well as the Marquis, whom he congratulated thereupon. The Master Cat, who went always before, said the same words to all he met, and the King was astonished at the vast estates of my Lord Marquis of Carabas.

Monsieur Puss came at last to a stately castle, the master of which was an ogre, the richest had ever been known; for all the lands which the King had then gone over belonged to this castle. The Cat, who had taken care to inform himself who this ogre was and what he could do, asked to speak with him, saying he could not pass so near his castle without having the honor of paying his respects to him.

The ogre received him as civilly as an ogre could do, and made him sit down.

"I have been assured," said the Cat, "that you have the gift of being able to change yourself into all sorts of creatures you have a mind to; you can, for example, transform yourself into a lion, or elephant, and the like."

"That is true," answered the ogre very briskly; "and to convince you, you shall see me now become a lion."

Puss was so sadly terrified at the sight of a lion so near him that he immediately got into the gutter, not without abundance of trouble and danger, because of his boots, which were of no use at all to him in walking upon the tiles. A little while after, when Puss saw that the ogre had resumed his natural form, he came down, and owned he had been very much frightened.

"I have been, moreover, informed," said the Cat, "but I know not how to believe it, that you have also the power to take on you the shape of the smallest animals; for example, to change yourself into a rat or a mouse; but I must own to you I take this to be impossible."

"Impossible!" cried the ogre; "you shall see that presently."

And at the same time he changed himself into a mouse, and began to run about the floor. Puss no sooner perceived this but he fell upon him and ate him up.

Meanwhile the King, who saw, as he passed, this fine castle of the ogre's, had a mind to go into it. Puss, who heard the noise of his

Majesty's coach running over the draw-bridge, ran out, and said to the King:

"Your Majesty is welcome to this castle of my Lord Marquis of Carabas."

"What! my Lord Marquis," cried the King, "and does this castle also belong to you? There can be nothing finer than this court and all the stately buildings which surround it; let us go into it, if you please."

The Marquis gave his hand to the Princess, and followed the King, who went first. They passed into a spacious hall, where they found a magnificent collation, which the ogre had prepared for his friends, who were that very day to visit him, but dared not to enter, knowing the King was there. His Majesty was perfectly charmed with the good qualities of my Lord Marquis of Carabas, as was his daughter, who had fallen violently in love with him, and, seeing the vast estate he possessed, said to him, after having drunk five or six glasses:

"It will be owing to yourself only, my Lord Marquis, if you are not my son-in-law."

The Marquis, making several low bows, accepted the honor which his Majesty conferred upon him, and forthwith, that very same day, married the Princess.

Puss became a great lord, and never ran after mice any more but only for his diversion.

CHARLES PERRAULT

THE RATCATCHER

(The Pied Piper of Hamelin)

A very long time ago the town of Hamel in Germany was invaded by bands of rats, the like of which had never been seen before nor will ever be again.

They were great black creatures that ran boldly in broad daylight through the streets, and swarmed so, all over the houses, that people at last could not put their hand or foot down anywhere without touching one. When dressing in the morning they found them in their breeches and petticoats, in their pockets and in their boots; and when they wanted a morsel to eat, the voracious horde had swept away everything from cellar to garret. The night was even worse. As soon as the lights were out, these untiring nibblers set to work. And everywhere, in the ceilings, in the floors, in the cupboards, at the doors, there was a chase and a rummage, and so furious a noise of gimlets, pincers, and saws, that a deaf man could not have rested for one hour together.

Neither cats nor dogs, nor poison nor traps, nor prayers nor candles burnt to all the saints—nothing would do anything. The more they killed the more came. And the inhabitants of Hamel began to go to the dogs (not that *they* were of much use), when one Friday there arrived in the town a man with a queer face, who played the bagpipes and sang this refrain:

> "Qui vivra verra:
> Le voila,
> Le preneur des rats."

He was a great gawky fellow, dry and bronzed, with a crooked nose, a long rat-tail moustache, two great yellow piercing and mocking eyes, under a large felt hat set off by a scarlet cock's feather. He was dressed in a green jacket with a leather belt and red breeches, and on his feet were sandals fastened by thongs passed round his legs in the gipsy fashion.

That is how he may be seen to this day, painted on a window of the cathedral of Hamel.

He stopped on the great market-place before the town hall, turned his back on the church and went on with his music, singing:

> "Who lives shall see:
> This is he,
> The ratcatcher."

The town council had just assembled to consider once more this plague of Egypt, from which no one could save the town.

The stranger sent word to the counselors that, if they would make it worth his while, he would rid them of all their rats before night, down to the very last.

"Then he is a sorcerer!" cried the citizens with one voice; "we must beware of him."

The Town Counselor, who was considered clever, reassured them.

He said: "Sorcerer or no, if this bagpiper speaks the truth, it was he who sent us this horrible vermin that he wants to rid us of today for money. Well, we must learn to catch the devil in his own snares. You leave it to me."

"Leave it to the Town Counselor," said the citizens one to another. And the stranger was brought before them.

"Before night," said he, "I shall have dispatched all the rats in Hamel if you will but pay me a *gros* a head."

"A gros a head!" cried the citizens, "but that will come to millions of florins!"

The Town Counselor simply shrugged his shoulders and said to the stranger:

"A bargain! To work; the rats will be paid one *gros* a head as you ask."

The bagpiper announced that he would operate that very evening when the moon rose. He added that the inhabitants should at that hour leave the streets free, and content themselves with looking out of their windows at what was passing, and that it would be a pleasant spectacle. When the people of Hamel heard of the bargain, they too exclaimed: "A *gros* a head! but this will cost us a deal of money!"

"Leave it to the Town Counselor," said the town council with a malicious air. And the good people of Hamel repeated with their counselors, "Leave it to the Town Counselor."

Towards nine at night the bagpiper reappeared on the market place. He turned, as at first, his back to the church, and the moment the moon rose on the horizon, "Trarira, trari!" the bagpipes resounded.

It was first a slow, caressing sound, then more and more lively and urgent, and so sonorous and piercing that it penetrated as far as the farthest alleys and retreats of the town.

Soon from the bottom of the cellars, the top of the garrets, from under all the furniture, from all the nooks and corners of the houses,

out come the rats, search for the door, fling themselves into the street, and trip, trip, trip, begin to run in file towards the front of the town hall, so squeezed together that they covered the pavement like the waves of flooded torrent.

When the square was quite full the bagpiper faced about, and, still playing briskly, turned towards the river that runs at the foot of the walls of Hamel.

Arrived there he turned round; the rats were following.

"Hop! hop!" he cried, pointing with his finger to the middle of the stream, where the water whirled and was drawn down as if through a funnel. And hop! hop! without hesitating, the rats took the leap, swam straight to the funnel, plunged in head foremost and disappeared.

The plunging continued thus without ceasing till midnight.

At last, dragging himself with difficulty, came a big rat, white with age, and stopped on the bank.

It was the king of the band.

"Are they all there, friend Blanchet?" asked the bagpiper.

"They are all there," replied friend Blanchet.

"And how many were they?"

"Nine hundred and ninety thousand, nine hundred and ninety-nine."

"Well reckoned?"

"Well reckoned."

"Then go and join them, old sire, and *au revoir*."

Then the old white rat sprang in his turn into the river, swam to the whirlpool and disappeared.

When the bagpiper had thus concluded his business he went to bed at his inn. And for the first time during three months the people of Hamel slept quietly through the night.

The next morning, at nine o'clock, the bagpiper repaired to the town hall, where the town council awaited him.

"All your rats took a jump into the river yesterday," said he to the counselors, "and I guarantee that not one of them comes back. They were nine hundred and ninety thousand, nine hundred and ninety-nine, at one *gros* a head. Reckon!"

"Let us reckon the heads first. One *gros* a head is one head the *gros*. Where are the heads?"

The ratcatcher did not expect this treacherous stroke. He paled with anger and his eyes flashed fire.

"The heads!" cried he, "if you care about them, go and find them in the river."

"So," replied the Town Counselor, "you refuse to hold to the terms of your agreement? We ourselves could refuse you all payment. But you have been of use to us, and we will not let you go without a recompense," and he offered him fifty crowns.

"Keep your recompense for yourself," replied the ratcatcher proudly. "If you do not pay me I will be paid by your heirs."

Thereupon he pulled his hat down over his eyes, went hastily out of the hall, and left the town without speaking to a soul.

When the Hamel people heard how the affair had ended they rubbed their hands, and with no more scruple than their Town Counselor, they laughed over the ratcatcher, who, they said, was caught in his own trap. But what made them laugh above all was his threat of getting himself paid by their heirs. Ha! they wished that they only had such creditors for the rest of their lives.

Next day, which was a Sunday, they all went gaily to church, thinking that after Mass they would at last be able to eat some good thing that the rats had not tasted before them.

They never suspected the terrible surprise that awaited them on their return home. No children anywhere, they had all disappeared!

"Our children! where are our poor children?" was the cry that was soon heard in all the streets.

Then through the east door of the town came three little boys, who cried and wept, and this is what they told:

While the parents were at church a wonderful music had resounded. Soon all the little boys and all the little girls that had been left at home had gone out, attracted by the magic sounds, and had rushed to the great market place. There they found the ratcatcher playing his bagpipes at the same spot as the evening before. Then the stranger had begun to walk quickly, and they had followed, running, singing and dancing to the sound of the music, as far as the foot of the mountain which one sees on entering Hamel. At their approach the mountain had opened a little, and the bagpiper had gone in with them, after which it had closed again. Only the three little ones who told the adventure had remained outside, as if by a miracle. One was bandy-legged and could not run fast enough; the other, who had left the house in haste, one foot shod the other bare, had hurt himself against a big stone and could not walk without difficulty; the third had arrived in time, but in harrying to go in with the others had struck so violently against the wall of the mountain that he fell backwards at the moment it closed upon his comrades.

At this story the parents redoubled their lamentations. They ran with pikes and mattocks to the mountain, and searched till evening to find the opening by which their children had disappeared, without being able to find it. At last, the night falling, they returned desolate to Hamel.

But the most unhappy of all was the Town Counselor, for he lost three little boys and two pretty little girls, and to crown all, the people of Hamel overwhelmed him with reproaches, forgetting that the evening before they had all agreed with him.

What had become of all these unfortunate children?

The parents always hoped they were not dead, and that the ratcatcher, who certainly must have come out of the mountain, would have taken them with him to his country. That is why for several years they sent in search of them to different countries, but no one ever came on the trace of the poor little ones.

It was not till much later that anything was to be heard of them.

About one hundred and fifty years after the event, when there was no longer one left of the fathers, mothers, brothers or sisters of that day, there arrived one evening in Hamel some merchants of Bremen returning from the East, who asked to speak with the citizens. They told that they, in crossing Hungary, had sojourned in a mountainous country called Transylvania, where the inhabitants only spoke German, while all around them nothing was spoken but Hungarian. These people also declared that they came from Germany, but they

did not know how they chanced to be in this strange country. "Now," said the merchants of Bremen, "these Germans cannot be other than the descendants of the lost children of Hamel."

The people of Hamel did not doubt it; and since that day they regard it as certain that the Transylvanians of Hungary are their country folk, whose ancestors, as children, were brought there by the ratcatcher. There are more difficult things to believe than that.

CHARLES MARELLES

THE THREE LITTLE PIGS

THERE WAS once upon a time a pig who lived with her three children on a large, comfortable, old-fashioned farmyard. The eldest of the little pigs was called Browny, the second Whitey, and the youngest and best looking Blacky. Now Browny was a very dirty little pig, and I am sorry to say spent most of his time rolling and wallowing about in the mud. He was never so happy as on a wet day, when the mud in the farmyard got soft, and thick, and slab. Then he would steal away from his mother's side, and finding the muddiest place in the yard, would roll about in it and thoroughly enjoy himself. His mother often found fault with him for this, and would shake her head sadly and say: "Ah, Browny! some day you will be sorry that you did not obey your old mother." But no words of advice or warning could cure Browny of his bad habits.

Whitey was quite a clever little pig, but she was greedy. She was always thinking of her food, and looking forward to her dinner; and when the farm girl was seen carrying the pails across the yard, she would rise up on her hind legs and dance and caper with excitement.

225

As soon as the food was poured into the trough she jostled Blacky and Browny out of the way in her eagerness to get the best and biggest bits for herself. Her mother often scolded her for her selfishness, and told her that some day she would suffer for being so greedy and grabbing.

Blacky was a good, nice little pig, neither dirty nor greedy. He had nice dainty ways (for a pig), and his skin was always as smooth and shining as black satin. He was much cleverer than Browny and Whitey, and his mother's heart used to swell with pride when she heard the farmer's friends say to each other that some day the little black fellow would be a prize pig.

Now the time came when the mother pig felt old and feeble and near her end. One day she called the three little pigs round her and said:

"My children, I feel that I am growing old and weak, and that I shall not live long. Before I die I should like to build a house for each of you, as this dear old sty in which we have lived so happily will be given to a new family of pigs, and you will have to turn out. Now, Browny, what sort of a house would you like to have?"

"A house of mud," replied Browny, looking longingly at a wet puddle in the corner of the yard.

"And you, Whitey?" said the mother pig in rather a sad voice, for she was disappointed that Browny had made so foolish a choice.

"A house of cabbage," answered Whitey, with a mouth full, and scarcely raising her snout out of the trough in which she was grubbing for some potato-parings.

"Foolish, foolish child!" said the mother pig, looking quite distressed. "And you, Blacky?" turning to her youngest son, "what sort of a house shall I order for you?"

"A house of brick, please mother, as it will be warm in winter, and cool in summer, and safe all the year round."

"That is a sensible little pig," replied his mother, looking fondly at him. "I will see that the three houses are got ready at once. And now one last piece of advice. You have heard me talk of our old enemy the fox. When he hears that I am dead, he is sure to try and get hold of you, to carry you off to his den. He is very sly and will no doubt disguise himself, and pretend to be a friend, but you must promise me not to let him enter your houses on any pretext whatever."

And the little pigs readily promised, for they had always had a great fear of the fox, of whom they had heard many terrible tales. A short time afterwards the old pig died, and the little pigs went to live in their own houses.

Browny was quite delighted with his soft mud walls and with the clay floor, which soon looked like nothing but a big mud pie. But that was what Browny enjoyed, and he was as happy as possible, rolling about all day and making himself in such a mess. One day, as he was lying half asleep in the mud, he heard a soft knock at his door, and a gentle voice said:

"May I come in, Master Browny? I want to see your beautiful new house."

"Who are you?" said Browny, starting up in great fright, for though the voice sounded gentle, he felt sure it was a feigned voice, and he feared it was the fox.

"I am a friend come to call on you," answered the voice.

"No, no," replied Browny, "I don't believe you are a friend. You are the wicked fox, against whom our mother warned us. I won't let you in."

"Oho! is that the way you answer me?" said the fox, speaking very roughly in his natural voice. "We shall soon see who is master here," and with his paws he set to work and scraped a large hole in the soft mud walls. A moment later he had jumped through it, and catching Browny by the neck, flung him on his shoulders and trotted off with him to his den.

The next day, as Whitey was munching a few leaves of cabbage out of the corner of her house, the fox stole up to her door, determined to carry her off to join her brother in his den. He began speaking to her in the same feigned gentle voice in which he had spoken to Browny; but it frightened her very much when he said:

"I am a friend come to visit you, and to have some of your good cabbage for my dinner."

"Please don't touch it," cried Whitey in great distress. "The cabbages are the walls of my house, and if you eat them you will make a hole, and the wind and rain will come in and give me a cold. Do go away; I am sure you are not a friend, but our wicked enemy the fox." And poor Whitey began to whine and to whimper, and to wish that she had not been such a greedy little pig, and had chosen a more solid material than cabbages for her house. But it was too late now, and in another minute the fox had eaten his way through the cabbage walls, and had caught the trembling, shivering Whitey, and carried her off to his den.

The next day the fox started off for Blacky's house, because he had made up his mind that he would get the three little pigs together in his den, and then kill them, and invite all his friends to a feast. But when he reached the brick house, he found that the door was bolted

and barred, so in his sly manner he began, "Do let me in, dear Blacky. I have brought you a present of some eggs that I picked up in a farmyard on my way here."

"No, no, Mister Fox," replied Blacky, "I am not going to open my door to you. I know your cunning ways. You have carried off poor Browny and Whitey, but you are not going to get me."

At this the fox was so angry that he dashed with all his force against the wall, and tried to knock it down. But it was too strong and well-built; and though the fox scraped and tore at the bricks with his paws he only hurt himself, and at last he had to give it up, and limp away with his fore-paws all bleeding and sore.

"Never mind!" he cried angrily as he went off, "I'll catch you another day, see if I don't, and won't I grind your bones to powder when I have got you in my den!" and he snarled fiercely and showed his teeth.

Next day Blacky had to go into the neighboring town to do some marketing and to buy a big kettle. As he was walking home with it slung over his shoulder, he heard a sound of steps stealthily creeping after him. For a moment his heart stood still with fear, and then a happy thought came to him. He had just reached the top of a hill, and could see his own little house nestling at the foot of it among the trees. In a moment he had snatched the lid off the kettle and had jumped in himself. Coiling himself round he lay quite snug in the bottom of the kettle, while with his fore-leg he managed to put the lid on, so that he was entirely hidden. With a little kick from the inside he started the kettle off, and down the hill it rolled full tilt; and when the fox came up, all that he saw was a large black kettle spinning over the ground at a great pace. Very much disappointed, he was just going to turn away, when he saw the kettle stop close to the little brick house, and in a moment later Blacky jumped out of it and escaped with the kettle into the house, when he barred and bolted the door, and put the shutter up over the window.

"Oho!" exclaimed the fox to himself, "you think you will escape me that way, do you? We shall soon see about that, my friend," and very quietly and stealthily he prowled round the house looking for some way to climb on to the roof.

In the meantime Blacky had filled the kettle with water, and having put it on the fire, sat down quietly waiting for it to boil. Just as the kettle was beginning to sing, and steam to come out of the spout, he heard a sound like a soft, muffled step, patter, patter, patter overhead, and the next moment the fox's head and fore-paws were

seen coming down the chimney. But Blacky very wisely had not put the lid on the kettle, and, with a yelp of pain, the fox fell into the boiling water, and before he could escape, Blacky had popped the lid on, and the fox was scalded to death.

As soon as he was sure that their wicked enemy was really dead, and could do them no further harm, Blacky started off to rescue Browny and Whitey. As he approached the den he heard piteous grunts and squeals from his poor little brother and sister who lived in constant terror of the fox killing and eating them. But when they saw Blacky appear at the entrance to the den their joy knew no bounds. He quickly found a sharp stone and cut the cords by which they were tied to a stake in the ground, and then all three started off together for Blacky's house, where they lived happily ever after; and Browny quite gave up rolling in the mud, and Whitey ceased to be greedy, for they never forgot how nearly these faults had brought them to an untimely end.

ENGLISH FAIRY TALE